Lair

James Herbert is not just Britain's No. 1 bestselling writer of chiller fiction, a position he has held ever since the publication of his first novel, but is one of our greatest popular novelists, whose books are sold in thirty-three other languages, including Russian and Chinese. Widely imitated and hugely influential, his twenty novels have sold more than forty-eight million copies worldwide.

JAMES HERBERT

Lair

PAN BOOKS

First published 1979 by New English Library

This edition published 1999 by Pan Books
an imprint of Pan Macmillan Ltd
Pan Macmillan, 20 New Wharf Road, London N1 9RR
Basingstoke and Oxford
Associated companies throughout the world

www.panmacmillan.com

ISBN 0 330 37619 5

3 5 7 9 8 6 4

A CIP catalogue record for this book is available from
the British Library.

Typeset by SetSystems Ltd, Saffron Walden, Essex
Printed and bound in Great Britain by
Mackays of Chatham plc, Chatham, Kent

If you go down in the woods today

You're sure of a big surprise . . .

Contents

Lair

Prologue

The rat had been trapped in the basement for five days. It had crawled into a dark corner behind a row of shelves to give birth to its litter and, when it had tried to follow the sound, the sound that buzzed through its head, it had found the way blocked by a heavy iron door. The sound had continued for five long days, almost driving the mother-rat and its tiny offspring mad with its incessant, monotonous pitch. But they had found food in abundance in the basement. The owners had ignored the government warning to leave all doors open so that every building could be cleared, for they knew that when the city's population returned from its short exile, food would be scarce for the first few days, and their shop would be ready to cash in on the shortage. The rat and its litter gorged themselves on the food, for the young ones seemed only to need their mother's milk for the first three days, finding greater replenishment in the food around them. They grew larger and sturdier day by day, dark brown, almost black hairs were already beginning to grow on their bodies. Except for one. Only a few white hairs sprouted on its pinkish white body. It seemed to dominate the others, who brought it food and kept its body warm with their own. A curious lump seemed to be growing on its broad, lop-sided shoulder, next to its head.

Patiently, they waited for the people to return.

Signs

1

'Bloody vermin,' Ken Woollard cursed aloud, raising his head to examine the 'loop' smears around the rafters of his low-ceilinged barn. The grease marks against the whitewashed walls had been caused by small furry bodies sliding under the beams into the recesses of the rough ceiling. And the only creatures he knew who did that were rodents. Mice and rats. The stains looked too big to have been caused by mice.

'Bloody cats aren't earning their bloody keep,' he said to himself. Turning and walking from the gloomy building, he examined the floor for droppings. He found none, but it was hardly reassuring. The vermin were there all right, the smears were proof enough. Well, the poison would go down tonight, no messing about waiting for serious damage to be done. Farming the land was hard enough without pests destroying anything edible they could find. Fluoroacetamide should do the trick, no sodding about with pre-baiting. A good dose of it, clear them out right away.

The bright October sunlight made him narrow his eyes as he paused at the barn door. Have to report it, I suppose, government law after the Outbreak. They'd gassed the buggers then, but they were still nervous it might start all over again. Still, that was the city, a great big filthy breeding-place for vermin – animal and human. Unfortunately, Epping Forest was close enough to London for them to get the willies again. They'd be down, snooping around, putting the whole bloody farm into quarantine until they were sure it wasn't *the* bloody rats.

Fuck 'em. Got no time for that nonsense. Get rid of them before all the fuss starts. Where's those bloody cats?

Woollard trudged through the mud of the small farmyard hissing through his teeth to attract the two cats he kept not as pets, but as working animals. Until now they had managed to keep the number of rats down – you could never keep them away altogether – but the vermin were now getting into the buildings, and that could lead to big trouble.

Woollard's weathered face was creased into deep trenches of anger as he turned the corner of an outbuilding, when suddenly he caught sight of a small white object lying in the mud. At first he thought it might just be a bird feather, but the tinges of red along one edge aroused his curiosity. He squinted as he approached, deciding it wasn't a feather at all but a tiny, obviously dead, animal. He was used to finding dead mice around the place, for his cats *usually* did their job well enough. This time, though, there was something odd about the furry corpse.

Stooping to examine the body more closely, he suddenly drew in a sharp breath. He reached for the object he now knew was not a dead mouse. Blood had matted the fur at one end and two of the claws at the other end were missing. He dropped the cat's paw in disgust.

Pushing himself erect, he quickly searched the area around him for the rest of the cat's body. The stupid bloody creature must have got tangled up in some farmyard machinery, or maybe some wiring, and had the paw torn from its body. It must have crawled away somewhere to nurse its wound – or die, most likely. It was then he saw the blood-streaks against the wall of the outhouse.

They stretched all the way along the wall's length, dark red, clots of black and brown hair sticking to the viscous surface. One of the cats – they had no names, he wasn't that sentimental – was black and brown, with white paws. Whatever had got hold of the poor bloody creature had dragged it along the wall, and the frantic red scratch marks gave evidence that the cat had still been alive at the time.

'Good bloody God,' the farmer said in a hushed tone. He followed the gory trail, anger quickening his strides. What manner of creature could do such a thing? A fox? Been none of them around here for years. Anyway, he'd never heard of a fox fighting with a cat before. Some bloody dog's done it! One of them belonging to someone living in the forest. Never kept their bloody animals locked up! Bad enough with horses trotting all over the place! Well this one'll get my bloody shotgun up its arse.

He reached the end of the wall and hurried round, anger blurring his vision so that he failed to see the object lying on the ground before him. His heavy boot crunched it down into the mud before he realized he had trodden on something hard. He stopped, turned, and once again stooped to examine the object on the ground.

Two sightless slits stared up at him, mud covering the lower portion of the crushed skull. He pulled at a pointed ear and the cat's head came free with a sucking sound, startling Woollard and making him throw the skull into the air. It landed in the mud again with a plop, and lay half on its side, a wicked, feline grin seeming to mock the frightened farmer.

The man crawled on his stomach through the damp grass towards the prone woman. She lay unaware of his stealthy approach, her face turned towards the sun, surprised and happy to receive its warmth so late in the year. She flexed her shoulders against the rough blanket, its thickness protecting her from the wetness of the grass which even the sun could not draw out.

The creeping man smiled and a gleam came into his eyes. A sound behind him made him turn his head sharply and he frowned at his two companions, silently urging them to remain quiet.

The woman sighed and raised a knee provocatively; the smoothness of her legs caught the man's attention. His smile widened and he felt the pressure of the earth against his loins. He was close now, close enough to reach out and touch that wonderfully soft body. He tried to control his breathing so that she wouldn't hear.

Bringing his arm forward, he snapped off a long blade of grass, then pointed its quivering tip towards the woman's face. She twitched as the fine point ran down the side of her nose, then twitched again as the tickling sensation persisted. She suddenly sat upright, vigorously rubbing at her skin as though to dislodge an errant insect.

'Terry,' she shouted when she saw his shaking body, and grabbed a handful of grass and threw it into his face.

The two children behind the man laughed excitedly, the small girl jumping on his back and pounding his head with the palm of her hand.

'Oi!' he yelped, reaching behind and toppling her over his shoulder. 'S'nough of that!'

The woman smiled as her husband rolled the four-year-old over in the grass. 'Mind her clothes, Terry. She'll get wet.'

'All right, monkey, you heard what your mother said.' Terry tossed the girl onto the blanket where she immediately jumped into the woman's arms.

'Game of football, Dad?' the boy asked, eyebrows raised in anticipation.

'Okay, Keith, get the ball. It's in the back of the car.'

The boy, seven years old, and ready to play for England – maybe West Ham would do – scampered off towards the red car parked fifty yards away on a hard piece of ground not too far from the road.

'This is nice, Terry,' the woman said, allowing her daughter to scramble free and chase the boy.

'Yeah. We should do it more often, you know.'

The woman looked at him meaningfully. 'We could always do it on weekends. It would be better than keeping Keith away from school for the day. Wouldn't do any harm to take them down to Southend now and again. They like the sea.'

Terry grunted noncommittally. He didn't want to make any promises just because he was in a good mood. 'Come on, you two, hurry up,' he shouted after the children.

The woman knew there was no point in pursuing the subject. 'When do you think you'll go back?' she asked.

Terry shrugged. 'When the Union says so, I suppose.'

'I don't know how they get away with it. It's a wonder the company don't go bust. It's the fifth dispute this year.'

'Sixth. We were on a go-slow last month.'

The woman groaned. 'How you get any cars out at all beats me.'

'Leave it alone, Hazel. I have to follow the Union rules.'

'Yes, you all do, don't you? You're all bloody mindless.'

'They get us more money, don't they? And better conditions.'

'And what are they going to do when there's no car plant left? When the Americans pull out?'

'Leave off. That'll never happen.'

'No, not until it does.'

The couple sat in silence for a few moments, each annoyed with the other.

'At least it gives me more time with the kids, don't it?' Terry said finally.

Hazel sniffed.

The two children returned, the boy kicking the ball ahead and the girl running after it, trying to smother it with her body. Terry leapt to his feet and ran towards them, kicking the ball away from the girl who shrieked with glee.

Hazel smiled at the three of them and pushed thoughts of strikes and unions and weekends spent indoors away from her mind. 'Lazy bastard,' she said softly, still smiling, as she watched her husband kick the football with his knee onto his head.

'Okay, Keith, in goal,' Terry told the boy who immediately pulled a disgusted face.

'I'm always in goal. Can't you go in for a change, Dad?'

'Yeah, I will. When I've scored three, all right? In between those two trees, go on.'

The boy slunk off and stood between two hornbeams, hands on his hips, facing his prancing father.

The girl tried to grab the ball from her father's feet and giggled when he pulled it away from her with the underside of one foot.

'No you don't, Josie. You're up against a pro here.' Terry kicked the ball clear of his daughter then gave it a hefty kick towards the makeshift goal. Keith met it with a kick of his own and sent it skimming back past his father.

'Show off!' Terry called out and ran after it, slipping and falling onto his back as he stretched a foot out to halt the ball's progress.

Hazel and the two children laughed aloud as Terry struggled to his feet, a rueful grin on his face.

'All right, you asked for it,' he called back to Keith. 'Get ready for this one!'

He retrieved the ball, placed it firmly on the ground, took a few steps back, then kicked it high and hard towards the goalmouth. Josie bravely jumped up and tried to catch the ball, but the boy was older and wiser: he ducked and let it sail over his head. The ball disappeared with a rustle of protesting leaves into the heavy clump of bushes behind the trees.

'Oh, Dad!' Keith moaned.

'Terry, that's too hard,' said Hazel, reproachfully.

'Well, go and get it, son,' said Terry, unabashed.

But Keith squatted on the ground, arms folded across his chest, a set expression on his face.

'I get it, Daddy,' Josie cried out, scurrying towards the bushes.

'Watch her, Terry, don't let her go out of sight,' Hazel said anxiously.

'She's all right, it didn't go far.' Terry stretched his arms and gazed at the greenness around him. 'Beats bloody working,' he muttered under his breath.

Josie peered into the bushes, then jiggled her body through the small opening she had found. She squirmed further into the undergrowth, her eyes darting from left to right in search of the lost ball. Her mother's voice followed her through the tangle of leaves and branches, but the girl's mind was too concentrated on her quest to listen. She squealed in excitement when she saw the white round object of her search nestling beneath a leafy bush, and pushed herself forward, wincing as the branches scratched at her legs.

She reached the ball in a final determined rush, then squatted on her haunches to retrieve it. Something moved just beyond the football. Something dark, hiding in the darker shadows of the thick undergrowth.

Josie's fingertips reached for the ball and flicked it free, rolling it back towards her. She hugged it to her chest and was about to rise when her sharp little eyes caught sight of the animal. She moved closer, ducking beneath the leaves to get a better view. The football was forgotten for the moment and left to one side, shiny and wet. Josie crawled forward on all fours, oblivious to the damp earth which muddied her hands and knees. In the dimness she could just distinguish a black, stiff-furred body and two close-set highlights reflected in the creature's eyes. It did not move, but waited for her to draw near.

'Good doggy,' Josie said happily. 'Come here. Come on.'

A thick branch blocked her way and she pushed at it impatiently, but it would not budge. She reached over, wanting to stroke the animal's head.

The pointed head jerked once, then stretched forward towards the approaching fingers. The girl giggled, overjoyed that the animal wanted to be friendly, and pushed even harder against the branch so that she could touch the furry body. Hot breath from the creature's mouth warmed her pudgy hand.

The sudden crash of broken undergrowth from behind startled her and she drew her arm back in a reflex action.

'Josie? Where are you?' came her father's concerned voice.

'Here, Daddy,' she called out. 'Got a doggy.'

Terry brushed the leaves and branches aside and found his daughter on her knees in the mud, the white football near her feet. Her face beamed up at him in excitement.

'You wait till your mother sees the state of you,' he scolded, and reached down to scoop her up in his arms.

'Dog in there, Daddy. Can we take him home?'

Her father peered into the gloom behind her, but when she turned to point to the spot where the animal had been hiding, it had gone.

The horse, chestnut in colour, cantered easily along the hoggin path, its rider immaculately clad in a light brown uniform and dark riding cap. Charles Denison, Head Keeper of Epping Forest, was content on this fine, October morning.

It was the season he loved best: the greens, yellows and browns of autumn gave the forest new life, changed its personality in a most beautiful way. The dying leaves replenished the earth, the golden, myriad carpet they formed on the woodland floor injecting the soil with fresh vitality which would be slowly processed through the winter months. The air was fresh, its sharpness exhilarating. And best of all, the people were gone.

The vast acres of woodland, rolling fields and agricultural land were a retreat for thousands upon thousands of Londoners or those living in the urbanized areas around the forest. The hordes invaded at weekends and public holidays in the summer months, scattering their litter, terrifying the shy forest creatures with their bludgeoning excursions into the wooded areas, shouting, laughing, mutilating trees and undergrowth. The public thought they owned the lush strip of land, assuming its upkeep came from the rates they paid; but it wasn't so. Private money preserved this sanctuary.

Still, they were gone now, leaving the forest to those who cared, those who loved the vast nature reserve for its peacefulness, its constantly changing pattern, its timid wild-life. Fewer squawling brats, less bawling transistor radios. Weekends were still busy – they always would be, whatever the weather – but, ah, weekdays. Weekdays, such as this, were a joy. Denison brought his mount to a halt to examine fresh markings at the base of a birch tree.

The bark had been stripped away by some small animal, revealing the virgin wood beneath, bright and naked, a fresh wound. He lightly kicked against the sides of his mount and urged it forward for a closer inspection. Squirrels, he told himself. Damned pests, despite their bushy-tailed precocious-ness. If he had his way, he would trap or poison the lot of 'em. The grey squirrel, usually in early summer, attacked trees, gnawing at the main stem for the sweet, sappy layers beneath the rough bark. A tree could often die from such attacks, particularly if completely ringed. The ordinary layman just did not understand the nuisance value of these tiny creatures, didn't seem to appreciate that they were rodents. Of course, there had been no sign at all of the red squirrel. The red had been ousted from the forest by the grey many years ago and the amount of greys had increased uncontrollably; but this year, strangely, their numbers seemed to be down.

He pulled the horse away from the birch, lifting its head up from the succulent grass. Guiding it back to the path, Denison gazed around him, looking for signs of further damage. A sudden flurry of movement to his left brought him to a halt again. A section of thicket across the path from him shook frantically, then settled into an uneasy stillness. It often happened in the forest – an animal or bird startled by the approach of man, a sudden attack by one animal on another – it was this that made the woodland so alive.

A sudden, spasmodic twitching of leaves and a tiny, almost inaudible squeal told him that a forest creature had fallen victim to a larger enemy. He felt no sympathy, for that was the law of nature, but he was curious to know who was prey and who was predator. He clucked his tongue at the horse and lightly kicked its flanks again. The chestnut took a few steps towards the thicket, then stopped, its neck and legs suddenly stiff.

There was no movement from the undergrowth, not even the rustle of unseen leaves beneath its many layers.

'Come on, girl,' said Denison, irritated at his mount's unexpected nervousness. 'On you go.'

But the horse refused to budge. It regarded the thicket with bulging eyes. Denison became impatient with the horse's inexplicable fear – and fear it was, for the keeper could feel the rising tension in the beast. He knew horses, knew their moods, and he certainly knew this mood. The horse was ready to bolt.

'Steady now, Bettina. There's nothing there to worry you.' He patted the chestnut's long neck, speaking in soft, soothing tones. Bettina was normally the most docile of animals, rarely spooked by the abrupt actions of startled wildlife. 'Calm yourself, girl, and we'll go on our way.'

The horse skipped from hoof to hoof, jerking its head up and away from the now silent thicket. The keeper exerted pressure with his left knee and pulled the reins towards the right, trying to steer his mount down the path and away from the menacing undergrowth.

And then the horse was off. There had been no other sound, no other movement from the thicket, but the tension inside the skittish horse had finally boiled over, and the mare fled away, hoofs pounding, digging deep into the path and throwing clumps of earth high into the air behind it.

Denison tugged at the reins, his legs stiff against the stirrups, his body thrown backwards in an attempt to control the chestnut's gallop. But the terror in the animal was stronger than the pull of its master's hands. Low branches came dangerously near Denison's face as the horse sped along the churned-up path, and he decided to let his mount have its head, to run itself out, to disperse its energy until its strength – and will – was more controllable.

They cleared the trees and Denison silently thanked God; open grassland was before them. The horse left the path and headed into the lush fields, the keeper praying that it would not step into a rut or a hole and break its leg. And possibly, his neck.

He tugged at the reins again and sensed some of the excitement leaving the horse now that it was out on open ground.

'Whoa, girl! Stop now, girl! Whoa, Bettina!' Denison tried not to shout the words, but it was hard to keep the urgency, the near-panic, from them.

A sudden dip caused the horse to stumble, but it managed to keep its feet, though one leg twisted badly. It staggered forward, the impetus of its wild gallop carrying its powerful body onwards; but the sudden check in speed threw the head keeper forward, almost over the beast's head. He clutched desperately at the long neck, his legs losing their grip on Bettina's flanks, his body slipping from the saddle. He was fortunate, for his feet touched the earth while he was still supported by the horse's neck. He clung to the horse, his riding boots scraping through the long grass, and his weight slowed the animal down even more. It came to a gradual halt, body twitching and eyes rolling, froth foaming from nostrils and mouth. Bettina's body gleamed with sweat as she tried to pull her neck free of the man.

'Steady, steady, girl,' Denison gasped, relieved to be still in one piece.

He let his legs take his full weight and continued to talk soothingly to the horse, stroking its head, calming it.

It proved difficult to settle Bettina, though, and from the way the animal favoured one leg, Denison realized it had injured an ankle. He rested his own head against Bettina's, telling her it was all right now, nothing could harm her, when a movement on a grassy slope not too far away caught his eye.

His face jerked away from the horse and he stared towards the hillock. He rubbed a hand across his eyes in disbelief and stared even harder. But the vision had gone.

'I'll be damned,' he said in a hushed breath.

There should have been no deer in this part of the forest – they were kept in a special compound on the other side, near Theydon Bois, where they were safe, away from cars, away from people. They were precious creatures to the forest, especially now in the rutting season. The numbers had been reduced so drastically over the past fifty years, that special measures had been taken to protect them. It was odd enough to see a deer running loose nowadays, but this was even more strange. It had been thirty years since a white buck had been seen in Epping.

And the superstitions and folklore of the forest were entrenched deeply enough in Denison for him to feel uneasy. He knew the sudden appearance of a white deer was a bad omen.

2

The car began to reduce speed as it approached the entrance to the laboratories, the driver easing his foot from the accelerator and using his gears rather than brakes to slow the vehicle. Crisp fallen leaves had scattered across the road's surface and, as the car turned into the long winding driveway that led through the trees up to the huge red-brick building, they formed a patterned surface on the road.

It was a pleasant location for a company involved in the control and destruction of pests, Lucas Pender mused as he kept the Audi down to the authorized speed limit. Deep in the heart of Surrey, surrounded by ten acres of lawns, fields and woodland, it would have made an ideal home for retired generals, or perhaps a health farm. It was difficult to guess from the building's appearance that its main function was the investigation of new methods in rodent destruction. Ratkill, the company he worked for, was involved in other operations, the building itself containing various divisions which handled woodworm and dry rot elimination, damp proofing, insulation, wood preservation and hygiene, manufacturing its own products for these particular markets; but the business it was renowned for, and the business that was responsible for its incredible growth over the past few years, was the extermination of rats. The massacres perpetrated by rats in London four years before had made companies such as this a growth industry. Ratkill had become the biggest and most reputable.

At the time of the Outbreak, as it had become known, Pender was an entomologist researching for a company dealing mainly with wood preservation. He had produced various papers on insect life, which was good for prestige, and contributed material for an encyclopaedia publisher, which was good for the pocket. His company had been based in Huddersfield at that time, so he had been fortunate to have missed the nightmarish invasion of London and the consequent evacuation. The rodents, a new breed of monster Black rats, had finally been gassed, rooted from their underground lairs by the use of ultrasonic machinery and, apart from a few more minor skirmishes with those that had somehow escaped the gas, the threat had appeared to be over. But it had proved difficult to convey that to the public at large, for the disease transmitted by rat-bite had meant death for hundreds. And the memory of those torn to pieces by the vermin was impossible to erase.

The government inquiry had laid the blame squarely on the shoulders of the ministry involved and as the minister directly responsible had himself been killed by the rats, the outcry had been neatly directed towards his negligence. No chances would ever be taken again: all sewers, underground rail tunnels, cellars, storage units were inspected, fumigated, and those thought to be a high risk potential, demolished. It was a massive operation and cost the ratepayers millions, but no one complained. The horror of it all had been too great.

Perversely, the greatest sigh of relief came when the first Brown rat was discovered. Always enemies to the Black and, until then, the dominant species, they had been ousted by the new breed of *Rattus rattus*, the Black rat, for these had become not only more powerful, but more cunning too. The return of the Brown rat was a good sign, for it meant the Black really had been vanquished. And, of course, these lesser creatures could be more easily dealt with.

The rodent companies had flourished, for it had become law that any signs of vermin had to be reported to the local council immediately, and they had the power to quarantine and investigate. The Ministry of Agriculture and the Department of the Environment worked hand-in-hand with the various control companies, but Ratkill had the biggest government contract, thanks to the determined efforts of Stephen Howard, a young researcher for Ratkill at the time of the Outbreak who had played a large part in the final defeat of the rats. He had made many friends in government circles at the time of the siege, impressing them with his drive and knowledge of the subject, and Pender suspected that his special contacts within the ministries had contributed more to his rise in the ranks of the Ratkill organization than his skills as a biologist and administrator.

Nevertheless, they were old friends from student days, Pender, at thirty-one, a year older than Howard. They had both studied zoology at university, but had lost close contact on leaving, going their separate ways and into different fields. A phone call now and again, a meeting once a year – that was all their relationship had boiled down to. But soon after the Outbreak, when the city had been cleared of infestation and life had returned to normal, they had made contact and Howard invited Pender down to London. By then Howard was Ratkill's Director of Research and business was booming because of a large government contract, and other countries were also plying Ratkill with commissions, for the fear in England had spread worldwide. Howard needed good men, fast, and Pender had his own reasons for wanting to join the organization. Within five weeks he had become what was known as a 'troubleshooter' for Ratkill, a rodent investigator. The public term was 'rat-catcher'. A high salary came with the job, for it now had an element of danger to it, and it hadn't taken Pender long to absorb the techniques concerning the tracing and destruction of vermin. He studied the animal itself, its life cycle, habits, preferences, and he learned of the various poisons used to eradicate them.

In the first year of his working for the company, only three groups of Black rats were discovered and these had been quickly and easily dealt with. No one was sure how they had resisted the ultrasonic soundwaves that should have drawn them into the gas-filled enclosures, but it was assumed they had been trapped somewhere below ground at the time the beams were emitted. It was a relief to everyone that the rats' normal reproduction rate had been hindered, for the sound-wave machine had inflicted a particularly heavy stress on the mother rats, causing their breasts to run dry, which resulted in the starvation of new-born rodents. The groups found were old and half-starved, and those captured alive soon died. It was the theory of many biologists that their brain cells had been permanently damaged by the high-frequency sound-waves, and this had upset their normal bodily functions. It seemed a reasonable assumption.

The startling fact about this new, now vanquished, breed was that they were a mutation. It seemed a zoologist, William Bartlett Schiller, had illegally brought back a rat – it may have been several, no one was sure – from an island near New Guinea. An island that had been used for nuclear tests. Their lair had been discovered in the cellar of an old house near London's dockland, a house that had been owned by the zoologist when he was alive. He had allowed the creature – or creatures – to breed with the normal Ship rat, or Black rat, as it was commonly called, introducing a new strain. Papers written by Schiller dealing with radiation effects and mutations were found in his study as well as drawings of dissected animals. The facts of the matter had been well-documented by the media and even the government inquiry findings were published in their entirety, yet ... Yet even in his many subsequent talks with Stephen Howard, Pender had felt something was being withheld.

He left the Audi in the estate's car park and entered the red-brick building, waving to the receptionist as he passed her desk.

'How was Cheshire?' she asked.

'Chilly,' he replied with a grin. 'Is Stephen Howard in his office?'

'Yes, but he won't be for long. A party is coming down from the Ministry of Agriculture and he'll be showing them around the laboratories before taking them off to lunch.'

'Right, I'll try and catch him before they arrive.'

Pender climbed the stairs and walked down the long corridor leading towards the back of the building, Windows overlooking the grounds were on one side and office doors on the other. The clatter of a typewriter greeted him as he approached an open doorway.

'Hello, Jean, is he in?' he asked, entering the office.

Howard's secretary looked up from her typewriter and gave Pender a beaming smile.

'Hello, Luke. How was your trip?'

'Okay,' he replied, non-committally. He inclined his head towards the door of the Research Director's office and raised his eyebrows.

'Oh, no,' said Jean. 'He's gone down to the laboratories to make sure everything's shipshape. We've got a visit from . . .'

'I know – the Min of Agro.'

She nodded.

'I'll just dump my briefcase then I'll find him. He wanted to see me, I believe.'

'Yes, he did. He's got another trip lined up for you.'

'Christ, I've only just got back. I've got to make out this last report yet.'

'It's only a quick job, I think, Luke,' the secretary said.

Pender sighed. 'I suppose I should be grateful for that. How's the boyfriend?'

'Around,' she said. 'I'm free for lunch.'

He walked to the door and grinned. 'I'll let you know,' he said, then ducked around the doorway to avoid the pencil hurled at him. He chuckled as he retraced his steps down the corridor, wincing at the one-word abuse that followed him.

He found two of his colleagues in the large office he shared with Ratkill's troubleshooter unit. Two were out in different parts of the country investigating pest complaints and the sixth had resigned the month before, sick to death of 'hairy little beasts'.

The two men, one an entomologist like himself, the other a biologist, waved their greetings and continued pounding at their typewriters. They, too, hated the paperwork involved in their job, but realized the only way to clear it was to get on with it. Pender opened his briefcase, took out several papers bearing his scribbled notes and placed them on his desk. Then he left the office and went off in search of Stephen Howard.

He walked through the downstairs laboratories, occasionally stopping to look into cages at the captive rats and mice. Many looked drowsy, for they were slowly being dosed with various poisons to gauge their reactions. Others seemed active and bright-eyed, pushing their quivering snouts through the thin metal bars, eager to be free. Pender glanced at several ultrasonic generators grouped together on a bench at one side of the laboratory. These had been sent by manufacturers from all over the world, keen to have Ratkill's seal of approval on their product. Most of them worked on the principle of driving vermin away from buildings rather than drawing them in, and the manufacturers claimed they were invaluable for clearing factories, shops and any other buildings with a pest problem.

He joined a technician at the bench who was carefully examining the inside workings of a machine.

'Any good?' Pender enquired.

The technician looked up with a start. 'Oh, hello, Mr Pender. Didn't see you.' He bent his head low to get a better look inside the machinery. 'No, none of them seems to do much. Their frequency's too low, really. I thought this Japanese model might be effective because it's got variable range and, at the top end, quite a high sound pressure. But the rats get used to even that after a while.'

'What area does it cover?'

'About 3,000 square feet. It has an intermittent transmitter which confuses the rats for a while. Eighteen kilohertz is the frequency the buggers hate most, but that's a bit unpleasant for the likes of me and you, too. The trouble with rats is that they adapt too fast, so even that frequency doesn't bother them too much after a time.'

'But it works for a limited period.'

The technician nodded. 'For a short time, yes.'

'And the ultrasonic machine that attracts them?'

'Same thing. It worked in London that time because it hadn't been used before – the rats had no chance to grow accustomed to the sound. It was just as well they were all killed first time round.'

'A few escaped.'

'Not enough to worry about. And they were soon finished off.'

'But if they had lived and continued to breed, they might have developed some resistance to the soundwaves?'

'It's a possibility.'

Pender shuddered inwardly. All things considered, London had had a narrow escape.

'Is Mr Howard around here somewhere?'

'He came down with Mr Lehmann about twenty minutes ago. They've gone out the back, over to the pens.'

Pender left the technician to his work and made for the laboratory's exit. He carefully closed the door behind him, then entered a long shed-like structure which had a 'Danger – Poisons in use' sign on the door. He walked through the building, the smell of straw and rat droppings pungent in his nostrils, occasionally seeing a dark streaking body in the enclosures on either side of the gangway. Feed-hoppers containing various compounds mixed with food were placed at strategic positions inside the enclosures, each a different attractant for the rat whose sensitivity towards odd flavours or odours made pre-baiting – encouraging the rodent to eat a certain food over a period of time before the lethal poison was administered – a difficult operation. The attractant compound most favoured by the rodents would be a valuable aid in their destruction.

The building was empty of humans and he assumed that Howard and Mike Lehmann, the laboratory's Chief Biologist, had gone through to the outside pens. He was glad to leave the shed; it was filled with the smell of death. A gravel path led him towards a garden area, then on to a grassy field beyond. He saw the figures of the two men ahead, both peering into a wide rat pen.

They turned at his approach and Lehmann, at least, looked pleased to see him. Because of their working relationship, Howard and Pender's friendship had cooled somewhat. Pender, Howard thought, sometimes forgot he was working *for* the Director of Research and not *alongside* him.

'Hello, Luke,' he said.

'Stephen, Mike,' Pender acknowledged.

'How'd it go, Luke?' Lehmann asked, enthusiastic for discussion as ever. By rights, Mike Lehmann should have become Director of Research, for he was a good deal older than Howard and had been at Ratkill for more than fifteen years. However he seemed to show no outward resentment towards the younger man, the man he had engaged in the first place, but every so often, Pender noticed a certain disdainful tone in his voice when arguing a particular technical point with his superior.

'Well, they're Warfarin-resistant all right,' Pender said, leaning against the fence surrounding the enclosure. 'No doubt about it.'

'So it's spreading?' Howard asked anxiously.

Pender looked at the Research Director and, not for the first time, was surprised at the way age seemed to be forcing its way into Howard's features. No, it was more that Howard *himself* was forcing age into his features, almost as if the added years would make him seem more appropriate for the position he held. The thinning hair was severely brushed back and a fine, blond moustache adorned his upper lip. Even the glasses he wore were heavy and unattractive. All you need now is a pipe, thought Pender, then directed his attention back to the question.

'Yes, it's certainly spreading. Montgomeryshire, Shropshire, Nottinghamshire, Gloucestershire and Kent used to be the only areas where rats resistant to the poison could be found – apart from a couple of places in Denmark and Holland, of course.'

'And our own labs,' Howard interjected.

'Yes, but they were specially bred to be resistant. These creatures acquire the resistance naturally. Anyway, they're in Cheshire now and a few weeks ago I found several groups in Devon.'

'But they were not the Black rat?' Howard looked almost hopeful.

'No, just the common Brown. No monsters there, but I think we'll soon need to find some new poisons if we're going to control them.'

Pender looked down at the earth around the concrete base of the fence. 'Someone trying to get in?' he asked, pointing at the burrows that had been dug.

'Yes, the wild rats from the fields,' Lehmann told him. 'They know there's plenty of food in there so they try to join their tame chums inside. Life as a prisoner can be a luxury. The concrete goes two feet down, though, so they can't get under.'

'I'm going to need your report as soon as possible,' said Howard. 'I've got the ministry people arriving at any moment – it's a pity I haven't got your findings to show them. The problem appears to require some more government investment.' He looked slightly miffed that the ratcatcher was unable to hand over his typed report there and then.

Pender smiled pleasantly. 'It took some time to gather in the facts, Stephen. I didn't think you'd want any wild assumptions.'

'No, no, of course not. I'm sorry, Luke. I didn't want to sound impatient, but it could affect the direction we take over the next few years.'

'Well, I don't think machines are going to be the answer.'

It was Lehmann who spoke and from his brusque tone, Pender guessed it was a point of conflict between the two men.

'Now you can't say that, Mike.' Howard did not try to disguise the irritation he felt. 'New generators are being sent to us all the time, and each seems to be an improvement on the last.'

'I know our Products Division has been spending a lot of time on it, using the best ideas from other manufacturers.'

The Research Director's face flushed angrily. 'We are in this business to make money you know, Mike. If we come up with a competent machine, then the government will make a substantial investment to mass-produce them.'

'That's if they ever will be really effective. What do you think, Luke, poisons or ultrasonic sound machines?'

Pender was not eager to be drawn into the argument, especially on a subject to which he didn't have the answer.

'I don't know, Mike. With our poisons beginning to fail, generators might be the only way. I think there has to be more study into the rat's communication system itself, though. We know they produce ultrasonics themselves and use echo-location for orientation, so there may be a way of using a machine against them rather than just trying to disrupt their endocrine system.'

'But alpha-chloralose, coumatetralyl and chlorophacinone haven't been fully tested against them yet,' Lehmann said.

'No, but they will be,' Howard interrupted. 'At the moment, we're exploring all avenues. Look, when can I have your report, Luke?'

'I could have started work on it today, but Jean tells me you've got another little "trip" in store for me.'

'What? Oh yes, I'd forgotten. Sorry, I would have sent one of the others, but Kempson and Aldridge are both making out their reports for me, and Macrae and Nolan are in the north. You're the only one available.'

'It's all right, I don't mind. What's the problem?'

'There's a Conservation Centre on the other side of London. They've seen evidence of rats around the place and the ordinary rodenticides don't seem to have had much effect. They don't think it's anything to worry about, but as the law says it has to be reported, they've done so. I'd like you to go out there today.'

'Surely you don't need me to investigate. Couldn't the local council do it?'

'I'm afraid not. London is still a sensitive area and our contract with the Ministry states that we'll send in an expert to look into any rodent problems within thirty miles of the city.'

'Why didn't they call us before they started messing around with poisons?' Lehmann said in an annoyed voice. 'That's how this whole Warfarin-resistance business started – amateurs not administering the right dosage, letting the rats build up a defence against it.'

'They didn't consider it a big enough problem. They still don't, but they're playing safe.'

'Just where is this Conservation Centre?' Pender asked. 'I've never heard of one that close to London.'

'It's been there some time,' Howard replied. 'It's in the green belt area, the woodland that starts somewhere on the outer fringes of East London. Epping Forest.'

3

The Reverend Jonathan Matthews watched the two men filling in the grave and mentally said his own personal prayer for the deceased. His was an unusual parish, for most of its members were forest people. The term could be used lightly; very few actually worked in the forest itself. The great woodland was surrounded on all sides by suburbia, the forest fringes cut dead by bricks and mortar. Less than ten miles away was the city's centre where better paid employment could be found. Some still worked the land, but they were few and far between, the work being arduous and offering little reward. Several forest keepers and their families attended his church at High Beach and he welcomed their patronage. They were a breed of their own, these forest minders, as he preferred to call them. Stern men, most of them, almost Victorian in their attitudes; but their commitment to the woodland and its animals was admirable. He felt their harshness came from the very harshness of nature itself; their open-air existence, whatever weather prevailed, and the constant struggle to maintain the correct balance in forest life despite its location, had given them a dourness which few people understood.

The Church of the Holy Innocents was ancient, its grey-stoned steeple badly in need of repair. A small building, its size adding to the historic charm, it was seldom filled to capacity. The Reverend Matthews had presided as vicar for more years than he cared to remember, and he deeply regretted the loss of a stalwart parishioner such as Mrs Wilkinson. At seventy-eight, she had been one of his more active church members, never missing Sunday service and always attending Morning Prayer; her work for the needy of the parish even in her latter years had been a shining example of true Christianity.

The funeral ceremony an hour before had been well attended, for Mrs Wilkinson had been a much-loved character in the community, but now the small graveyard adjoining the church was empty apart from himself and the two grave-diggers. Their shovels dug into the soft mound of earth beside the open grave with dull thuds and the soil falling onto the coffin lid caused a shiver to run through the vicar's thin body. It had the sound of finality. It represented the end of life in this world, and no matter how much he told his flock of the glorious life to come after, he, himself, was afraid.

The doubts had come of late. His faith had once been unshakeable, his love for humanity unscathed through all the bitter times. Now, at the time when his own life was drawing towards its concluding years, be they five or fifteen, his mind was troubled. He had thought he understood, or at least accepted, the gross cruelties of the world, but his body had become fragile, and his faith with it. It was said man was reaching a new point in civilization, yet the atrocities continued and, if possible, seemed more hideous than before. His personal trials had been overcome but, rather than strengthening his spiritual self, had progressively undermined it, leaving him vulnerable, exposed. A question often asked of him by grieving parishioners was how could God allow such madness? His answer that no one understood the ways of

God, but ultimately they were just, had given them little comfort; and now it gave him little comfort.

Those such as Mrs Wilkinson and his dear departed wife, Dorothy, would surely find their spiritual reward, for they epitomized the goodness that still existed. But the heavy sound of earth on wood somehow diminished the ideal; it gave death a stark reality. What if their God wasn't as they thought? He wiped a hand across his forehead, swaying slightly. His parishioners must never know of his doubts – they needed his firm guidance. His misgivings were his secret and he would overcome them with prayer. The years had taken their toll, that was all. He would regain his old beliefs, vanquish the sinful questions, and soon. Before he died.

The two workmen were breathing heavily by now, their task almost completed. He turned away, not wanting to gaze at the shallow indent, death's seal of earth, and looked around at the quiet, sunny graveyard. The constant rustle of the surrounding trees was more comforting than the sounds of the gravediggers. But he was in a depressed mood and he wondered if it was this that made the forest seem so oppressive. The vicar felt he was being watched. Or was he merely exhausted mentally? Could that be why there seemed to be dozens of eyes watching from the shadows beneath the leafy trees, stripping away his façade, looking deep into his guilt?

He shook his head, knowing he had to repress this dreadful feeling before it broke him. Yet the forest did have a different atmosphere lately. None of his parishioners mentioned it, but he had caught certain looks in the eyes of the forest keepers. An uneasiness as they studied the undergrowth.

He searched the distant foliage and tried to penetrate the dark areas. Was that a movement? No, just a fern stirred by the breeze. He had to snap out of this destructive mood, had to get a grip on himself. Epping Forest and its inhabitants were his life. He loved the forest. Why then did it seem so menacing?

Brian Mollison was a broad-shouldered, deep-chested, thick-thighed man of forty who hated his mother and detested the children he taught. If he had married – if his mother had *allowed* him to marry – he might well have overcome his problem. Love and sexual fulfilment might have smothered or at least diverted his unnatural inclination. But not necessarily.

It had started in his late 'teens and he had managed to keep his odd tendency to himself. Lonely, quiet places – places free of people – were best, because then there was no danger. As the years went by he found it wasn't enough. Something was missing. Then he discovered exactly what that something was, and it was, of course, the danger. Or, more precisely, the excitement of danger.

His problem was that he liked to expose his body, or again, more precisely, his genital area. Exposing himself to the elements in secluded places sufficed at first, but exposing himself to people proved to be much more thrilling. He discovered this one day at a new school in which he had been appointed games master. His mother – stupid cow – had neglected to mend the elastic in the trousers of his tracksuit and when he had demonstrated to the boys – it was a boys' school – just how to jump into the air from a squatting position thirty times without a break, the trousers had slipped to his knees revealing all to the delighted pupils.

It could have been the beginning of a persecuted career – at least in that particular school – but he had cracked down hard on them. His rage had been more to cover his embarrassment than real anger at the boys, for he realized after he had whipped up his trousers again that his body was responding to the secret pleasure he had experienced. It was just as well the tracksuit was a loose-fitting, baggy garment. Whether he would have been just as nasty to the boys and his future pupils had the incident not occurred was debatable for he was already of an unpleasant disposition, and if his mother hadn't loved him, then he would have been unloved.

Through the years he was very careful with his perversion, for he needed the job as PE instructor to keep himself and his semi-invalid mother – silly bitch – and the slightest hint that he might be in any way *peculiar* would mean an abrupt end to his career. Not that *he* considered himself peculiar. It was more of a hobby.

To stand on a crowded tube train in the rush-hour wearing his loose-fitting raincoat, the one that had bottomless pockets, would almost make him faint with excitement. The thrill of knowing that only a thin layer of material separated his monumentally erect organ from the female body crushed up against him would make his knees grow weak. It was his breathing he had to control. They often realized what was happening – the rod of iron pressure against them could hardly be mistaken for anything else – but they usually just flushed with embarrassment and moved away at the next stop, or turned to give him a scathing look which he returned with a stalwart stare. His hard features – the short-cropped hair, the heavy jaw, the nose twisted slightly from his boxing days – always won the day. He wasn't a man to be tackled lightly.

Cinemas were good, sitting there in the dark with his trousers gaping, his raincoat across his lap ready to be slid aside at odd moments.

Public lavatories he didn't care for too much. He'd tried standing there at an urinal, penis in hand, but the presence of other men engaged in the same activity, whether devious or normal, disturbed him too much. Twice he'd been approached and that really frightened him.

Railway platforms were good if he could find a solitary woman on a lonely bench. To stand in front of them and watch their bodies freeze with fear was extremely pleasant, then, to slowly unflap his raincoat was a joy beyond compare. Of course, he had to make a quick getaway, but that was half the fun. That really set the heart pounding.

He would never try it in a railway carriage again, though. It had been quite a successful pastime for a while, changing carriages at each stop until he found one occupied by a lone female. They were usually shocked rigid and he always jumped off at the next stop before they had a chance to raise the alarm. But one night, the startled passenger had had bloody hysterics! He'd nearly jumped out the window in fright! Pleading hadn't prevented her from tugging at the communication cord, and falling on top of her when the train had lurched to a grinding halt hadn't soothed the situation. She'd really panicked then. He could still hear those shrill screams ringing in his ears to this day! Christ, it was no wonder some of them got bloody murdered.

He'd had to jump from the compartment there and then, hurting his knee as he'd stumbled in the dark. He was lucky he hadn't been knocked down by a passing train! He'd managed to escape, but it had been a long walk home because he hadn't dared use British Rail again that night. He hadn't gone out for a fortnight after that. He'd been too shaken. Mother – sodding bag – had fussed and fretted and wanted to get the doctor in, thinking he was really ill, but he'd told her he was only run down, and that a few days in bed would soon put him right again. When the recuperation period stretched into the second week she'd reverted to her usual quaveryvoiced nagging, and in the end he had been relieved to go back to school. Sometimes he wondered where such a frail little woman found the energy for such unceasing ranting. And sometimes he wondered if she suspected something. He'd caught her giving him strange looks lately. No, she couldn't know. He'd always been careful, always scrubbed the inside of his raincoat after each trip. She was just getting older and more senile, that was all. Afraid he might leave her.

The incident had made him more cautious than ever and after that he avoided enclosed places where he might possibly be trapped. Epping Forest became his most invigorating haunt.

He was surprised he hadn't used it as a location in his earlier years; it was such a natural. There were so many lonely spots where foolish women strolled with their dogs, or young girls rode on horseback, or children played football; and there was so much undergrowth to hide in, so many trees to skulk behind. You had to keep a wary eye out for the forest keepers of course – some of them didn't even wear uniforms – and police cars often patrolled the quiet lanes. But a man in a tracksuit was hardly a suspicious character in such an open environment. It was a perfect place for his particular activity, a paradise for flashers. And it was healthy, too.

He had left his car, a battered Morris 1100, in an area just off the main road, the drive from their small, terraced house in Leytonstone not taking much more than ten minutes or so. It was his afternoon off from school and he had decided to take advantage of the clement weather: standing around in the pouring rain and exposing your organs to the cold wasn't much fun. Bad weather also made it more difficult to find a viewer and just doing it on your own took away much of the joy. He had caught a bad chill last winter.

Today was a good day for picnickers and strollers because it was a weekday. There wouldn't be many sightseers around, but there was always the bored housewife with her non-schoolable offspring to be found. It just required a little patience.

He drew in a sharp breath as he realized that his patience was about to be rewarded. In the distance, strolling casually and quite alone, was the figure of a woman. The stretch between them was open grassland, but she was using a path that led towards the trees. He knew the path and was aware it ran through a heavily wooded area. If he was fast he could skirt the edge of the open grassland, duck into the woods and reach a secluded point in the trail ahead of her; and at times like this, or when running away, he could be very fast. He sprinted off, his aroused penis acting as a pointer.

Making his way as swiftly and quietly as possible through the trees and undergrowth, Mollison kept well away from the path itself. If she heard him or caught sight of his running figure, she might turn back. When he judged he was some distance ahead of her he cut back towards the track at a slower and more cautious pace, quickly finding an ideal spot. The path widened into a relatively large clearing, several other paths leading off from it. He could hide in the bushes opposite the point where she would emerge and catch her completely unawares. Perfect! He crouched in the bushes, gasping for breath after his hard-paced run, and was disappointed to discover that his erection had become somewhat subdued. A little manipulation soon corrected that matter, but his breathing became even more laboured.

His lungs had settled down to a heavier but more steady rhythm by the time she came into view. He drew in an excited breath: this was more than he had hoped for – she was a good-looker! Although she was still some distance away he could see she had a good figure, rounded but not plump, short brown hair, nicely shaped ankles. In her late-twenties, early thirties? Hard to tell at this distance, but certainly not older. He was sure she was pretty.

The woman had reached the edge of the clearing now and, for some reason, she paused. Had she seen him? No, not possible – his cover was too good. She was looking to her left, slightly ahead of her, and seemed to be listening. Bloody hell, she was good-looking! This was an added bonus: it wasn't often you found a stunner. He couldn't afford to waste this one; he decided to give her the full works.

Trying to control his rising excitement, he pulled the tracksuit top over his head and lay it on the ground behind him. He peered through the bushes and saw she was coming forward again. He licked his lips and cleared his throat of juices. She stopped again and this time he, too, heard the rustle of undergrowth from a point to her left. Mollison frowned and tried to see into the thicket. Must be an animal in there. Come on, you silly cow, it can't hurt you! He tugged at the trousers of his tracksuit, pulling them down his legs, the elasticated bottoms catching at the heels of his plimsolls. Sod it! he said to himself. No time to work them free, she'll be off down another path in a minute!

His whole body was trembling now, a light sheen of perspiration covering his well-developed muscles. He began to rise but suddenly fell back, his trousers tangled in a root. Spiky leaves scratched at his buttocks and he pushed himself up, ignoring the sharp jabs as his hands were prickled by brittle foliage, knowing she must have heard him by now.

He leapt from the hiding-place, his arms outstretched and legs out as far as his fallen trousers would allow, a wide grin on his face and pelvis thrust forward, all in an announcement of his enlarged organ.

But she was gone. He just caught sight of her retreating figure as she scurried off down the path.

His surprise gave way to disappointment and then to resentment and frustration. He looked down bitterly at his fast-shrinking member and swore. She couldn't have reacted that fast to the noise he'd made when he'd stumbled! Then he heard the other sound again and realized it came from the same spot as before. The bushes were rustling as though something was moving through them. Oh Christ, there was someone else hiding in there.

He hoisted his trousers, hastily retrieved the jacket, and ran off in the opposite direction.

The children called excitedly to each other as they lowered their long-stemmed nets into the murky water. It wasn't very often that their school organized a day out at Epping Forest's Conservation Centre, so it was a special treat for them. All under eleven years of age, not many truly appreciated the lessons on the woodland's abounding wildlife taught by the Centre, but with the ever-growing threat to the natural environment, it was judged to be a worthy aim to instil in them a respect for nature rather than a deep knowledge of it. That was why the Centre was prefixed with the title 'Conservation' and not 'Nature'. Outside pressure from primary schools and colleges whose pupils attended the Centre meant lessons had to be orientated towards future examinations, but the tutors' main purpose was still to make the children more ecologically aware.

Jenny Hanmer was one of the Centre's four tutors, and it was her class that had gathered around one side of the water's edge. Because a whole section of the pond was overshadowed by the forest, the bottom was choked with dead leaves covered with a purple scum due to sulphur bacteria, making its depths very dark and its vegetation restricted to algae and a few clumps of starwort. Nevertheless, the oxygen-scarce water still contained many forms of life: water-lice, tubifex worms and blood worms; mosquito larvae and rat-tailed maggots; pond skaters, water crickets and water beetles. Jenny had described all these creatures to the children in the classroom. Now she wanted her pupils to discover them for themselves in the much bigger, outdoor classroom. It was exciting for them to 'fish' in this way and even more fun when they studied their samples under a microscope back at the Centre.

'Careful now,' Jenny called out to one adventurous nine-year-old whose name she didn't remember, and who was stretching out precariously over the water in order to net an interesting looking insect. She regretted never getting to really know her pupils individually, but it was almost impossible with so many different schools visiting every week, each class made up of twenty-five to thirty-five children. Some of the older groups, those taking 'O' levels or CSE exams, would take longer and often concurrent day courses, and it was possible to build up something of a relationship with them; but not with the younger pupils, although she found them more fun.

'It's all right, Miss, I can reach,' the boy said, his net extended to its limit.

'Patrick, will you step back!' The sharp command came from the boy's schoolteacher, a small, round woman whose eyes never seemed to agree in which direction to look; Jenny could have sworn she was talking to a boy innocently standing well away from the pond's edge.

The guilty Patrick took a grudging step backwards, disappointment evident in his face. 'I won't be able to get it now,' he complained.

'Look,' Jenny said, pointing at a small insect skimming across the surface of the water. 'That's a water skater, the one I told you about back in the classroom. We won't be seeing much more of him now the colder weather is on its way.'

She smiled as the children followed her pointing finger with their eyes and exclaimed triumphantly when they caught sight of the swift-darting insect. It was fine to talk about such animal life in the detached atmosphere of a classroom, but it certainly added a new dimension when the children could see that life for themselves in its natural surroundings. Five nets were immediately plunged into the water to capture the startled skater.

'No, children,' Jenny said, laughing. 'We're looking for algae. Remember I told you about the rootless, flowerless plant? Volvox is what we're after. Let's see if you can spot it.'

The children stopped tormenting the insect which had the sense to head towards the centre of the pond.

'Come on, boys and girls, do as Miss Hanmer says,' their stray-eyed teacher said heartily. She clapped her hands as if to emphasize the command and the giggling children scattered around the pond's muddy bank.

'Keep to this side!' Jenny called out anxiously.

'Keep to this side!' their teacher instructed.

'Thank you, Miss Bellingham,' said Jenny, inwardly amused. 'They're very well behaved.'

Miss Bellingham gave a small, self-conscious laugh, both eyes defiant of one another as they singly followed the children running off in different directions. 'You have to keep them under control, mind.'

Jenny nodded, blinking and shifting her gaze from the teacher's undisciplined eyes. 'They seem to enjoy coming out here,' she said.

'Oh, yes, it's a great lark for them!' Miss Bellingham

quickly realized her slip. 'And so *educational*,' she added. 'How long have you been with the Conservation Centre, Miss Hanmer?'

Jenny had to think hard; the time had flown by. 'Nearly a year, I think. Yes, about eight months. I was with the Juniper Hall Field Centre in Dorking before.'

'It must be a lovely life, my dear. *Very* interesting,' Miss Bellingham enthused.

'It is, most of the time. I had planned to be a geologist, but I somehow got sidetracked into ecology. I'm not complaining, though.' Jenny dug her hands into her loose-fitting cardigan and looked around, checking that the children hadn't got into any awkward situations.

Miss Bellingham was about to ask another question, her interest aroused by the attractive young tutor, wondering why she should choose what seemed to her an almost monastic existence at the Centre, when a shout from their left distracted her attention.

'Look, Miss, look over there!' One of the children, a coloured boy, was pointing towards the shaded side of the pond. 'What's them?'

Jenny and Miss Bellingham looked towards the spot, the rotund teacher's eyes swivelling past and taking several seconds to settle back onto a moving object in the water. 'What is it, Miss Hanmer?'

Jenny wasn't sure for a moment; she moved further down the bank for a closer look.

'There's three of 'em, Miss,' shouted the sharp-eyed boy.

At first the tutor thought they might be water-vole, but remembered that voles usually swam beneath the surface, and rarely in a group like this. These swam in an arrowhead formation.

As they entered a sun-lit area, she saw only their long,

pointed heads above the surface, the water barely disturbed by their progress. They ignored the excited clamouring of the children and continued on their way, making for the bank on Jenny's left. The boy who had first seen the creatures picked up a thick piece of rotted bark and hurled it towards the centre of the pond, a point just reached by the three animals.

'Darren, you naughty boy!' Miss Bellingham was outraged by the youth's action. Jenny felt a good clout from the teacher might be appropriate. She quickly turned her attention away from the culprit and back to the pond. The bark had landed with a loud splash directly in front of the animals and she was relieved none had been hit. They had merely changed direction and were now heading for the shadowed bank directly opposite.

Their sleek, black heads glided through the murky water at an almost leisurely pace and Jenny's eyes widened as they emerged on the other side. She recognized the creatures, but something told her she must be wrong. They were too big. The long, black-haired bodies, shiny with water, were far too large for rats!

Their tails, slimy and grey-pink, slivered from the water behind them and the tutor suddenly felt repulsed: the tails alone must have been a foot long. Without waiting to shake themselves free of water, two of the creatures disappeared smoothly into the gloom. The third, the one that had been leading, turned to face the group across the pond. It squatted there and Jenny shuddered as she felt herself being observed. Several of the children began to cry and the young tutor knelt down to comfort the nearest.

When she looked up again, her attention diverted for no more than a few seconds, the rat – if the creature had been a rat – was gone. The forest, and the pond, were perfectly still.

4

Pender pushed his foot down hard on the accelerator pedal, glad to be free of the city again. The journey from the Ratkill laboratories in Surrey had taken him through London's vehicle-choked centre and the constant frustration of stopping, starting, waiting, avoiding, had made his mood grim. Although he didn't regret moving back down to the south again he often missed the more open country of the north. Huddersfield had provided a splendid base for trips into the surrounding counties, and, although he was city-bred, he appreciated their coarse beauty. Perhaps the people-crowded years had heightened his respect for the countryside's seclusion. The car gathered speed and, as the woods on his left thickened, so he began to relax. Soon it was woodland on both sides of the road.

Pender knew the area, but not too well. The Epping New Road ran straight through the forest, but he would have to turn off onto one of the quieter roads branching into the forest itself. The car was doing seventy-five when he slowed for the roundabout ahead. He saw the sign for High Beach and swung into the narrow winding road leading from the roundabout. The trees almost met overhead, the bright sun sparkling through dying leaves, and he felt the last ounces of tension drain away. Another narrow road to his right took him past a small church into a slightly wider road, and then the scenery opened out as if the car had been squeezed through a funnel.

The high ground fell away to his left down into a vast green valley, its lower slopes filled with trees of every kind, stretching for miles into the distance. Beyond them Pender could see the hazy suburbs, glints of sunlight reflected here and there off glass surfaces. He stopped the car for a moment to take in the vista, feeling heady with its abrupt freshness. Driving along the winding road, he hadn't realized the swift ascent the car had been making. He remembered reading once, long ago, the theory of how the rolling hills of Epping Forest had been formed. A great sheet of ice had slid down eastern England at the end of the Ice Age and split in two on a high bank north of the forest, each section scouring out two valleys on either side of the bank and, as they pushed forward like the pincers of a giant crab, the soil was squeezed between them into rugged contours. From his vantage point he could see the truth of the theory.

A few cars were parked on a muddy area on the rim of the valley, their occupants gazing out at the view through windscreens, as though to leave their metal cocoons and make contact with fresh air would shrivel their bodies. Pender drove on, looking for a sign which would tell him the location of the Conservation Centre.

A huge public house stood on his right, a lofty and cold perch at the top of the long, grassy slope, and beyond that he saw the sign pointing towards his goal. He drove down the curved road, almost doubling back in direction, and came upon the entrance to the Centre. Passing through the narrow gateposts, he found a small, gravel car park. He sat and studied his surroundings before leaving the car.

The white-bricked single-storey buildings were set in a square horseshoe shape around a close-cropped lawn, a ribbon of gravel cutting across the grass from the car park towards a glass-doored entrance to the building on his left. The low-ceilinged building had no windows – at least, not on that side – and a sign in front of him indicated it was the school section. An arrow, pointed in the same direction as the path, bore the heading: INFORMATION DESK. Directly ahead and slightly apart from the main building was a continuous row of chalet-type structures joined at right angles by a similar row leading back in his direction. They were of the same neat, functional design as the school and reception section and Pender guessed they were the staff's living quarters. Stephen Howard had briefed him on the Centre before Pender had left, explaining that the Warden, as the principal was ominously called, and his tutors were resident at the establishment. Trees loomed up darkly behind the Centre, dwarfing the buildings, making them seem more squat than they really were. He crossed the lawn, keeping to the gravel path, and entered the reception area.

The rectangular hall was cluttered with single-panelled exhibition stands displaying pictures of various animals and plants, accompanied by written information on each subject. The area was empty but there was a reception window to his right. He peered into the room beyond; a woman was at one end typing busily and a man sat reading a book at a table nearest the window. The man, youngish, intense-looking, glanced up at Pender.

'Yes, sir, can I help?' he asked.

'My name's Pender. I've come to see Mr Milton.' Pender had learned to be discreet about his profession: people were still nervous of ratcatchers.

'Oh yes. From Ratkill, aren't you?'

Pender lifted his eyebrows in surprise.

The man grinned as he got up from the desk and came

over to the window. 'It's all right, there's no secrets among the staff. I'll just see if he's in his office.'

The young man disappeared through a door and re-appeared a few seconds later.

'Yes, he's there. If you'd like to go through the door round to your right, I'll take you to his office.'

Pender followed the instructions and was met in the corridor beyond.

'I'm not sure we really need you people,' the young man said as he led the way. 'We've seen signs of vermin, but they haven't done any bad damage yet. It's just the, uh, law, you know?'

Pender nodded and went through the door which had been opened for him. The Warden of the Conservation Centre stood and offered his hand across the desk as Pender entered.

'Mr Pender? I'm Alex Milton. Didn't take Ratkill long to get someone up here, did it?'

Pender shook the proffered hand and sat in the seat opposite.

'Thank you, Will,' Milton said to the man at the door. 'I'll see you about the arrangements for tonight's lecture a little later on. Would you like some coffee, Mr Pender?'

The ratcatcher felt like something stronger after the wear-ing drive, but he smiled and said, 'Coffee'll be fine.'

'Would you mind asking Jan for me, Will?'

'Right.' Will closed the door behind him.

The two men faced each other across the desk, Milton smiling and slouched back in his seat. He seemed to have forgotten why Pender was there.

'Interesting place you have here,' the Ratkill man said, breaking the silence.

'Yes, it is,' the Warden agreed enthusiastically.

'Have you been here long as Warden?'

Milton thought for a moment, his smile still beaming. 'Just over two years, I think. The Centre itself – the Epping Forest Conservation Centre, to give it its full title – was only opened nine years ago, so it's still in its youth.' He gave a small almost embarrassed laugh. 'In fact, most of my staff are rather youthful – apart from myself and my wife, of course.'

Pender nodded politely, smiling at the man's self-deprecating humour. He hoped the Warden would soon get to the business in hand. 'Tell me about your rodent problem,' he prompted.

'Oh yes. Mustn't waste your time.' The Warden leaned forward, elbows on the desk, his face serious and his tones hushed. 'It started a couple of days ago, actually. Nothing much, just signs, you understand.'

'What kind of signs?'

'Well . . .' A light tap at the door interrupted the Warden's next words. 'Yes, come in,' he called out.

The door opened and a small, thin girl, clad in jeans and sweater, entered the room. She carried a tray bearing two coffees, milk and sugar, which she placed on the Warden's desk.

'This is Jan,' said Milton and the girl pushed her gold-framed glasses back towards the bridge of her nose, giving Pender a nervous smile.

'Jan saves our lives every day by cooking our meals and providing us with gallons of coffee,' the Warden said as Pender smiled back at the young girl. 'She's only filling in a year between school and agricultural college, actually, but I must say, she'd make an excellent chef. Perhaps we can persuade you to remain one, eh, Jan?'

The girl shook her head and said in a quiet voice, 'I don't think so, Mr Milton.' She left the room, keeping her face low to hide a blush. Pender hadn't seen a girl blush for quite some time.

'You were saying?' he said as Milton handed him a coffee from the tray.

'Saying?'

'About the rodent signs.'

'Oh, yes, forgive me. Yes, the signs. Well, we keep examples of forest wildlife in pens outside the classrooms – the children love to see the animals, you know. Rabbits, hares, squirrels – even had a fox until recently. A couple of nights ago, the pens were broken into.'

Pender poured milk into his coffee, then looked steadily at the Warden. 'Were the animals killed?'

'Good gracious, no! Nothing like that.'

Pender relaxed in his seat.

'No, it was just their food that was stolen. But the animals, when we found them next day, were in a state of shock, do you see? Absolutely terrified. Hadn't even attempted to escape through the holes in the wire left by whatever broke in.'

'It could have been anything. Maybe the fox you had before returned – it would if it knew it could find food here.'

'Oh, no, the fox died.'

'Then another.'

'Yes, it could be possible. There are about fifty foxes that we know of still living in the forest. But we found droppings, you see. And they certainly weren't those of foxes.'

'Did you keep them? Can I see them?'

'Of course you can. That's why you're here. I'll take you along to the laboratory in a moment.'

'What shape are they?'

'Roundish, spindle-shaped, I'd say.'

'Were they in groups?'

'Yes, yes. Small groups.'

Milton could read nothing in Pender's expression.

'Anything else?' the ratcatcher asked.

'We have an outhouse round at the back of the buildings where we keep the refuse. All the kitchen waste is put there. Yesterday morning we found the bottom of the door had been gnawed through.'

Pender sighed. 'Yes, rats would do that.'

'Of course. But you must understand we are in the middle of the forest and are used to night-time marauders. The Centre was built to keep out our more persistent friends. The bottom of the outhouse door is reinforced with a metal strip. A corner of the strip had been completely pulled away.'

Pender sipped his coffee.

'The metal was securely attached to the door, Mr Pender. It would have taken a crowbar for a man to tear it loose.'

'I'll have a look at it. Have you laid any poisons?'

'No, we thought that best left to you. The rule is to inform the Ministry immediately rodent signs are found. We're still not sure it's rats, of course, but we thought the two unusual events warranted investigation, don't you agree?'

Pender nodded. He placed his coffee cup back on the Warden's desk and began to rise. 'I'll look at those droppings . . .'

The loud rap at the door startled both men. It burst open without waiting for a reply from the Warden, and a young girl dressed in denims and a loose-fitting cardigan entered the room, closely followed by the man called Will. The girl looked breathless and she leaned with two hands on the Warden's desk, her long dark hair falling across her face. Milton was too surprised to speak.

'I've seen them, Mr Milton,' the girl said, trying to keep her voice calm. 'They're down by one of the ponds.'

'What are, Jenny? What are you talking about?'

'Jenny's seen the rats, Mr Milton,' Will said anxiously.

Milton glanced at him, then back at the girl. 'You have?'

'Yes, yes. I'm sure they were rats. But they were so big,' the girl said, her face earnest.

'Sit down, Jenny, and just tell us exactly what you saw.' The Warden indicated a chair opposite Pender's and as she sat, the girl noticed the ratcatcher for the first time.

'It's rather opportune, really,' Milton said. 'This is Mr Pender, Jenny. He's been sent from Ratkill. I'm sure he'd very much like to hear what you have to say. Jenny Hanmer is one of our tutors.'

Pender looked at the girl and, now that he could see her face fully, realized she was very attractive, not at all 'tutorish'. She brushed her shoulder-length hair back and gave Pender a faint smile, her mind too busy with what she had just witnessed to pay him much attention.

'Now, Jenny, tell all.' Milton smiled benignly at the tutor.

'I took my class down to the small pond – the one before you get to the Wake Valley Pond. We'd only been there a few minutes when one of the boys saw something swimming across the water. I couldn't make out what they were at first, but there were three of them.'

'Not necessarily rats, then?' said the Warden.

'We got a better look at them when they were climbing out. The boy threw something at them and they changed direction and made for the bank. We saw their whole bodies then.'

'But it is rather, er, gloomy down there, isn't it? I mean, are you sure they weren't some other animal? A water-vole would be the obvious choice.'

'That was my first thought. They were too big, though.'

'Big enough to be dogs?' said Pender. Black dogs, mistakenly taken as the giant Black rat, had caused several scares over the past few years.

'No, I'm sure they weren't,' the girl said, looking directly at Pender. 'They had long pointed heads, and their ears were long too, and pink. Their tails . . . their tails were horrible.'

'Did the children see them?'

'Yes, and their teacher, Miss Bellingham. I didn't imagine them, Mr Pender.'

'Where are the children now?' The Warden had a worried look on his face.

'I brought them back right away. Miss Bellingham's with them in Class Two. It's all right, they're not frightened; we played it down, told them they were coypus.'

Pender grinned. 'And they believed you?'

'Most of them did – it *was* rather shady down there. It's not so unlikely anyway. Coypus live mainly in Norfolk and Suffolk, so it's not improbable that some should find their way south. A few of the children were a bit doubtful, though.'

'I think I'll just go along and have a word with them,' said Milton, rising. 'We don't want them spreading false rumours about the forest until we've checked this out.'

'We may have to stop people coming into the forest anyway,' Pender said quickly.

'Stop them? That would be impossible, Mr Pender. Have you any idea how wide an area the forest covers? And what about those who live here?'

'They'd have to leave.'

'Now just a moment, let's not jump the gun. Let's find out if these monsters really do exist first.' Milton looked down apologetically at the girl. 'Not that I doubt your word at all, Jenny. It's just that you may have been mistaken.'

'I wasn't. They were rats and they were over two feet long.' The tutor's face was set firm.

'Yes, well, that's what Mr Pender is here to find out. I'll have to inform the Superintendent of the Forest, Mr Pender. No doubt he will want to see you.'

'Fine. But first I'd like you to take me back to this pond, Miss Hanmer.' All eyes turned towards Pender.

'Do you think that's wise?' asked the Warden.

'These . . . animals, whether they're rats or not, haven't attacked anyone yet. I don't think there's any danger in going to the spot where Miss Hanmer last saw them – they'll be well away by now. We might find some evidence which would help identify their species.'

'It's up to you, Jenny,' the Warden said.

'I'll take Mr Pender there, I know the pond,' Will volunteered.

'It's okay, Will,' Jenny said. 'I'll go. I can show Mr Pender the exact place.'

'I'll go with you then,' the young man offered.

'No, you'll have to take charge of Jenny's class,' said Milton. 'I really don't want the children or their teacher to think there's a problem.'

'But Miss Bellingham . . .' Jenny began to say, before Milton interrupted.

'I know Miss Bellingham quite well. I don't think her eyesight is all that reliable, do you?'

Jenny was lost for words for a moment. 'Now just wait a minute . . .'

The Warden held up a restraining hand. 'Please, Jenny, let me handle this. You go along with Mr Pender, will you?'

The tutor stood, glanced at Pender, and walked from the room. Milton grinned feebly and Pender followed the girl.

She was halfway down the narrow gravel path before he caught up with her.

'Just wait a minute, Miss Hanmer,' he said, taking her arm and bringing her to a halt. He selfconsciously dropped his hand when she pointedly looked down at it. 'He is right, you know. These things can snowball into panic if they aren't handled carefully.'

'But I saw them,' she said resolutely.

'No one's doubting that. But it has to be checked out before the alarm bells go off.'

She began striding down the path again and he kept pace, walking on the grass beside her.

'Look, ever since the Outbreak people have been panicking over real or imagined rats. Usually, the ones we've found have been normal, either Black or Brown, but no giants. More often than not, they've been animals of a completely different species. Bad light, optical illusions, over-nervous people – all sorts of things account for the sightings. It's become as popular as spotting UFOs.'

'I am not over-nervous. Nor do I imagine things. Nor do I believe in flying saucers.'

'Then you're a better person than I am.'

'Possibly.'

He grinned at the sarcasm. 'Probably,' he said.

She stopped and faced him. 'I'm sorry, Mr Pender . . .'

'Luke,' he told her.

'Luke?'

'Short for Lucas.'

'Lucas?' She couldn't help smiling.

'Not my fault. Parents. I was conceived on honeymoon in a place in lower Italy. Lucania.'

She laughed aloud.

'I was lucky. They could have gone to Ramsgate.' His smile broadened as she laughed again.

'You sound like something out of a bad western,' she said.

'The way certain people regard my profession, I sometimes feel like it.'

'Okay, I'm sorry, Luke. I didn't mean to get huffy with you.'

'It's all right. You've had a shock.'

Jenny frowned. 'I meant it, you know, I wasn't mistaken.'

'Let's check it out, then, eh?'

They began walking again and the tutor glanced down at Pender's feet. 'You're going to get awfully wet.'

'I've got boots in my car, and an old leather jacket. I have to be prepared to get mucky in this job.' He pointed towards his Audi and they headed in that direction.

'How did you get into rats?' the girl asked as he opened the back of the car and reached in for a pair of hefty high-ankled boots.

'I wouldn't say I'm into them, exactly,' he replied, removing his shoes and lacing up the boots. 'It's just a living. I was an entomologist until an old friend of mine from Ratkill told me rodent control was the thing of the future. Big money, he told me, and all the vermin you can eat.'

Her reserve was beginning to break down. People were usually wary of him because of his profession, even though he and his colleagues had become latter-day heroes due to the 'dangerous' work they carried out, but he sensed a natural wariness in this girl, as if she rarely took people at face value. Maybe she had learned not to the hard way.

'And is it? The thing of the future?' she asked.

He took off his coat and reached for the short, worn leather jacket inside the boot. 'Well, it's big business now, but I suppose the fear of rats will fade with time.'

'It'll be a long while before people forget what happened in London.'

'Yes, it will. But that was a freak. They'll forget it eventually.'

'Unless it happens again.'

He said nothing and lifted up a folded bundle of silver material that lay on the floor of the boot. He pulled out two pairs of large gloves made from the same tough fabric and handed one pair to the tutor who looked quizzically at him.

'Just a precaution,' he told her. 'If by any chance we do run into your friends, slip these on. They'll give you some protection.' He saw the fear in her eyes. 'Don't worry. It really is just a precaution; nothing's going to happen. If I thought there was any real danger I'd make you put the whole suit on here and now.'

'I hope to God you're right.'

So did he.

'Over there, the other side of the pond.' Jenny pointed towards the opposite bank and Pender scrutinized the area.

'We'll have to go round,' he said. 'Get a closer look.'

The tutor wasn't happy about the situation, but nevertheless she followed him as he skirted the pond, their boots sinking into deep mud at the water's edge. As they walked, he pulled on the heavy gloves and told Jenny to do the same. The undergrowth was much thicker on that side and he trod warily, brushing aside foliage and examining the ground before him as he went. Jenny kept close behind.

'It's just a little way ahead, I think,' she said, looking over towards the side they had just come from to check their position. 'Look, you can see where they disturbed the reeds when they climbed out.'

Pender approached the spot with even more caution and crouched down to examine the mud for tracks. The splayed claw marks told him what he wanted to know. 'Let's see where they lead to.' Keeping low, he pushed his way through the undergrowth, but soon he stood upright. 'The tracks have run out – too many fallen leaves, I'm afraid.'

'I want to go back.'

Pender turned to study the girl. She stood there, body stiff, eyes shifting uneasily from left to right. Her face was drained of colour.

'What's wrong?' he asked taking a step towards her.

'Can't you feel it? The forest – the forest is standing still.'

The remark puzzled him, but as he looked around he began to sense it too. It was an eerie sensation, for the forest had become quiet, hushed, the normal chatter of birds, the discreet rustle of timid animals – even the sound of the breeze hissing through the trees – were gone, leaving an unnatural, foreboding silence. It seemed to weigh down on him, a heavy thing. An oppression.

'Let's go,' she said again, her voice very quiet.

Pender was reluctant, despite his unease. 'I've got to find some evidence of them, Jenny. Those tracks back there could have been made by any number of animals.'

She knew he was right, but the anger still flared in her eyes. She was about to reply when a sudden crashing of branches made them both jump. Pender scanned the area ahead, looking for the cause of the noise, and he saw the swaying bush, its thin branches weighed down by something that must have fallen from the tree overhead. The object looked like a red scarf, but from the way the bush was sagging, it had to be something heavier than loose material.

He made his way towards the bush and Jenny said, 'Don't,' but he ignored her. She followed, not wanting to be left alone.

Pender swallowed hard when he realized what the object was. The animal's body had been torn apart, its insides exposed and half-eaten. The rising steam told Pender the creature had not been dead long.

He felt the girl's presence beside him and heard her breath sharply drawn in. 'It must have run up the tree to get away,' he said. 'Whatever did this followed.'

'Rats climb don't they?' Her voice was faint.

'The Black rat does.'

Only the animal's head and tail were intact, its fur shredded and covered in blood. He tried to identify it from the pointed skull and dark markings on its tail.

'It's a stoat,' Jenny said, and she walked away, round to the other side of the tree.

Pender looked up into the branches overhead, suddenly aware that whatever had killed the animal might still be there. He found it hard to believe a rat could have done this, for usually the stoat was the hunter. But then a group of giant Black rats could tear a human to pieces. Jenny's sudden cry startled Pender and anxiety swept through him when he failed to see her.

He crashed through the undergrowth, brushing past the bloody corpse which fell from its resting place, and swung round the tree, one hand resting against its rough bark. She was standing with her hands up to her face, her whole body trembling and knees beginning to sag. He rushed forward and held her to him to prevent her from falling.

'Jesus Christ,' he said when he saw what had caused her shock.

The tree was hollow, the opening facing him. And the hollow and the area just outside were soaked in blood, small lumps of wet flesh lying all around, tiny, disjointed bones, smeared red, scattered in the dirt. There were no recognizable animal parts among the debris; the stoats must have either been dragged off or eaten whole there and then. Pender cleared his throat uncomfortably.

'There must have been a family of stoats,' he said. 'The rats must have slaughtered all of them.'

The girl did not reply and he realized she was weeping against his chest. He looked around at the undergrowth nearby, seeing the short trails of blood disappearing into the shadows. They were darker now. The sun was beginning to dim and early evening was approaching. The trees around them suddenly seemed black and threatening.

'Come on,' he said gently, 'I think I've got all the evidence I need. Let's get back to the Centre.'

He led her back through the darkening forest, his eyes wary and searching.

5

The walls of the large house glowed pinkly as the last rays of the fast-setting sun reflected off the white surface. Pender had left his car in the small car park at the entrance to The Warren and made his way up to the house on foot. He had passed two attached cottages which, he assumed, belonged to forest keepers or whoever maintained the grounds of The Warren, and taken a lane branching to the left. He approached the house from the rear, the rough road winding round till it formed a circle enclosing a centre lawn set out before the house itself, another road leading off from it towards the estate's main entrance. Before Pender had branched off, he had noticed the sign pointing towards The Warren's offices and realized the forest's administrative staff were kept separate from the main house in which Edward Whitney-Evans, the Superintendent of Epping Forest, lived.

His own shadow was cast darkly before him as Pender strode past three high windows, their glass reaching down to the ground. White-painted lattice-work covered with deep green foliage clung to the lower half of the house, rising up on either side of the windows and joining above them. If the house came with the job, then the Superintendent's lot was a happy one, Pender thought as he rang the doorbell.

The door opened almost immediately and a small, waspish woman peered out at him.

'Mr Fender, is it?' she said and before he had a chance to correct her, she ushered him in. 'Mr Whitney-Evans is waiting for you.'

She moved aside to allow him entrance and he stepped through the porch into the main building.

'Through there, sir,' she said, indicating a door on the left of the hallway. He thanked her and entered the room finding it empty. He walked over to one of the deep windows and gazed out; the grounds sloped away from the circular lawn and, even in the dusk, Pender could see the estate was beautifully situated. The Epping New Road, with its heavy traffic, was completely screened from the house by trees and shrubbery. Beyond he could see the hills of woodland and it was hard to consider he was so close to the world's largest city.

'Ah, Fender.'

He turned to see a man in a dark grey suit standing in the doorway.

'Pender, actually.'

The man looked puzzled for a moment. 'I thought Milton said Fender over the phone. Not to worry. Tell me what this is all about, Pender.' He strode forward and settled himself in an armchair and indicated a chair for Pender. He was a squat man, who appeared to be in his late fifties; a few streaks of hair were combed carefully across his bald head, compensated by wispy locks curling around his ears and resting on his shirt collar. Enlarged eyes stared out at Pender through thick lenses.

Slightly irritated by the man's gruff, no-nonsense tone, Pender sat and deliberately took his time in answering. There was silence for a moment or so, each sizing up the other, the superintendent finally becoming impatient.

'Well?' he said.

Pender cleared his throat. 'I was sent to the Conservation Centre by Ratkill to investigate complaints by Mr Milton . . .'

'Yes, yes, I know all that; Milton discussed it with me first. When I spoke to him a little while ago on the phone he said you'd found some evidence. That's why I asked him to send you over here. I thought you might have got here sooner – the Centre's only five minutes away.'

'I wanted to examine the rat droppings Mr Milton had collected first. Also, I wanted to see the door of the refuse building that had been broken into.'

'And what did you deduce from all this?'

'I'd say it's fairly certain that you have the Black rat living in this forest.'

Whitney-Evans frowned in displeasure. 'Fairly certain? What does that mean? You're either sure or you're not.'

Pender struggled to keep his voice even. 'I said fairly certain because I haven't yet seen the rat itself. All the evidence points to it being the Black, though.'

'But you could be wrong. It could be another type of rodent.'

'One of the tutors at the Centre, Jenny Hanmer, saw three of them.'

'Yes, the Warden told me that. He also said the pond in question is extremely shaded and the only other adult witness has questionable vision.'

'But I went down to the pond myself with Miss Hanmer.'

'And you found evidence that a family of stoats had been slaughtered.'

'Torn to pieces.'

'Yes, yes, but by what? You, yourself, did not actually see the assailants.'

'No, but there's enough evidence now to assume . . .'

'No, Pender. We mustn't assume anything. Do you realize the harm such an assumption could bring to the forest?'

'That's not the point. If people are killed . . .'

'Of course we don't want anybody to be killed by these creatures – if they exist. But first, let's make sure they are a reality. Surely you can – you must – investigate further before you reach such an extreme conclusion.'

'Look, Mr Whitney-Evans, I can appreciate not wanting to spoil the image of your beautiful forest, but if lives are in danger, there is no choice in the matter. Epping Forest will have to be cleared of people.'

'Impossible!' The Superintendent stood, his face flushed red. 'Don't you realize how densely populated Epping Forest and its neighbouring forests are? You can't just suddenly shift all those people on the slight evidence you've produced.'

'The evidence is enough for me,' Pender replied.

Whitney-Evans walked to the window. Silent for a moment, he then turned to face Pender again. 'It may be enough for you, but will it be enough for your superiors? Or the Ministry?'

'I think they'll listen. They wouldn't want to risk another Outbreak.'

'I'm sure they wouldn't; that is not under debate. What I – and I'm sure they will take the same view – am questioning, is your evidence.'

'Look, I don't understand this. Why are you resisting my attempts to avert a dangerous situation?'

Whitney-Evans regarded Pender coolly. 'Have you any idea how much it costs to maintain Epping Forest?' he said finally.

'What? What's that got to do with . . . ?'

'It costs over £100,000 a year, Pender. Money, I may add, that does not come from the government, nor the public. It comes from private City funds.'

'I don't see what that has to do with this matter.'

'The forest is governed by the Corporation of London; they

are the Conservators. The actual management is carried out by a committee of twelve, all an elected representative body of the City of London; they are joined by four Verderers.'

'Verderers?' Pender asked, wondering where the sudden lecture was leading.

'They are members elected by the public to represent local interests. The committee meets several times a year and, in fact, there is a meeting due to be held in two weeks' time. I intend to ask for a considerable increase in the funds allocated to the forest.'

'I still don't understand how that affects . . .'

'Can't you see, man?' Whitney-Evans' face had flushed red again. 'Can you imagine the cost of evacuating the whole forest? The cost of quarantining 6,000 acres of woodland? Do you think they would even consider a rise in management allocation knowing the cost of such an operation as you are suggesting?' He raised a hand when Pender tried to protest. 'But even worse, do you imagine they would even consider taking on such a huge responsibility? Absolutely not! It would be passed on to the government, who have tried unsuccessfully for years to gain control of this green belt area. Can't you see what they, the great bureaucratic *they*, would do with this land? It would become one vast concrete estate! Not all at once, I grant you, but a little at a time under the guise of economic necessity! Do you realize the value of this land so close to the City? My God, man, they'd eat away at it until there was nothing left! Oh, a few parks scattered here and there just for cosmetic purposes; but it wouldn't be a nature reserve anymore.' The Superintendent began to pace the room in his anger and it seemed as if he had forgotten Pender's presence for a moment.

'Look, I can appreciate your worries, Mr Whitney-Evans, although I feel they're a little exaggerated.'

The Superintendent stopped his pacing. 'Exaggerated? I can assure you they are not. I can show you countless court cases we've had in the past over the acquisition of forest land, not to mention the constant battle with the government who want to dissect and destroy the woodland with their monstrous motorways.'

'All the same, the law is quite clear on this: rat-infested areas have to be sealed off immediately.'

'Infested? What evidence do you have of that? You've seen a few signs that rats may be living in the forest and you can't even say for sure they are of the Black variety. Don't you think if the place were infested, the forest keepers would have discovered them by now?'

'I don't know. There may just be a small group at the moment.'

'That, even if it's true, would hardly justify putting the whole damned forest into quarantine.'

'Or,' Pender continued, undaunted, 'there may be hundreds of them. Remember, after their near-extermination in London, those that survived would have become even more elusive than usual.'

'Those that survived the extermination would have died of old age by now.'

'But their offspring would have inherited the fear. The monster Black has developed incredible intelligence according to all the reports: they would certainly know how to keep themselves hidden.'

'Then, if that's the case, there can be no immediate danger, can there?' Whitney-Evans' voice had taken on a new tone, softer, almost coaxing. Pender decided he liked the man even less than before.

'Then why this sudden evidence of them?' he said firmly. 'Why are they suddenly losing this timidity?'

'Just a combination of circumstances, Pender. If – and that's a big *if* as far as I'm concerned – if they do exist, they still haven't attacked a human, have they?'

'Not yet. But they might.'

'Look, Pender, I've stated my case quite frankly to you. Now, I'm not trying to prevent you from doing your duty, Lord knows I haven't that power, but I am asking you to reconsider your action. Why not investigate further before you recommend evacuation and quarantine? I have a staff of over seventy who I'm sure would be only too pleased to assist you in any way possible. My forest keepers and woodsmen could help you in your search. I'm not saying you shouldn't inform the Ministry, of course, you must do that, but all I'm saying is, don't jump to hasty conclusions. By all means, bring your people in, but surely we can keep – what's the expression? – yes, a "low profile" on this. Until you're absolutely sure. What do you say?'

Pender shook his head wearily. 'I'm sorry, Mr Whitney-Evans, I really am. But the risk is too great. If anything nasty should happen while we're still searching, then it would be my responsibility.'

The Superintendent's tone was acid. 'No, not your responsibility, Pender. Your company's. But I wonder what they would say about this inflexible attitude of yours?'

'Well, you can find out.' Pender rose and made for the door. 'Why don't you ask them?' He paused and looked back at the Superintendent, whose face was, yet again, flushed bright red.

'I'll do just that, Pender. I also have some very good connections in the Ministry of Agriculture – we work closely together, you know. I'll see what they have to say about the matter.'

Pender could not be bothered to reply. He resisted the urge to slam the door behind him, and made his way out of the house.

'Bloody idiot,' he allowed himself to say as he crunched his way back down the lane.

By the time he got back to the Conservation Centre, phone calls had been made. His intention had been to inform the Warden of his decision, then to get in touch with Stephen Howard at Ratkill, who would advise the appropriate authorities. But Alex Milton was waiting for him in the reception area of the Centre, a concerned look on his face.

'Ah, Mr Pender,' he said, striding forward to meet the ratcatcher. 'We weren't sure if you'd return to the Centre this evening. We thought you might go straight back to your company to make your report.'

'No, I wanted to have a word with you first. Can we go into your office?'

'Of course. In fact, I've just had your Research Director on to me. He said he'd like you to ring him immediately if you showed up here.'

Pender looked at the Warden quizzically.

'He said it was important,' Milton said somewhat lamely.

Pender had his suspicions before he even picked up the phone. He dialled the Ratkill number and asked to be put through to Stephen Howard.

'Stephen? It's Luke.'

'Ah, Luke. Good. Now what have you been up to there in Epping Forest? Seems you've stirred things up.'

'Meaning?'

'Well, I've just had old Thornton from the Ministry of

Agriculture on to me. Says you've been upsetting a chum of his by the name of Whitney-Evans. Superintendent of the forest, isn't he?'

'Oh, for Christ's sake! The man wants to do a cover-up. He doesn't want the forest to be evacuated.'

The Warden looked both embarrassed and startled. He sat down.

Howard's voice on the other end of the phone was sharp. 'Evacuate. That's a bit drastic, isn't it? What makes you think the Black rat is in the forest?'

Pender quickly told him what he'd seen, been told, deduced. The phone buzzed with static for a few moments.

'Sorry, Luke, I'm afraid that's not enough.'

'Not enough? You've got to be kidding.'

'No, old boy, I'm not. Look, I'm going over there for a meeting. Thornton's already set something up with this Whitney-Evans for nine o'clock. Can you hang around until then?'

'Yes, I can hang around.' Pender felt a heaviness dragging him down. Howard had obviously been asked to soft-pedal by Thornton, who was a Private Secretary in the Ministry of Agriculture, Fisheries and Food, and a major contact between Ratkill and the government. Ratkill had always worked closely with the Ministry's Safety Pesticides and Infestation Control Division, even though the Ministry of Defence had become involved in the London Outbreak, and in the subsequent years after the supposed elimination of the Black rat, they had become even more united in their joint work. Howard was unlikely to go against the wishes of one of the Ministry's private secretaries, and it was obvious Thornton was one of Whitney-Evans' 'good connections'.

'Are you still there, Luke?' Howard's voice interrupted Pender's thoughts.

'I'm still here,' he said.

'Right. The meeting will be held in the Conservation Centre itself. Apart from the Warden, I'd like this girl, the tutor who says she saw the rats, to attend, as well as the forest's head keeper. Dugdale from the Safety Inspectorate will also be there. Don't worry, Luke, we'll soon sort things out.'

'We'll need to. Fast. You know how the situation in London got out of hand.'

'Of course I do. I was in the thick of it. But look, I feel certain this is just an isolated case.'

'I wish I shared your confidence.'

'I don't want you to discuss this any further, Luke, not until the meeting.' The forced lightness had left the research director's voice.

'In case I upset anybody else?'

'No, because the matter must be treated in the strictest confidence,' came Howard's curt reply.

'A party of schoolchildren and their teacher saw the rats, too.'

'Yes, but I understand they've been convinced they saw something completely different.'

'Oh, have they,' Pender said flatly.

'Until later then, Luke?'

'Okay.' Pender replaced the receiver and found himself looking into the eyes of Milton. 'I need a drink,' he said.

'I wish I could join you,' Milton replied, smiling apologetically. 'I'm afraid I have a lecture due to begin shortly and I have to greet our guest speaker.'

Pender nodded and left the Warden's office, suppressing the anger he felt. If anything disastrous happened while they wasted time . . . And yet, he could see their point of view. It would be a massive operation to clear the whole woodland area, and would undoubtedly send waves of panic, not just through that green belt area, but through all the surrounding districts. London, itself. And if it did prove to be a false alarm . . . He pushed the thought of consequences from his mind. The girl had seen the rats, and she didn't seem the type who would put the fear of God into everyone if she thought there might be some doubt.

He walked the length of the corridor and entered the reception area. Jenny Hanmer, talking to a tall, bearded man, saw him and gave him a smile. The bearded man turned at Pender's approach.

'Hello, Luke,' Jenny greeted him. 'This is Vic Whittaker, our Senior Tutor.'

Pender nodded. He judged the tutor to be in his late-thirties, prematurely grey hair streaking his close-cropped, black beard. Whittaker looked fixedly at the ratcatcher.

'I'm rather disturbed at what Jenny tells me, Mr Pender,' he said.

'It's something to be disturbed about,' Pender replied. He turned to the girl. 'There's going to be a meeting tonight, Jenny, here at the Centre. The powers-that-be want you to attend.'

'But aren't they going to do something right away?' Jenny asked.

'They'll decide exactly what to do at the meeting. First we've got to convince them there really is a threat.'

'That's ridiculous! Surely . . .'

'I know, I've just been through all that. I suppose it's sensible to hold an inquiry before they decide on a plan of action. So far, you're the only reliable witness, so it'll be up to you to assure them you're not just over-imaginative. The other evidence we have will help.'

'Do you think they will be convinced?' asked Whittaker.

Pender paused before he spoke. 'To tell the truth, I just

don't know. My guess is that they'll play for more time. All I want to do now is to get a bite to eat and a beer. Care to join me, Jenny?'

Jenny said, 'Yes, I would,' and Pender caught the sharp look the senior tutor gave her.

'What about the lecture this evening? Aren't you coming to that?' Whittaker said.

'I don't think I'm really in the mood for "A Naturalist's Journey to Iran and the Persian Gulf" at the moment, Vic,' she replied. 'After what I saw today, I could use a stiff drink myself.'

'I'll see you later then.' Whittaker turned and strode off down the corridor leading to the classrooms.

Pender ignored the exchange. 'Okay,' he said, smiling at Jenny, 'lead me to a pub.'

They drove past the huge public house close to the Centre and headed south, using the car's lights at full-beam because of the total darkness that had descended on the forest. The road had sudden dips and Pender kept to its centre because of the rough banks on either side, adjusting his headlights and pulling over to the left when the occasional car approached from the opposite direction. He noticed they passed several high, bricked walls which he guessed hid some large properties. In a clearing to his left he saw lights shining.

'That's a forest keeper's house,' Jenny told him. 'There are quite a few scattered throughout the woodland.'

'And what's that coming up on the right?' he asked, pointing to a sign ahead of them.

'That's the Suntrap Field Study Centre.'

'Anything to do with your place?'

'Not really. We work together from time to time.'

The moon suddenly appeared from behind rolling clouds and the landscape was bathed in its silvery light. They passed a farm, and then the road swung hard to the right and they found themselves ascending a steep hill, more houses on their right, a riding stable on the left. The public house was on the top of the hill, opposite a group of buildings surrounded by a high wire fence. 'What's that?' Pender asked.

'Oh, that belongs to the police. It's a training camp for cadets. They also have a firing range and a place for training their dogs.'

Pender turned the car into the car park at the rear of the pub and stopped. He shivered in the cold night air as they crossed the tarmac, heading for an entrance to the bars. Looking around, he saw they were quite high above the forest, gentle fields leading down into dense woodland below them. But what he saw in the flattened area immediately next to the pub brought him to a halt.

'What is that, Jenny? What are those buildings?'

Jenny followed his gaze. 'It's a mobile homes estate. You know, like caravans but with no wheels.'

'Do you know how many houses there are?'

'There are two estates over there, one of about twenty, the other about thirty or forty. They're separated by a farm. Another one is at the end of Hornbeam Lane, but not many people know about it – it's very secluded. I think there are twenty homes on that.'

'Christ,' he said. 'I didn't realize the forest had such a heavy population. It may make us look silly, Jenny, but I just hope-to-God we're wrong about the rats.'

As he spoke, a heavy cloud covered the moon's brightness and he suddenly felt vulnerable to the night. He took Jenny's arm and guided her into the welcoming warmth of the pub.

Onslaught

The creature shifted position in the bed of straw and damp earth, obese body making movement difficult, legs no longer able to support the great weight comfortably. Others moved around in the darkness, mewing sounds and the slivering of bodies occasionally breaking the silence of the black, underground chamber. They did not approach the creature in the corner, fearing its wrath, knowing to approach could mean the tearing apart of their own grey, swollen bodies. Not by the creature itself, but by the three black-haired guards that crouched nearby.

Tiny bones lay scattered around in the darkness and occasionally they would be picked up and ground to a fine powder by powerful jaws. There was a restlessness among the sluggish bodies and the creature in the corner sensed their mood. A gurgling sound came from its throat and it was joined by another, similar noise, close by, almost from the same point in the darkness. All movement stopped. They listened.

The gross body thrashed around in the straw and the other creatures flattened themselves against the ground, pushing themselves into the rubble and exposing their fleshy necks in a ritual of self-abasement.

It was old now and did not remember the journey to this place, the long journey through the underground tunnels, crouching, terrified in the dark, as the huge things thundered over their heads, urging the others on with high-pitched squeals, keeping them together, fleeing from where they were hunted, where the extermination of their species was taking place, instinct for survival their only ally. They had been freed from the cellar and had slain their liberators, eating the bodies before venturing forth.

Inherited knowledge drove them below ground, for they had no adult to lead them; they had devoured their mother in the final days in the cellar. The creature had dominated its brothers and sisters from the beginning; although they were part of the same evolvement, its body was different from theirs. They were dark, covered in a blackish-brown fur. It was not.

It had led them through the tunnels, resting only when they were completely exhausted. The two weakest had been used for sustenance and had hardly protested their deaths. The group had gone on, following the tracks, cautious when they heard human voices, knowing this was the enemy, these were the hunters. The fresh biting air that reached their nostrils had shocked them and they had cowered in the darkness. But the dominant one had ventured forward and the others had followed. The night sky was above them and they clung to the shadows.

The others had wanted to leave the tracks then and go out to where there were houses and living flesh, but it would not let them. They were still in the city, and that meant danger. They hid when daylight came, trembling, fortunate to have found another tunnel further on. Then with the night, they found something completely new to them, and they welcomed it.

They had never experienced the long flowing grass before, but they relished its softness and the cover it afforded them. It teemed with small, living things and because they were still young, they forgot their fear and wanted to play. But their leader would not let them; it knew that danger was all around. It led them up the grassy embankment, away from the railway track, away from the tunnels in which the trains sped beneath the city, and into the woodland, a new world where they could breathe the air and run free. It could sense that the humans were still there, but the further they went into the woodland, so the presence became less noticeable. They crossed hard, concrete strips, fearful of the racing monsters whose eyes shone far ahead into the night, and eventually, as dawn approached, they rested. They were still afraid, but it seemed the badness was over.

The group soon adapted to their new life and they never lost their cunning. They grew to a size that made them fearful to the other animals of the forest, and they mated. But the one whose body was different from the others would not rest; it could not adapt as the others had, for it knew they were not yet safe. And it missed something. It felt unprotected in the open.

They journeyed further, always at night, always in a tight-packed group, flowing through the grassland and skulking in dark places when the sun rose. They found the heart of the forest, and the dominant one found the resting-place it needed, somewhere it could feel safe, where it could hide its deformed body in constant darkness. It had found the perfect lair.

It had grown old, living twice the normal life-span of the creatures it was derived from; and it had mated, creating offspring that were in its own image. Not many completely of its kind lived, and those that survived were weak and not always able to fend for themselves. Yet they dominated the others of the litter, the dark-furred ones, and the two strains lived together, the latter foraging for food and bringing it back to the lair for the leader and its natural heirs.

It never left the confines of the lair now, for its misshapen body had become too heavy, too bloated. It still ruled over them all, but it could sense the mounting tension. Its followers were becoming increasingly restless, both the black and those more like itself craving for something they could not understand. Although they were now many in numbers, they had remained hidden for several years, their inborn fear of what lay beyond binding them to the woodland, away from the eyes of humans. But it was as if their numerical strength was making them bolder, giving them a courage they had not possessed before. And the craving grew stronger each day, the forest animals they killed failing to satiate their strange yearning.

The thing in the corner knew what that craving was, for the group hunger came from their leader. The creature hungered for something tasted before, long ago.

Its two heads weaved to and fro in the darkness and a stickiness drooled from the mouths as it remembered, after so many years, the taste of human flesh.

6

'Can't we stay in the car, Alan? It's so cold out there.' The woman pulled her coat tightly around herself and hunched down into the passenger seat.

'Come on, Babs, it's not that cold. I'll soon warm you up.' The man leered across at her, and slipped a hand around her shoulder, pulling her towards him.

'It's creepy,' the woman complained.

'We're too near the roadside here, Babs. There's too many passing cars.'

'Well, drive a bit further in.'

Alan tried to keep the irritation from his voice. 'I can't do that, darling. The car might get stuck in the mud. I won't be able to see the ground properly in the headlights. I might get jammed on a tree root or something.'

The woman sighed with resignation. Why bother to protest? Alan always got his way in the end. And she had to admit, she usually enjoyed it when he did.

Alan Martyn was an estate agent, his offices in the nearby Loughton area, and Babs – Mrs Newell in the office – was his secretary. At twenty-nine, he was up and coming; at thirty-five, was down and hadn't been coming enough. Fifteen years of marriage and raising two sons who were now teenagers had almost smothered any overt desires in her; her lifestyle had reached its level and the sudden bumps, the rises and falls, were only slight. She should have been content, for she was married to a good, if dull, man, and the boys had grown into fine, if boisterous, young men. The house was nice – perhaps a little small, but nice – and they had a colour telly. Even the dog was obedient.

Sometimes she could have screamed with the niceness of it all.

Reg, her husband, was solid, salt of the earth, A GOOD MAN. He didn't wear carpet slippers around the house, nor did he smoke a pipe – he wasn't *that* bad. But he did roll his own to save the expense of buying cigarettes; and he did keep rabbits in the back garden; and he did bath every Sunday and Wednesday, without fail; and he did always find time to help the boys with their homework or answer their questions; and he always took the dog out for a walk in the evening, no matter what the weather; and he always offered to wash the dishes, even if she wouldn't let him; and he always left his muddy shoes outside the front door; and he had never raised a hand to her; and he always made love on Saturday morning without fail; and he never asked her to try a new position; and he never used anything other than his penis on her; and she had never caught him masturbating.

Oh Reg, why are you such a fucking bore?

Alan's lips brushed against hers, roughly, greedily. Alan was bad, selfish, but he excited her. Babs was aware that it was his difference to safe, reliable Reg that made him so attractive. He was a bastard, beyond doubt, and he used her just to fulfil his own lusts. But that was all right; that was how she used him.

She would never leave her husband and the boys – she loved them dearly. But she was a woman, and she needed more than just cosy affection. Reg had his rabbits, she had – this.

Babs had always wanted to return to work, missing the contact with outsiders, people whose lives she knew little of and therefore would find more interesting than her neighbours or relations. Housework was humdrum, hard but unchallenging, and the house no longer held any stimulation for her. But outside work had come by as a necessity rather than an indulgence: Reg's salary had become steadily worth less week by week, inflation became the master of household decisions. Reg, as a production controller in an advertising agency, had no union behind him to make sure his earnings kept reasonably level with the ever-increasing price rises and so, at the instigation of Babs herself, it was decided she should take a job again. The boys were now old enough to be less dependent on her, so there was no great problem in that respect, and Reg was sensible enough to realize his wife needed an outside interest.

'Come on, darling, it's been a long time since we've done it out in the open.' Alan pushed his hand against the rough material of Babs' coat, kneading her plump breasts in a circular movement. 'I'll get the rug out of the back so you won't get damp.'

She felt the excitement in her, a flush spreading across her chest beneath her clothes. 'What if someone comes along, Alan?' she asked, but her tone told her weekday lover she was willing.

'Don't be daft, Babs. There won't be anyone walking in the forest when it's this dark.'

'I won't be able to stay too long.'

He looked at the luminous dial on his watch. 'It's only ten-to-eight. What time did you say you'd be in?'

'About half-past. I told Reg we'd be going over the books tonight. He said he'd do the boys' dinner.'

'Good old Reg,' Alan said distractedly, his lips finding and moistening Babs' ear and, equally distractedly, he thought, fucking idiot.

Babs' breasts were rising and falling as though air was being blown into them, and she squeezed her thighs tightly together, feeling the moistness between them. Alan was such a good lover, so thoughtful, so unselfish And – she shivered with pleasure – so demanding. Babs wondered if he was as demanding with his young wife.

'Come on then, Alan,' she said, an urgency in her voice now. 'Let's find a sheltered place, though.'

He was out of the fawn-coloured Capri in a flash, opening the boot and reaching for the rug inside. Babs stepped from the car, closing the door behind her and making sure it was locked. It was one of the things Alan was serious about, his car. She looked around, the chill night air almost quelling her excitement, and thought the forest looked very unreal in the moonlight.

'Okay, Babs?' Alan was beside her and she knew his shortness of breath was due to excitement. He loved to experiment, did Alan, loved to try new things all the time. In the seven months she had known him – six of them carnally – they must have investigated every position there was. Even though she was the more mature in years, she had come to it as a young girl, eager to learn, almost desperate to experience. Lunch-times in the office, when the others had gone out and she and Alan had pretended to work on, they had disappeared into the back room where the records of all their clients were kept and made love among the filing cabinets – on the floor next to them, up against them, even on top of them. He had beaten her buttocks with a belt, used her anus as a vagina, bitten her breasts until she screamed, almost choked her with his spurting semen. She had sat on his face and made him drink her juices, had painfully bound his penis and testicles with his own tie and yanked him yelping around the filing room, had straddled, ridden and raped him, had smeared him with face cream and manipulated him. He had loved it all. And she had loved it all.

On the few occasions they had managed to get away together – to Reg it was business conventions, to the office, who were not fooled, it was coinciding holidays or, surprise, surprise, mutual illnesses – they indulged themselves to the full, rarely leaving the hotels they had booked into. Masochism and sadism were attempted but only by mutual consent and only at amateur status; neither liked to hurt or be hurt that much. Bondage was fun but it made the wrists chafe. Wearing each other's underwear was okay if the lights were off. After a while, when their imagination for new experiences seemed to have become exhausted, they both realized there was more enjoyment in normal intercourse. It just depended on where you did it. Neither cared to look into the future, to where their relationship was leading, for their excitement was always in the present, never tomorrow or the day after. They were not in love, but they loved what they did, and when it ended, that would be the end.

The moon suddenly disappeared and they were plunged into darkness.

'I don't like this, Alan,' Babs said, nervously.

'It'll be out in a minute, don't worry. Come here, and have a cuddle.'

He pulled her to him and pressed his body hard against hers, his eyes staring over her shoulder into the darkness. He didn't care too much for the dark himself. He breathed a silent sigh of relief when the moon appeared once more.

Taking her hand, he pressed on farther into the undergrowth, pushing the higher foliage away with his hand, the rug draped over one shoulder.

'Not too far, Alan,' Babs pleaded.

'No, darling, just a bit further. It's nice and thick just ahead. It'll screen us from the road.'

A scuttling noise made them stop.

'What's that?' Babs whispered.

Alan listened for a few moments, but heard nothing more. 'Must have been an animal. We probably scared it.'

He moved on and she meekly followed.

'This'll do,' he said leading her down into a slight dip, wondering why he had whispered. He stamped on the grass, trampling any gorse that might be there, then threw down the rug, pulling each corner straight.

'Okay, lover?' he said, his face faint and white in the moonight.

'I'm not sure, Alan,' she answered, but he knew she wanted him as much as he wanted her. He pulled her down on the rug and began to unbutton her coat and she forgot about the forest and night creatures. Babs' plumpness was of the firm, springy kind, her figure rounded provocatively rather than flabbily, and Alan's excitement grew when her breasts and stomach became exposed to the moonlight. He bent his head and kissed her neck, lowering himself so his lips brushed against the tops of her breasts which threatened to spill over the silky material of her bra. His tongue drew a slivery trail over her stomach, sudden goose-pimples making her flesh hard and brittle.

Although the cold made her shiver, it seemed to add a new dimension to their lovemaking, the chill numbing her on the outside, warmth flooding through her on the inside. And the stars above her, the air around her, gave the feeling that they were being observed and that added to the thrill. The goose-pimples made her body lose its numbness, made it tingle, tickle when he touched her. He pulled her arms free of the coat and began to slip the blouse from her shoulders.

'No, Alan,' she protested, 'it's too cold for that.'

He kissed her lips and ignored the protest, pulling the blouse free. He looked down at her white, bare shoulders, at her face staring up at him, yearning yet innocent, and, for a moment, he almost loved her. Almost, and only for a moment: desire quickly overwhelmed emotion. He reached behind her and undid the clasp holding the bra together, then slid it down along her arms. He pushed her back onto the rug and began to tug at the skirt. After the initial struggle over the hips, it pulled away easily from her legs. Her tights came next, along with her shoes. He took his time with the panties, touching her first through the flimsy material, making her squirm and causing her to grab his hand to guide it more skilfully, urging his fingers to reach inside. He pulled away, knowing her pleasure would take her too far, upset their timing.

Her body looked like white marble as he stood and gazed down on her: soft, yielding marble that could absorb his own body. Her hands hooked into the sides of her panties and pulled them down over her hips, over her ankles, over her feet. She delicately placed them to one side, then lay back on the rug, her legs slightly apart, a small black triangle the only contrast against her pale skin.

Alan quickly threw off his clothes, letting them fall in an untidy heap, knowing he would regret it later when he would be scrabbling around in the dark searching for them and feeling the cold; but for now, it hardly mattered. All he cared about was being joined with that wonderfully passionate body lying at his feet. He fell to his knees, then smothered her with his own body, pressing against her, moving and sliding, squeezing and caressing.

Her arms encircled his waist, moved up to his shoulders, back down to his buttocks, pulling him against her, sinking her fingers into the fleshy parts. Her knees rose on either side of his thighs and she hooked her heels around his calves, using her legs to pull him in tighter.

His mouth encircled a nipple and he drew his breath in, making the nipple erect and angry red. He sought her lips, his hand giving the abandoned breast rough comfort. Soft moans of pleasure were escaping her now and he had to control his own murmurings, not wanting to make too much noise just in case there really were others in the forest. But as their movements became more frantic, so their appreciation grew louder.

Babs reached down for him, wanting him inside her, no longer prepared to prolong the foreplay. She found his penis and heard him groan, then she pulled it towards her, her legs spread wide, heels off the rug now and making indents in the earth. He jerked his hips back, when he felt the lips of her vagina, and kept his organ there, teasing her with its touch.

'Alan, please,' she implored, and he was smiling in the darkness and she was smiling too, wanting him inside but wanting the game to go on. He deliberately pushed himself away and changed her small cry of disappointment to one of delight when he sank his head between her thighs and thrust his tongue into the deep moist passage. Her hips rose from the rug, her whole body moving frenziedly, and he had to hold her in a tight grip so he would not lose her. She thrust her body out to meet his teasing lips and tongue and he brought his knees forward to support her weight more easily. He lifted one thigh so it was over his shoulder, then the other, her legs closing around his head in a grip he thought might flatten his ears permanently. He was finding it difficult to breathe, but she refused to loosen her hold, using her hands and the backs of her legs to draw him in further, her neck and shoulders supporting the weight of her upper body.

Alan thought he might suffocate and was ready to panic when he felt her body go stiff and taut in the last paroxysms before orgasm. Her hand, reaching beneath her buttocks and finding his penis erect in his lap, encouraged him to make the final effort and he plunged as deeply as he could, stretching the retaining tendon at the base of his tongue until he thought it might tear, her moving hand causing the pleasure in his lap to mingle with the pain in his head and lungs, the pain somehow enhancing the pleasure, the pleasure somehow nullifying the pain.

She failed to hold back her cries and, at that stage, didn't care; Alan's flesh-enclosed ears did not even hear. Her arched back became wet from him as both bodies convulsed with their separate releases, and their figures created a bizarre, trembling sculpture in the moonlit clearing. They became locked rigid for the last dying seconds of orgasm, then their bodies slowly crumpled to the ground. Lying there breathless, chests heaving, they allowed their frantic hearts to slow before moving together again.

Alan pulled her coat over them and they huddled together, their bodies warm but aware that the chill would soon bite its way in.

'Alan, Alan, thank you,' Babs said when her breathing had become more controlled. 'It was lovely.'

Alan could only grunt, the sound muffled, for his head was snuggled against her breasts beneath her coat. He felt utterly exhausted and his lips were sore.

Babs ducked under the coat and lay her head close to his. 'Didn't you think it was lovely?' she said.

Alan stretched his legs down and the grass tickled his feet. He quickly drew his knees up again. 'Yes, Babs, terrific.' But now, satiated and beginning to feel cold, he thought about getting home; he'd told Marjie he wouldn't be too late.

Babs lifted her head to kiss his cheek, then turned and lay on her back, limbs stretched akimbo, a contented smile on her face. Her body was still warm from their lovemaking and even her exposed feet refused to acknowledge autumn's frigid presence. Something prickled one foot and she moved it away, closer to the other.

'Darling,' she said, watching a cloud swallowing the moon, 'have you ever wondered why it's so good – with us, I mean.' She lifted the edge of the coat and looked down at him, waiting for an answer.

'No, Babs,' he replied.

She returned her gaze to the heavens. 'It's never been this way with Reg, not even when we were first marrried.'

The top of Alan's head appeared as though he were testing the air before emerging fully. 'I suppose we're just physically compatible,' he said. 'Some people are. Some are compatible mentally, others physically. Me and you are physical.'

'Not just that, Alan.' She was a little hurt at the suggestion.

'Oh, no, not just that, Babs,' he quickly assured her. 'It's just that some people are more, er, more energetic than others. But I think our minds are tuned in as well. We do seem to understand each other.' He wondered if he could sneak a look at his watch without her seeing.

Babs tucked her arms beneath the coat, the chill beginning to reach her. Why fool herself? Alan wanted one thing from her and she wanted one thing from him. Sex was also a thing of the mind, and that was where they both tuned in mentally. She wondered if Reg had given the boys their dinner yet.

Something prickled her foot again and this time, her senses beginning to lose their dullness, she became alarmed.

It might not just be a leaf, or grass, or a twig touching her; it might be an animal.

'Alan!' she said sharply and began to sit up, the coat falling and revealing her ample breasts. It took a fraction of a second to register the pain, then she screamed and jerked her leg up, reaching for her injured foot, and she screamed again, louder, when she felt the two bloodied stumps that were left of her toes.

Alan jumped up, frightened by her cries, and looked around, trying to see what had happened, what had hurt her.

'Babs, what is it?' He grabbed her shoulders and tried to hold her still. 'What happened? *Tell me!*' His own voice had risen to a shriek.

'My foot! Something's bitten my toes off!' she screeched.

'Oh God! It's all right, Babs. Calm down. Let me have a look!'

But there was no time to look, for the rat, excited by the blood, ran forward and attacked her foot again, sinking its incisors deep, through the hand that clutched the injured limb, and into the foot itself. Alan shrank away when he saw the black creature, not knowing what it was, thinking it must be a wild dog because of its size. The moon suddenly burst from its cloud covering and dread hit him as he recognized the beast. The pointed nose, the long sleek body with its hunched lower back, the stiffened tail – it was a Black rat!

Babs' screams startled him from his paralysis; he grabbed the rat at a point near its neck and pulled. The screams reached a new pitch as Babs' flesh was ripped and Alan fell backwards, the struggling creature still in his grasp. It twisted its head and bit into Alan's thigh, gnawing at the flesh and swallowing blood as it burrowed deeper. The main artery was severed and more blood gushed into the rodent's throat, almost choking it, forcing it to withdraw its head. The blood jetted from the wound in a high arc and the air was full of its smell.

'Oh, no, no!' Alan cried, for he knew damage to that artery could be fatal. He clutched at the leg to try and stem the flow, but the blood spurted through his fingers and splattered his face. The rat, squirming between his legs and expelling Alan's blood from its throat, turned and leapt at his chest, raking the skin down to the bone with its claws. It clung there and, as Alan toppled backwards, it began to snap its way into his throat. The others, those that had been more hesitant, crept out from beneath the clearing's surrounding undergrowth, still cautious, for the fear of man was inbred, but becoming bolder as the sweet blood aroma aroused them.

Through tears of pain, Babs saw the approaching black shapes, and she too knew their meaning. She wanted to help Alan, but she was too afraid; she wanted to run, but her fear made her freeze. All she could do was bury herself beneath the coat, her knees tugged up into her chest, her hands clutching at the material, holding it tight around her. The pain in her foot was excruciating and the terror in her mind incapacitating. She prayed, the words tumbling from her lips in a garbled flow, that the creatures would leave them, would fade back into the night, would return to the hell they had come from. But Alan's screams told her they wouldn't. And the tugging at the coat, the sudden sharp, exploratory nips, told her the rats wouldn't leave until she and Alan had been devoured.

As the bites began to puncture her flesh and the agony made her body unfold and writhe, she saw Reg and the boys sitting around the dinner table, Kevin, the youngest, saying, 'Mum's late, Dad . . . Mum's late . . . Mum's late . . .'

*

It was past midnight and no sounds had come from the inside of the tent for at least an hour. It stood alone, like a canvas sentinel, in a corner of the wide field, the forest a dark backdrop. Liquid, almost frozen, clung to the stiffened blades of grass around the tent, but inside it was snug and warm, heat from the boys' bodies providing its own central heating. A small night-light glowed weakly in the centre of the floor space, the seven slumbering boys and their supervisor spread around it in giant cocoon shapes, dreading the cold dawn which would force them to shed their sleeping-bag skins.

Gordon Baddeley, the supervisor, slept to one side, a one-foot gap between him and the nearest boy as though the dividing line were a wall behind which authority rested. Gordon maintained that such abstract symbolism was important.

The boys, their ages ranging from twelve to fifteen, were all from a Barnardo's home in Woodford, and this was their outdoor 'survival' week. There hadn't been much to survive, for the nearest shop was under two miles away, and wild lions, tigers and crocodiles were not reputed to inhabit that part of Epping Forest. The younger boys, however, did believe bears roamed free in that particular area. The field was empty of any other form of life, for it was not one of the official forest camp-sites, but a certain benevolent Lord Something-or-Other – the boys could never remember his name – allowed the Woodford orphanage to use that corner of a field on his estate for camping purposes. As he did not live on the estate any longer but rented the land out to local farmers, he was only a mythical figure to the boys, vague and aloof, like God.

Gordon Baddeley had been a Barnardo boy himself a few years before and was, so everyone said, a shining example of the goodness and honesty that could come from an orphanage background. After only three years in the outside world, working in a supermarket as a shelf-filler, winning promotion to assistant on frozen meats, he had returned to the orphanage that had reared him, turning his back on success because he wanted to help those like himself, the underprivileged. The home had been proud to accept him, although it wasn't common practice to take back those who had left, for Gordon had been an exceptional boy. Well-mannered, soft-spoken, hard-working, no outward emotional problems – he was a boy the staff could point at and say: 'You see, it works. Even though we can't give them the love and affection of true parents, we can turn out well-balanced young people like this.'

Not that Gordon was regarded as soft by the other boys; on the contrary, he was looked upon as 'a tough nut'. He was friendly but firm, could be rough but not unkind, funny when he wanted to be and serious when others wanted him to be. No chip on his shoulder, no nurtured grievances; he seemed to like most people and most people seemed to like him. All in all, they said, he was the perfect Dr Barnardo boy. And after three years on the outside, he had come to realize that was all he ever wanted to be.

The world frightened him. It was too aggressive and too big. There were too many strangers. When out on the streets, he ran everywhere; it was as though he were naked and that by moving swiftly he could shorten the period of exposure. It was a common enough syndrome among fledgling orphans, that awkward reaction to the world in general, but most managed to overcome their uneasiness in time. But not so Gordon; he missed the home and its security to a distressing degree. The orphanage had found him a bedsitter in the house of a friendly and tight-knit family, and their very closeness towards each other had made him feel even more the intruder. They tried to make him feel welcome and he accepted their hospitality with due gratitude, but the more time he spent with them the more he was aware of what he had missed in his own upbringing; he felt no resentment, but he did feel different.

Girls were a problem, too. He was attracted to them and several in the supermarket where he worked were kind towards him, yet again he felt there was a barrier between him and them, that he could only watch their world through an invisible glass screen. Given time he would have joined the people inside, but the loneliness of the interlude between became too hard to bear. Inside the home he had been someone; outside he was nothing. He returned and they turned his defeat into triumph. The home was his home, and it was there he wished to stay.

Gordon turned in his sleep and his eyelids twitched, then opened wide. He stared at the tent's sloping ceiling for a few moments, his dream-thoughts tumbling over themselves to disperse. The night-light gave the slumbering shapes in the tent an eerie, green tinge as he looked around to see if anyone was awake. He listened for the tell-tale and not uncommon sob in the night, the sudden spasmodic jerk from a curled-up form beneath a tightly clutched covering, but the snores and sighs of the sleeping boys assured him all was well. Then what had caused him to awaken?

He lay in the gloom and listened.

The soft scratching noise made him turn his head towards the canvas wall of the tent and the sound stopped. He held his breath.

Something pushed against the coarse material, something low, near the ground. The bulge was at a point near his hips and it suddenly began to move towards his head. Gordon carefully slid his sleeping-bag encompassed frame away from the protuberance and the movement outside came to a halt.

It was as though whatever was out there had sensed his presence, had been aware of the movement inside.

Gordon had to restrain himself from crying out and leaping away from that side of the tent. It would frighten the younger boys, he told himself. Besides, it was probably only a fox or some other curious night animal and it would never penetrate the tough canvas. He slowly unzipped the sleeping-bag and eased out his arms.

The bulge began to move again, upwards, towards his face, and he saw it was at least a couple of feet long. It had to be a fox! Maybe, but not likely, a badger? Whatever the creature was, it wasn't very tall. Or was it just crawling along on its stomach? It could be a dog. The movement stopped again and the bulge seemed to press even further in. Gordon drew his head away, but it was still less than a foot from the straining canvas, and he had an uncanny feeling that the creature beyond could see through the material, could smell his fear. Gordon's free hand groped down towards his side and scrabbled around for the torch he always kept close by when camping. The boy nearest to him stirred restlessly as Gordon's hand brushed against his sleeping-bag, but the searching fingers finally closed around the cold tube of metal. The torch had been pushed to one side by Gordon's sliding body and had come to rest against the nearest boy's sleeping form. Gordon gripped the handle tightly, then froze as the thin, scratching sound came to his ears once more.

With a barely suppressed cry he swung the heavy torch in an arc and struck hard at the swelling and the canvas became slack again, the creature obviously having fled. He thought he heard a high-pitched squeal as the makeshift weapon had struck, but couldn't be sure – it could have been the screaming inside his own head.

Gordon switched on the torch, keeping it low, his own

body screening the light from the rest of the dimly lit interior, and studied the bright, circular shape of canvas before him. He settled back into his sleeping-bag, but kept the torch on, studying the loose material to see if the creature's scratching had caused any damage. No, it was still intact; it would take more than a nosey old fox to make a hole in such tough canvas. His body began to relax and his breathing became more even; his thumb moved against the switch to turn off the harsh beam of light, and it was then that a heavy weight threw itself at the tent's side, the bulge showing clearly in the centre of the circle of light.

The scratching sound became frantic and Gordon gazed on, mesmerized as a small tear appeared in the canvas and a long curving claw pushed its way through. The rent tore downwards in a violent movement, then the claw disappeared to be replaced with tiny, scrabbling protuberances on either side of the hole. Gordon screamed as the two sets of claws broke through and ripped the material to shreds before his eyes. The black, bristling-furred body that launched itself through the gap lunged at Gordon's exposed face and sank its teeth deep into the open jaw, knocking him backwards, rolling with him onto the startled boys trapped inside their sleeping-bags.

They cried out in alarm, not realizing what was happening to their supervisor, the thrown torch shining uselessly into the folds of a sleeping-bag, the dim night-light not strong enough to explain the writhing shapes. The boy nearest the torch managed to push his arm free and make a grab for it. He shone the beam towards the screaming figure, but none of the boys understood just what clung to their supervisor's bloody face. A boy near the tent's wall shouted as he saw something black scramble through a gaping hole in the canvas, and the boy with the torch shone it in that direction.

Gordon choked on his own blood as he tried to push the creature away from his face, its claws raking his chest into a bloody mess. Its teeth were locked into his jaw bone and he could not tear them loose. He knew the animal had the strength and the weapons to kill him, but what he saw made him react almost automatically, as though once more he was viewing life through a glass window. This time, though, he was on the inside – he was part of that life – and the others, the black creatures, were breaking through the glass to reach into his world. He knew he had to stop them.

The pain was blinding, yet it meant little as he rolled his body towards the gap, dragging the creature with him. He could feel the bone in his jaw splintering and cracking, and the blood was running down inside his body, hindering his breathing, but his mind seemed almost apart from it, telling him one thing over and over again: Stop them coming through, block the hole with your body.

He knew he was there, knew his back covered their entrance, preventing them from pouring in. And he knew they were eating him, their teeth gnawing into his back, snapping around his spine and pulling. He knew the creature at his face was trapped by its own teeth at his jaw, but nevertheless was busy sucking his blood, draining him of life's fluid.

But he didn't know that other bulges were appearing all around the tent's walls, the scratching sounds mingling with the panic-stricken cries of the boys inside, and the canvas material puncturing in long, tearing gashes.

Dawn had begun to tip the treetops with a golden rim as the rising sun decisively cut its way through the mists. It was not unusual to find the Reverend Jonathan Matthews trudging down the lane from his vicarage towards the old church at such an early hour for, in recent years, sleeping had played a less important part in his life. The first rays of light projecting their leafy pattern onto his bedroom wall had become an increasingly welcome sight as the approaching day gave relief to the night's loneliness. Since his wife's untimely death eight years before, the vicar had had no one to confide in, no one to give him comfort. He had often considered speaking to his Bishop of his latter-day doubts, his spiritually debilitating fear of death, but had decided he would fight the battle alone. God would surely give him the grace to overcome his lack of faith.

He pulled the scarf concealing his clerical collar tighter around his neck, his frail body all too vulnerable to the morning dampness. Again and again he asked himself why such troubles of the mind should plague him in his later years when his beliefs had been so strong before? He felt somehow it was connected with the forest itself. In his imagination the brooding menace in the surrounding woodland seemed to represent death's constant presence, always there, lurking just out of sight, watching and waiting for the precise moment in which to reveal itself. For him, the forest had once been a place to love; now it had become a symbol of his own trepidation.

The vicar entered the covered gateway to the church and paused to gaze up at the ancient building's steeple. It wasn't high, the pinnacle barely topping the highest branches of the surrounding trees, yet it reached upwards in solid defiance of its earthly base as though it could pierce the heavens themselves, and feed through its funnel shape the souls of the faithful. Its spiritual brashness gave his heart a sudden uplift. Doubts were a part of serving, for if there were none there would be no searching for answers, no obstacles to surmount – no tests to be judged by. This was his time of testing and when it was through he would have sturdier faith, a stronger belief in God.

The little church always gave him this sudden surge of optimism, which was why he often visited it so early in the morning. The negative thoughts of the night had to be swiftly allayed if he was to survive the day, and a quiet hour at the altar helped him build his barrier. His feet crunched along the narrow gravel path running between the gravestones towards the church porch, his eyes avoiding the slabs of grey on either side, and it was only when his hand was on the circular metal handle of the door that he heard the scrabbling sounds that came from the rear of the building.

He slowly turned his head in that direction, a curious coldness stiffening his spine. Listening intently, he tried to place the sound. It was as if earth was being scattered, the sound of someone or *something* digging. It would have to be an animal of some kind, for he could not recognize the familiar thud of a spade biting into the earth, nor the dull clump as the tossed soil struck the ground in one loose lump. This was a ceaseless barrage of scattered dirt.

The splintering of wood made him jump.

Dread rising in him, he left the porch and continued on down the path, his footsteps loud, wanting to warn whatever was behind the church of his approach, wanting the area to be deserted before he reached it.

'Who's there?' he called out and for a moment, there was silence. Then the scrabbling noise began again.

The vicar reached the corner of the church, the ground beside the path dropping away to a lower level, stone steps leading down to the grass-covered graveyard. From there he could see the freshly opened grave.

It was the plot in which old Mrs Wilkinson had been laid

to rest the day before, untidy piles of earth lying in scattered heaps around the rough, circular hole. The gnawing of wood told him the worst.

Rage made him tear down the steps. What animal would burrow into the earth for the flesh of a human corpse? He reached the edge of the hole and cried out at the sight below.

The hole was wide and deep, a pit with acute sloping sides. At the bottom was a mass of squirming, black furry bodies. He could not recognize the animals at first, for the pit was darkly shadowed, the sun still hidden behind the trees, but as he watched, he began to establish individual shapes. Even then he wasn't sure what the creatures were.

One emerged from the writhing mass, its mouth full of dried meat, and scrambled over the backs of the others towards the side of the pit. Just before the gap it had left behind was closed by other eager bodies, the vicar saw directly into the damaged coffin. The sight of white broken bones stripped of all flesh made him sink to his knees, bile clogging his throat to be expelled onto the undulating mass below. He wanted to run from the terrible scene, but the convulsions wracked his body painfully, causing him to sway precariously, his fingers digging into the soft earth. He knew these creatures now – they were the harpies of his own conscience, come to torment him, letting him know death was not sacrosanct, the body could be further defiled.

The Reverend Matthews hadn't noticed the other rats in the graveyard, hidden in the grass, behind the trees, crouching beneath gravestones; those that had silently watched him enter the church grounds, followed his progress along the path with black, evil eyes, creeping forward, their bodies close to the earth. He wasn't aware that they were all around him, moving closer, haunches quivering in anticipation. It took long seconds for him to realize what was happening when the first one bit into his ankle, calmly eating into his flesh without haste or aggression.

And by the time he had screamed and struck out at the rat it was too late, for the creature's companions were already launching themselves at his body, landing heavily against him, teeth snapping and claws scratching for a hold, toppling him over, down into the pit among the others, who welcomed the new, warm meat and the satiating blood that ran from it.

In an effort that was brought about by terror overriding all pain, he gained his feet and tried to scramble up the steep incline, long black bodies clinging to him and pulling him back, but there were still more waiting for him up there. His hands grabbed at the grass, trying to haul himself from the pit, and the rats bit off his fingers one by one, the small bones proving no problem for the razor-sharp incisors. Unable to grip, he slid back down, one foot falling into the open coffin, sinking in the remnants of the old woman's now masticated flesh.

One of the creatures followed him down and for a few seconds he gazed into its black eyes, the twitching pink nose only inches away. The rat slid onto him, its jaws opening wide. The vicar's body was smothered by other giant vermin, the pit filling and brimming over with their agitated, struggling bodies, and his screams were muffled. He wondered why it took so long to die for he could feel a rat inside him, one that had eaten its way beneath his ribcage and was now gorging itself on his heart. Surely he should be dead by now? The pain had stopped moments before – or had its intensity become subliminal? Why did he still wonder? Why did the questions, the doubts, persist? Surely now there would be an answer? But no revelations came. There was only the awareness that he was being eaten. And then he realized his body *was* dead, that only his thoughts remained, and . . .

The rat fed on his brain, its pointed head buried deep into the open skull, swallowing cells and tissue that no longer functioned, the impulses finding no receptors and fading to nothing.

Sunlight pushed its way over the treetops and bathed the church and its grounds in a fresh, vibrant glow; but no birds greeted its arrival. The only sound to be heard was a faint scuffling noise from somewhere behind the ancient building. Soon, even that was gone.

7

Pender was tired. He and the head keeper, Denison, had spent the morning touring Epping Forest, visiting various farmsteads, private dwellings and official organizations within the area, looking for rodent signs, questioning the many occupiers. Most had had some trouble with vermin at one time or another, but none was of a serious nature and they could all identify their particular pests.

The day had started early for the investigator and the night before had ended late. He found himself biting into his lower lip in frustration as he mulled over the outcome of the previous night's meeting at the Conservation Centre. He knew Stephen Howard had become more of a businessman than a technical researcher, but hadn't realized to what extent. Ratkill's director of research had patiently listened to both sides of the somewhat heated argument that had continued between Pender and Whitney-Evans, his face impassive, occasionally nodding in agreement at points made by either protagonist, but rarely adding his own comment. Pender soon guessed Howard was waiting for a reaction from Thornton, the Private Secretary for the Ministry of Agriculture, Fisheries and Food, before he, himself, allowed his views to be known. Pender had seen Howard take this noncommittal line often in company meetings where superiors were involved and it had always mildly amused him; but now there was much more than private ambitions involved and the research director's attitude irritated Pender. It became obvious that Whitney-Evans and Thornton had discussed the matter before the meeting when the private secretary suggested that matters should proceed with the utmost caution, that he would refuse to recommend a full-scale operation until it was proved conclusively that the Black rat was breeding in the forest.

Stephen Howard agreed that more evidence was needed before such drastic and costly action was taken; besides, the Black rat, if it did still exist, had been pretty inactive up until now and it was fairly safe to assume it would remain so during the few days it would take to firmly establish its presence. He could see no reason to ring alarm bells at this time.

Jenny had lost her temper then, her eye-witness report having been dismissed almost out-of-hand, and the theory that it might indeed have been a group of coypus she had seen emerging from the pond seized upon and used against her. Pender, seated next to her in the Centre's library which was being used as the conference room, clasped a hand over her arm beneath the table to calm her, knowing her rage would be wasted on men like Whitney-Evans, Thornton and Howard. He, too, was angry, but he had long ago learned to control anger and direct it purposefully. He had begun to tell them of the dangerous consequences procrastination might bring. He had made a detailed study of the London Outbreak and he reminded them of the mistakes made at that time, the underestimation of the rats that had cost the lives of hundreds, the inadequate measures at first used against the vermin, the warnings that had been ignored beforehand. Would they take the responsibility for another 'Outbreak'?

Eric Dugdale, of the Safety Inspectorate, agreed with Pender: the risk was too great to take any chances. The head keeper, Denison, was unsure. None of his men had reported any strange happenings in the forest, although he had noticed a certain unease in them lately; his own sighting of a white deer, traditionally a bad omen, had disturbed him greatly. Thornton and Howard had smiled openly at that, but Whitney-Evans' reaction was more sober – he was too knowledgeable of forest folklore to scoff. Nevertheless, he still felt absolute proof of the Black rat's existence was vital before the ultimate decision was taken. Alex Milton, silent until then, reluctantly agreed. Thornton nodded. Howard had leaned forward and spoken gravely for the next ten minutes, explaining to the group his considered plan of action, how his team, organized by his head biologist, Michael Lehmann, and Pender, would search every square inch of the forest, discreetly but painstakingly, until they were sure the Black rat was not alive and well and living in the wooded suburbia of Epping Forest. At the slightest evidence that the rat was there – provided it was sufficiently substantiated – the panic button would be pushed without further delay. They were all aware of the seriousness of the situation but he felt sure they were also all aware of the panic they would cause if they made their decision for evacuation too soon. He had looked towards Thornton for approval and the private secretary had given it with a further lecture on the merits of caution.

Pender knew he had lost and further protestation was useless. The next two hours were spent discussing how the search would be set up and how the Superintendent's staff could coordinate with the Ratkill people. All would be sworn to secrecy, of course, and Thornton would personally inform the Home Secretary of the proceedings. It was decided that Pender would conduct a superficial search of the area the following day, accompanied by Denison, who would act as guide and introduce him to the many residents of the forest to be questioned. The questions would be asked under the

guise of a census on pests in the area; if anything was
seriously amiss, the locals would certainly mention it without
pointed prompting. Pender would then be able to organize a
more thorough search in specific areas – the more likely ones
– which could then spread into more widespread locales.

Throughout, Jenny sat in silence and Pender could feel
her disappointment in him. Over their drinks earlier that
evening, they had relaxed in each other's company. It had
been a pleasant interlude and both had left the pub reluctantly
to attend the scheduled meeting. He had soon become
involved in the plans for the next day's perfunctory, but
necessarily so, search, and on the few occasions his eyes had
met hers, the friendliness seemed to have disappeared from
them. He could understand her resentment towards the meeting in general, but was puzzled as to why she had turned cold
towards him. A mental shrug had tucked the question neatly
away and he had concentrated on plans for the search; after
the meeting, she had quietly slipped off without giving him
the chance to talk to her.

He had driven back across London to his flat in Tunbridge
Wells that night, set his alarm for 5.30, and wearily sunk into
bed.

Now he was back in the forest, having met Denison at the
Centre in the early hours of the morning. There had been no
sign of Jenny, but they had talked briefly with Alex Milton
and the senior tutor, Vic Whittaker, explaining the areas they
would cover and in which order, just in case the Centre
needed to contact them urgently. Steaming coffee had been
supplied by Jan Wimbush, the student-cum-cook, before
Pender and Denison had set off, both men refusing the offer
of a full breakfast.

By midday, they had become a little tired of repeating the
same questions to the forest residents, and the apprehension

caused by brief explorations of the quieter glades of the woodland, knowing the danger from the vermin they sought, had set their nerves on edge.

Pender studied the woodland on either side of the road as the Land-Rover trundled along at a steady speed. It had become another fine, clear day, the mists having vanished as the sun rose higher and, when on an open road like this and within the safety of the vehicle, Pender found it almost impossible to imagine there could be anything sinister lurking out there in the trees. He looked quizzically at Denison as the Land-Rover turned off from the main road into a wide, muddy track to be confronted by rusted iron gates. Tall, brick columns supported the gates and on either side stood two more single gates, apparently to allow access for anything on foot. It was obviously the entrance to some kind of estate, and he assumed the two gatehouses on opposite sides of the road inside were inhabited by whoever maintained the grounds. The road continued beyond, cutting through a forest of pine trees.

'What is this place?' he asked as Denison brought the Land-Rover to a halt.

'It's the Seymour Hall estate,' Denison replied, jerking on the handbrake. 'Nobody lives here now, not since the main house was gutted by fire over sixty years ago, but the grounds are cultivated for lumber, the fields rented out to farmers. It's a sizeable estate.'

Leaving the engine running, he pushed the door open and got down from the vehicle. It took considerable effort to swing open the iron gates.

'If you want to look down the road awhile, I'll question the people living in the gatehouses,' Denison called out, walking back to the Land-Rover.

'Okay,' Pender said as Denison climbed back in and drove through the entrance. 'Who lives in these places? Keepers?'

'No, they're privately rented, nothing to do with the estate now.' He stopped the Land-Rover again, turned off the engine and jumped out.

Pender joined him and looked around. 'It's quiet,' he commented.

Denison nodded. 'Private land. A public footpath goes through the property, but not many know about it. They see the gates and assume there's no access.' He walked over to one of the houses, its yellow-grey bricks faded and crumbled. 'You go ahead,' he said, turning back to Pender, 'I'll catch you up.'

Pender began the journey up the long, straight road, constantly glancing into the pine forests on either side. He soon felt completely alone and more than once he turned to see if the head keeper was back there in the distance. He had the same sensation as the day before when he and Jenny had gone off in search of the creatures she had claimed to have seen – that same feeling of being watched. He smiled at his own fears. It was the isolation that exaggerated everything, the quietness of the forest, the leafy screen that hid so much animal life. His upbringing had been in cities, among people, nothing ever still in his vision; here only the breeze seemed to make things move. He froze when he heard a scuffling noise to his right and then dropped into a defensive crouch as something broke free from a thicket a few yards away.

Pender straightened and grinned, shaking his head sheepishly at himself as the pheasant shot across the muddy road and disappeared into the trees on the other side. The investigator shoved his trembling hands into the side pockets of his green combat-jacket and resumed his journey.

Jesus, he said to himself, this is really getting to me. Was there a genuine tension in the air or was it imagination? Maybe he was over-reacting to Jenny's statement. But still, there had been the rat's droppings and the chewed-up door back at the Centre. And the stoats that had been slaughtered; if rats hadn't done that, then it must have been something pretty fearsome. Yet the local farmers he'd questioned that morning hadn't reported anything unduly worrying, and if the Black breed really were in the area, surely they would have been detected by now? Unless, of course, they had developed a new kind of cunning. He shuddered at the thought.

The trees gave way to his right and the land sloped gently away from the road; lush, bordered fields dipped, then rose into the horizon. A perfectly shaped round tree copse, about a hundred yards in diameter, stood in the nearest field and for some curious reason it made him feel uneasy.

He reached a low, farm-style gate and leaned his elbows against it, a frown creasing his forehead. The ground rose upwards beyond the gate and on the crest of its hill he could see a huge mansion. He assumed it was Seymour Hall itself, but from this distance it was hard to tell the building was only a shell. He counted six square-shaped chimney-stacks silhouetted against the sky, the building itself having three levels. Only the black glassless windows gave any hint of the ruin inside. But the real cause of Pender's puzzled expression was the land between the gate and the house.

The road leading up to the mansion was made of rubble and the field it ran through was completely barren, the dark earth churned and pitted as though any worthy soil had been scoured away, leaving only the ugly, rock-strewn crust below. It was an unpleasant sight among the lush forestland, and Pender wondered what could have caused such destruction. His eyes narrowed.

He had seen something moving in the distance, up near the house itself. An animal of some kind. Something pink. Something bloated.

His hand gripped the top of the wooden gate and he unconsciously held his breath. It was too far away to make out any discernible shape. It moved slowly towards the house, having appeared behind some nearby shrubbery. It was difficult to tell its true size from this distance.

The sound of the Land-Rover's engine made him snap his head around. Denison saw the curious look on the rat-catcher's face as he brought the vehicle to a halt.

'What's up?' he asked urgently, jumping out. 'Have you seen the rats?'

'I've seen something, but I'm not sure what it is.' Pender pointed towards the house, his finger searching for the pink, slow-moving creature. But it was gone.

'What's the matter, Pender? What did you see?'

Pender shook his head in bewilderment. 'I don't know. It's disappeared.'

'Well what in God's name did it look like, man? Was it a Black rat?'

'No, no, it was pink, bloated. It moved as though its body was too heavy for its legs. It was somewhere near the house.'

To Pender's amazement, Denison burst into laughter. 'What is it?' Pender asked. 'What's so funny?'

The head keeper controlled his laughter and leaned one hand on the gate, the other against his hip. 'Pigs,' he said.

'What?' Pender looked at him with curiosity.

'Pigs, old man. The place is alive with 'em.' Denison grinned at Pender, enjoying the man's confusion. 'This field is let out to a local farmer for his free-range pigs. It's his bloody animals that have made such a mess of the land here; they've sucked and chewed every living thing from it.'

'Pigs,' Pender said flatly.

Denison, still smiling broadly, nodded. 'They've got a shelter up by the house – used to be stables. You usually get them all over this field, but I suppose they've gone in for their afternoon snooze. Nothing deadly about those old boys, Pender.'

The investigator was forced to smile at his own error. 'Guess I'm in a spooky mood today,' he admitted.

'Well, there's one thing for sure,' Denison said, looking up at the house. 'There won't be any rats up there, not with the pigs around. They don't tolerate vermin too well, y'know.'

'Yes, you're probably right. We'll have to check it out later, though, just in case. Where to next?'

'Well, there are a couple of farms and private homesteads on the estate. We'll have a look . . .'

Both men's attention was caught by the beeping of a car's horn. They looked back down the long road leading from the entrance gates and saw a green van approaching at an unwise speed for the rutted track. Pender recognized it as the Ford Transit belonging to the Conservation Centre, yellow lettering painted on its sides giving it its official title.

He saw the driver was the young tutor he'd met at the Centre the day before – Will, he thought his name was. As the van slid to a halt, the passenger door flew open and Jenny Hanmer sprang lightly to the ground. There was no reserve in her eyes this time as she ran towards Pender, and there was a fear in her voice that made him want to reach out to her.

'Luke,' she said breathlessly. 'You've got to come back to the Centre immediately! They've found something up at the old church! Something – something terrible.'

He looked down into her tear-blurred eyes and then he did reach out to her, holding her close, just for a moment.

8

Brian Mollison jogged past the fawn Capri and glanced into the interior. He felt disappointment on seeing it was empty. The woodland area was a well-used copulation centre for the romantic and the desperate, and cars parked on roadside clearings in the forest often offered stimulating views of thrashing, half-naked limbs.

He continued running, a light sheen covering his skin beneath the tracksuit. The day before had been a frustrating failure for him: he had failed to expose himself to anyone, the shock of nearly being caught having subdued any further inclinations for the rest of that day. It was a pity, for the woman he had been about to show himself to had been a stunner. Who the fuck had been in those bushes? Had it been an animal? Or some bloody deviant lurking there? If he hadn't had his tracksuit trousers around his ankles he'd have sorted them out. He had to admit, though, he had been a little alarmed. Running and dressing at the same time was no easy thing and by the time he'd reached his car his whole body was shaking. It was a wonder he hadn't killed someone with the reckless way he'd driven home. His mother – Christ, he'd love to stop her prattling once and for all – had got short-shrift from him for the rest of that day!

School had been unbearable the following morning. He wasn't sure if it was because the woman had been such a good-looker or because his secret pleasure was making stronger demands on him, but his frustration was extremely upsetting. In fact, he knew he would have to do something about it or his unbesmirched record at the school would be ruined, which accounted for the quick drive out to Epping Forest in the lunch hour.

The journey had taken twenty minutes, but he had a free period after lunch; he would have plenty of time. It would mean not eating, of course, so his mother – God, one day he'd show her – had better have a decent dinner for him that night! Or else!

The grass had made his plimsolls damp, but he had a spare pair back at the school and he wasn't unduly worried. He would have to find someone fast – couldn't afford to be choosy today. Even an old woman would do – as long as she didn't resemble his mother. He headed for a wide track frequently used by strollers, keeping a steady pace, antici-pation already causing a stirring inside his tracksuit. Some-times he likened his penis to a bloodhound's nose – it seemed to sense its quarry from miles away.

He stopped when he heard the sound of laughter coming through the trees ahead. Knowing he was close to the track, the PE instructor trotted forward with more caution, keeping his body low and avoiding brittle-leaved bushes, slowing to a walk when the dead leaves at his feet gave warning of his approach. The laughter came again and then a woman's voice, calling. The trees and undergrowth thinned out and he found himself at the edge of the grassy track. He stepped back out of view and waited.

It wasn't long before a child of about four came scooting by, chased by another, slightly younger. A boy and a girl. The mother wouldn't be far away. He crouched behind a stout oak and his breathing became more laboured.

They came into sight a few seconds later, two of them, two women. And they looked quite young – late twenties, both of them. One was quite plain and dumpy, but the other wasn't bad. A bit sturdy, perhaps, but no, not bad at all. Let them go by, follow them for a bit, make sure they haven't got a dog with them, as well – dogs could be a bloody nuisance.

He clasped a hand to his mouth to muffle the sound of his breathing and let several seconds lapse.

All clear? Good. No one behind them. Have to be fast with this one. Do a bit in front of them, then off into the trees, finish off in private. Then straight back to school. One on her own would have been better, but beggars couldn't be choosers: two would have to do. They were braver when they weren't alone, and more inclined to complain to the authorities afterwards. Two had thrown stones at him once. Taught him to keep away from gravelly paths. Still, he wouldn't hang around. Quick flash, little jiggle, then off. Christ he'd show them something!

He crept forward, his hand reaching inside his tracksuit and squeezing as though assuring himself his erection was still there. He had been foolish to wonder. A high bush blocked his view and he stood straight, peeking over the top. It was unfortunate that one of the women – the plain, dumpy one – happened to glance round at that moment. He saw her jaw drop open and her body go stiff just before he ducked down again. Through a chink in the bush he saw her say something to her companion, who looked towards him, her body stiffening. Abruptly they turned and began marching briskly down the track away from him, calling to the children in tight voices as they went. He knew he would have to act fast, the element of surprise now gone.

Leaping into the centre of the wide track, he quickly dropped his trousers and pulled his tracksuit top up with both hands, calling out his greeting of 'Want a fuck?' to catch their attention. They stared in horror which quickly turned to disgust. Loathing even. The children beyond stared in fascination.

'Piss off, you dirty bastard!' the short woman shouted and her companion looked at her as though she had committed the greater offence.

Well used to the rudeness of such females, the PE instructor wriggled his buttocks from side to side, his swollen penis swaying like the boom of a sailing boat in a shifting wind. He only became aware of the little pale blue and white Austin's presence behind him when he heard a burly voice call out, 'Just a minute you!'

The police officer in his Panda patrol car had been too stunned to move at first. He had been on routine patrol through the forest, enjoying the tranquillity, heading for his favourite lunch spot where he could have his sandwiches and flask of soup in peace, and perhaps get his head down for twenty minutes or so. Travelling almost silently down the bumpy track at little more than 5 mph he had been amazed to be suddenly confronted by a pair of white, naked buttocks. The man's trousers were around his ankles and his upper clothing pulled upwards, revealing a broad, hairy back. It was so unexpected, even though the purpose of his patrol was to seek out such offenders, that his initial reaction was to sit and stare, wide-eyed and open-mouthed, until his foot slipped off the clutch and the car jerked forward as the engine stalled. The movement galvanized some action.

'Just a minute you!' he bellowed as he pushed open the door, failing to find words more appropriate to the situation.

Brian Mollison turned his head and this time it was his turn to be horrified. The thing he had dreaded most, the thing he had constant wide-awake nightmares over, had happened. Caught in the very act! Oh my God, what would mother say? Oh my God!

He dropped his hands and stooped, tugging at his trousers and trying to run at the same time. It was fortunate for him that he stumbled, for the policeman was grabbing for his shoulder at that moment and found himself clutching thin air instead. The momentum carried the uniformed man forward and he tripped over the PE instructor's scrambling body, landing heavily on his elbows.

In his panic, thrashing limbs and shrivelling genitals, the instructor endeavoured to push himself away from the heavy, mean-looking policeman, and his fitness allowed him to gain his feet before his adversary. He shrieked when he saw the two women bearing down on him, the short, plump one wielding a stout tree branch, a determined look on her face.

He was running before she had a chance to use it on him. But she did manage to hurl it just before he disappeared into the trees and he let out a yell of surprise rather than pain as the rough wood struck his still bare backside. It did spur him on, however, and soon he had been swallowed up by the forest; the two women could hear his crashing progress through the undergrowth.

Mollison knew the policeman would give chase and his eyes blurred with self-pity. What if he were caught? It would mean the end of his career. He'd be reviled. His mother would never forgive him! Could he go to prison for such an offence? They would certainly send him to a psychiatrist. The shame of it! One more chance, dear God, just one more chance. I'll never do it again. Oh please, please!

He staggered as a hidden root, obviously on the side of the Law, tripped him. He fell to his knees and stayed there in a crouched position, hands clasped together in his lap as though in prayer, drawing in deep breaths and trying to listen over his heartbeats for the sounds of someone giving chase. Oh please, God, don't let them follow. I'll do anything you say from now on. I'll be good. The fact that he had never been to church nor said a prayer since he was ten years old did not embarrass him and he certainly didn't think it was worth mentioning at that particular point in time. Besides, God welcomed repenting sinners. The crashing of undergrowth somewhere behind told him he wasn't as welcome as he'd have liked.

On his feet again and wiping tears from his face with a rough hand, he pressed onwards, his feelings of shame, unjust persecution and basic fear being replaced by one overriding objective: survival. He knew in which direction his car lay and he headed for it. No fucking flatfoot who spent the day on his arse driving around the countryside would catch him! Not on foot! He ran on, still afraid but confident he could outdistance the policeman. Yet when he turned once, just to see if he had lost his pursuer, he nearly collapsed at the sight of the blue uniform gaining ground. Extreme panic returned and once more he was a blubbering wreck, all running rhythm gone, pace spasmodic. A message beat its way through his jumbled senses as he caught sight of a yellowish-brown speck in the distance. The Capri! The fawn Capri he'd passed earlier, near the roadside, not far from his own car! He had a chance now. If he could –

His thoughts were cut off as he fell headlong into the dip, sliding down to the bottom, his face and hands torn by clutching brambles. Oh God, he was finished! The Law had him now! He buried his head into his hands and began to sob quietly.

But the policeman ran by. The PE instructor could hear the thudding footsteps, the swishing as thin branches were brushed aside, the muffled cursing as the law officer became confused. Then all noises receded as the policeman passed his position and ran on towards the road. It was unbelievable! The man had missed him completely.

Mollison realized he must have been screened from his pursuer by trees or bushes before he'd slipped into the dip. He was surprised the policeman hadn't heard him fall, but guessed the man had been making too much noise himself. And the dip had been shielded by more undergrowth around its edges. It was a perfect spot to hide in, a perfect place for lovers. Yes, someone had obviously used it already for clandestine purposes – there was a torn old blanket, twisted and leaf-strewn not three feet away from his very nose. And unless he was mistaken, that was a woman's shoe . . .

His eyes widened as the objects scattered around the small, hidden clearing became recognizable. There was torn, mangled clothing, another shoe – a man's this time – what looked like a pair of women's tights hanging loosely from a twig. A gold wristwatch. Why would someone leave a gold – ? Whatever had caused the mental delay, it was gone now and he realized the full horror of what surrounded him.

Deep red bloodstains smeared everything: the ripped clothing, the blanket, the shoes, the earth – even leaves on the undergrowth were discoloured. He knew the white gleaming objects were bones and the lumps of mushy substance that clung to them were flesh, but he could not understand why the bones did not form a recognizable shape; he failed to see that they had been torn apart, that the deep indents and the jagged endings had been caused by gnawing teeth.

He opened his mouth to scream but, partly because he was too stunned and partly because he still wanted to escape, no sound emerged. Instead, he began to sob again and, when he finally found the courage to take his hands from his face and look around once more, an irrational question entered his mind and he began searching the clearing. Although their bones were scattered, they could still be pieced together and buried complete; but after a while he gave up. He couldn't find them. He sat and wondered where the heads had gone.

Ken Woollard trudged across the muddy farm towards the farmhouse. His usual ill-tempered disposition had been worsened by the unwelcome visit from the 'authorities'. One of them had been the head keeper, Denison, a busybody if ever there was, and the other a man from Ratkill, the pest exterminators. Asking bloody fool questions, meddling. Of course he had problems with bloody vermin – what farmer didn't? But nothing he couldn't handle himself. He'd laid down poison two days before, immediately he'd discovered the remains of one of his cats. Lord knows what had happened to its companion – he hadn't seen hide-nor-hair of it since. Anyway, the fluoroacetamide hadn't been touched and he'd discovered no new evidence of rats in the area, so why should he report any trouble to the two snoopers? The cat could easily have been killed by dogs. Or maybe a fox had been crazed enough to have a go. Or a badger. He didn't know of any badgers in this part of the woodlands, but with Epping Forest, anything was possible; new breeding grounds were always springing up. Some said they'd even seen a white deer roaming free in the forest lately. Yes, a badger could have caused the damage to the cat. Violent bloody creatures they were, when aroused. Powerful. There were rats around, all right – the loop smears in the barn were proof enough of that – but not the big ones, not the Black rats. No, he'd have seen 'em. Big as dogs, they said. No way they could run around without being seen.

Nelly had wanted him to report the trouble, but then she

always panicked, the silly woman. She was a countrywoman, born and bred, and had never feared any living creature. Until the London Outbreak, that is. That had shook her bad. She couldn't even stand mice after that. Just as well the two snoopers hadn't gone up to the house and asked her questions! She'd have told 'em, all right. She'd have blurted out everything. A good strappin' was what she wanted. That'd make her hold her noise. Been – what? – seven years since he'd given her a strappin'. Ten years since he'd given her a good layin'. The land took it out of a man.

No, no trouble 'round here, misters, he'd told 'em. Nothing he'd call trouble, anyway. Of course he'd contact The Warren at any signs of unusual vermin activity. Be in his own interests, wouldn't it? The two men had departed satisfied, leaving the farmer sitting on his tractor staring thoughtfully at their backs.

Well, more poison would go down tonight, and a stronger dosage, at that. He'd take all the necessary precautions, but he wouldn't be panicked by them who knew nothing about working the land. He could take care of his own. Thing to take care of now was his belly. He was starvin'.

The farmer stomped his boots down hard on the cobbled yard, unloading the mud clinging to the undersoles. He wouldn't mention the two men and their questions to Nelly, she'd only get into a tizz and start naggin' again. He tramped across the yard, muttering to himself, wondering why he hadn't had the sense to pack up farming thirty years ago when he was a young man. His two sons, miserable bleeders both, had gone off as soon as they saw the sense of it. Merchant navy, the two of 'em. Should have been here helpin' him out. That's what education did for you. He paused at the front door of the farmhouse, an aged and crumbling two-storey building, and lifted one booted foot, a hand held against the door-frame for balance. With a grunt, he jerked off the boot and let it fall to the ground.

It was while he stood there, balanced on one leg, that he became aware of the unusual silence in the farmyard. Not that farmyards were noisy places, but there was usually some activity going on. Now there wasn't a sound. Not even from the birds. Except . . .

His head swung round to the door and he stared at the wood panelling. Except . . . for the faint scuffling noise from inside the house.

Curious, he placed his ear against the wood and listened. More scuffling noises, the sound a cat makes when scuttling across the floor after a ball of paper. Or after a terrified mouse. Perhaps the surviving prodigal cat had returned. Yet the noise was too great to have been made by one animal. Woollard stood erect and cursed himself, annoyed at the silly way he was behaving. He was acting like an old woman, listening at bloody doors! It was those two snoopers – they'd put the wind up him with their bloody stupid questions about bloody stupid rats! He grabbed the door handle and pushed hard, barging into the narrow hallway without further thought.

'Oh, Lord God . . .' he said quietly, for once his anger overwhelmed by what he saw. The hallway was filled with black, furry bodies that wriggled and climbed over each others' backs, that scuttled in and out of doorways, that leapt up at the walls as though trying to escape from the squirming, tightly pressed mass, that ran up the stairs and tore flesh from the bloody shape that lay sprawled there.

Nelly's eyes stared down into her husband's, but there was no life in them. A hand still clutched at the bannister rails and held her in that position, halfway up the stairs, on her back, as though she had slipped while fleeing, turning and grabbing for a rail as the rats dragged her back down, nipping at her legs, running up her body, sinking their teeth into her breasts.

Even as he watched, her fingers began to open as one creature ate its way into the tendons of her wrist, and she began to slide down, the dark bodies coming with her, refusing to let go of their prey. Her head was held up as though she was unwilling to take her eyes off him, but he saw it was because of the rat burrowing under her chin, pushing up the jaw as it worked its way inside.

She slumped to the bottom of the stairs, her knees high, feet held by the mass of bodies in the hallway, her head now rolling sideways, mercifully breaking the spellbinding gaze on him.

The farmer ran forward, his anger finally breaking forth, the one boot he wore stomping down on the vermin's backs. He slipped, for there was no firm footing, the floor a moving carpet of bristling fur, and his hands clutched desperately at the walls for support. He was on his knees, trying to crawl forward through the creatures, but they struck out at him with sharp incisors, clinging to him as their companions had clung to his wife.

The farmer moved forward, slowly, painfully, his exposed foot already torn and shredded. He tried to keep them away from his face, but his hands were weighed down by bodies and he was unable to even lift them from the floor. He became motionless, resting there in the hallway on hands and knees, unable to see his wife beneath the sea of black creatures. Soon the weight of the rats on his back crumpled his body into a heap and he too disappeared beneath the ever-moving mass.

9

Pender looked into the open grave and shuddered. The remains of what were once two human beings lay down there, their bones stripped almost clean. The identity of the skeletal corpse still half-inside its coffin was known to the group of people in the graveyard – it was an old woman who had been buried the day before – but they could only guess the identity of the second. It was an educated guess though, for the vicar of the Church of the Holy Innocents could not be found.

Blood had soaked into the walls of the grave giving the soil a rich viscous quality; the shattered wood of the coffin lid was stained red. Pender wondered how it had happened. Had the vicar, on his way to his early morning devotions inside the church, heard the noises coming from the graveyard and gone to investigate? Had he fainted when he had seen what was happening and fallen into the grave? Or had he been pushed into it? Could rats, no matter how large, have caused this? Pender shook his head in disbelief. Rats were not burrowers; they wouldn't dig into the earth to reach a corpse. At least, *normal* rats wouldn't.

A voice broke into his thoughts. 'Mr Pender? I'm told you can throw some light on this.'

Pender almost smiled at the policeman's solemn optimism. 'I'm not sure,' he said. He turned away from the grave and walked towards the single, foot-high railing that bordered the church grounds, the uniformed policeman following. Pender squatted on the iron bar and ran a hand across his rough chin. He could see the group of people near the entrance to the graveyard, all eyes turned away from the open grave. Whitney-Evans was there, so was Alex Milton, both deep in conversation. Denison was talking to Eric Dugdale, the safety inspector, obviously making a report of their fruitless questioning that morning. There were several other figures that Pender did not recognize but assumed were staff from The Warren offices. Jenny was being consoled by the senior tutor from the Centre, Vic Whittaker, who had an arm around her shoulders and was talking to her quietly. Why didn't he get her away from this bloody place, Pender asked himself.

'Can you help, sir?' the policeman hovering over the ratcatcher prompted.

Pender looked up at him and shrugged. 'We think it was rats,' he said.

The uniformed man paled visibly. 'Do you mean Black rats? The ones that were in London?'

Pender nodded. 'It seems likely.'

He stood once again and faced the policeman. 'Look, I think you'd better get whoever's in charge of your station down here right away. Things are going to start happening and the sooner the local police are involved the better.'

'I'll get on the radio now. But is there any more you can tell me before I do?'

'Only that I'm from Ratkill and at the moment investigating evidence of Black rats in the forest. I think this confirms it beyond all doubt.'

'Bloody hell! Why weren't we informed?' The colour had returned to the policeman's face with his anger.

Pender held up his hand in apology. 'Sorry, but nothing was confirmed until now. We didn't want to cause a panic.'

The policeman turned away in disgust. 'All the bloody same, you lot,' Pender heard him say as he stomped off.

'Just a minute,' he said, bringing the policeman to a halt. 'You're not to mention what I've told you to anyone.'

'If you think . . .'

'*Not to anyone*. I'll speak to your inspector when he gets here. Clear?'

The policeman's answer was unintelligible, but it was obvious he understood.

'Now,' Pender went on. 'Who discovered the . . .' the word was hardly appropriate but he used it anyway '. . . bodies?'

The policeman pointed towards an elderly man standing uneasily on the fringe of the group near the gate. 'The old boy over there. He maintains the grounds around the church. It's frightened the life out of him.'

'I'm not surprised. Where did he report it from?'

'The rectory. He went there to tell the vicar. Fortunately, Mrs Paige, the housekeeper, was in. She told us she hadn't seen the vicar all morning – that's why we think it could be him down there.' He nodded towards the freshly dug pit.

'Okay. You'll have to keep them both quiet for the moment.'

'Are you kidding? Half the forest knows by now. Mrs Paige has probably been on the phone all morning. The bloody forest superintendent was up here almost as soon as we were.'

'All right, but they don't know about the rats yet, do they?'

'Of course not.'

'Then that's the way it has to stay for the moment.'

'Until when?' The policeman's tone was belligerent.

Pender sighed. 'Until we start moving the people out. Look, I know how you feel. I'd like to get this out into the open right now, myself; but things have to be organized first.'

Recognizing the frustration in the ratcatcher's words, the stiffness left the policeman's voice. 'Fair enough, Mr Pender. We'll do our best.' He strode off towards his patrol car.

Pender walked over to Jenny and Whittaker, conscious of the shock they were in. The girl managed a weak smile as he approached.

'Will they do something, Luke?' she asked. 'Will this make them act?'

'Yes, Jenny, they'll do something more constructive now. They'll have to.'

'What happened, Pender?' asked Whittaker. 'Could rats really have done that?'

'I think the Black rat could. It's obvious they were after the dead body, although how they knew there was a fresh corpse down there beats me. The other person – if it was the vicar – presumably disturbed them and they got him too.'

'But, rats – digging?'

'I know. I've never heard of it either. But it sure as hell wasn't the vicar digging the body up – no spades around.'

'Pender, may we have a word?' It was Whitney-Evans' voice calling.

'Be right there,' Pender answered. Then he turned back to the two tutors. 'Why don't you take Jenny back to the Centre,' he said to Whittaker. 'She should rest after a shock like this.'

'I'm okay, Luke,' the girl said.

'He's right, Jenny.' Whittaker looked concerned. 'Let's get away from here.'

She reluctantly agreed but gazed up earnestly into Pender's face. 'Will you be coming back, Luke? I'd like to talk to you.'

Pender nodded. 'You'll be seeing a lot of me from now on, Jenny.'

Whittaker frowned, unsure of the meaning in Pender's words. 'Come on Jenny, let's go,' he urged, and gently led her away from the church grounds.

'Pender.' Whitney-Evans again.

'Coming,' the ratcatcher said wearily, and walked over to the superintendent and the Warden of the Conservation Centre.

'What caused this?' Whitney-Evans demanded to know.

'What the hell do you think caused it?' replied Pender, anger broiling.

'You think it was the rats?'

'I'm bloody sure it was.'

'There's no need to adopt that tone, Pender. I'm only asking your opinion.'

'My opinion didn't count last night.'

'Of course it did. We took the correct action.'

'We could have avoided this.'

'Perhaps. I still maintain, from the knowledge we had at the time, that we took the appropriate action. Now, is there definite proof the Black rat was involved in this terrible business?'

Pender stared at him in disbelief. 'No,' he said deliberately. 'I believe there's a tribe of cannibals living in this forest and last night or some time this morning, they decided on a little feast.'

The superintendent's face became outraged. 'There's absolutely no need for your ill-manners, Pender. Just who do you think you are to talk to me in this way?'

Pender controlled his anger and ignored him. He turned to the Warden. 'I suggest we set up an operational HQ at the Centre immediately, Mr Milton. If you could start by sending any classes you may have back to their schools, I'll get things organized from the Ratkill end. I've asked the constable to get his station inspector over here – I think he should be put fully in the picture . . .'

'Aren't you exceeding your authority?' Whitney-Evans interrupted.

'My job is to prevent another Outbreak, *Mr* Whitney-Evans, and I answer only to my organization and the government in times of emergency. *My* authority overrides that of any outside bodies. If you want me to produce the official papers giving me that power, they're in my car. I can . . .'

'That won't be necessary. But I think there should be another meeting before you put any plans into action.'

'Oh, we'll have another meeting all right. And another. Then another. But while we're talking, I'm going to make sure something is happening. You can help by calling in all your staff. Anyone connected with the forest, not just the keepers. Someone, *somewhere*, in the forest must have seen signs of these rats. I want to know when and where.'

This time Alex Milton spoke up. 'Why, Mr Pender? How will that help?'

'We have to find a pattern. We have to know their haunts, their hunting-grounds. Rats are scavengers and if they find a good source of food, they'll stick to it until it runs out.'

'But we've had no reports of damage or losses,' said Whitney-Evans. 'Not serious losses, anyhow.'

Pender shook his head. 'No, that's what I don't understand. I'll need to speak to the farmers I questioned this morning again. I think one or two may not have been exactly honest.'

'Surely not?' said Milton. 'The farmers know how serious the vermin problem is.'

'Yes, and they know how serious it is to have their farms put in quarantine. They'd suffer heavy losses.'

'What then?' asked Whitney-Evans. 'What if someone admits they have had trouble?'

'Then we can start pinpointing locations on a map. We already have three – the Centre itself, the pond and this graveyard. We can begin to work out their boundaries, trace their movements. It'll give us a more defined area to work in. You see, to eliminate the rats, we have to find where they're coming from, we have to rout them out. So our priority is to find their lair.'

10

It was early evening before the meeting finally got under way and the Centre's small lecture hall, though less than full, seemed crowded to Pender. He quickly scanned the many anxious faces, estimating there were over thirty people present. Personally he would have chosen a more select gathering; in his experience, the bigger the crowd, the more confusing the outcome. He supposed, however, each was necessary to the operation to be discussed.

He recognized the Private Secretary for the Ministry of Defence, Robert Shipway, talking with Antony Thornton from the Ministry of Agriculture, at a long table hastily brought in for the occasion from the Centre's library. Beside them sat the Director-General of the Forestry Commission with one of his commissioners and someone from the Department of the Environment – Pender could not remember his particular title, nor the names of any of the three. Whitney-Evans was seated next to Stephen Howard, Alex Milton sitting slightly away from the table. The police commissioner for the Essex area occupied the other end of the table, together with Mike Lehmann and a major from the Armed Forces. It was to be a high-powered meeting and Pender could already see that Stephen Howard was revelling in it.

The others in the room sat facing the select group at the table in the lecture hall's rows of rising seats, Pender among those in the front row. Eric Dugdale of the Safety Inspectorate was there with two members of his staff; several local councillors spoke together in hushed voices; the inspector from the area's nearest police station sat in deep silence; Charles Denison, seated next to him, equally silent; Vic Whittaker and an attractive, middle-aged woman introduced earlier to Pender as Alex Milton's wife, Tessa, sat immediately behind. Other seats were taken up by several men referred to as Verderers of Epping Forest, and a few members of the community considered important enough to be invited along. Thankfully there were no journalists present, but Pender knew it would not take long for the story to break.

The general low-voiced din was interrupted by Antony Thornton tapping sharply on the table top with the blunt end of his fountain-pen.

'Gentlemen, I think we should proceed with the meeting without further delay. I believe everybody who should be here is here.' He looked around at the forest superintendent and Stephen Howard for affirmation. Both men nodded.

Thornton continued. 'This is just a general meeting to let everyone who will be concerned with the operation know exactly what is happening. Details will be discussed in subsequent smaller gatherings by those directly involved.' He paused and looked around, his voice losing some of its briskness. 'Most of you have some idea of why you were called here, but for the benefit of those who haven't, I'll start at the beginning. Over the past few days, damage has been done that suggests a powerful vermin is at large. Droppings have been found which indicate the vermin is the Black rat.'

A buzz of voices broke out behind Pender. Thornton held up a hand to still them.

'Yesterday, three of the creatures were sighted by a tutor of this Centre. It was not a definite sighting . . .' Pender flinched '. . . so we thought it wise to investigate further before pushing the panic button.'

'Where were they seen?' a voice from the back asked.

'Quite near here.' Thornton looked towards Whitney-Evans who said: 'A small pond near the larger Wake Valley Pond.'

Thornton continued. 'Ratkill had already been notified and a rodent investigator, Lucas Pender, was at the Centre examining damage caused by these creatures when the sighting took place. He immediately searched the area around the pond and discovered the remains of a family of stoats; they had been slaughtered. He also examined the droppings left by the vermin at the Centre and his conclusion was that there was, indeed, a strong possibility that the Black rat was inhabiting a certain part of the forest.'

Pender smiled grimly.

'However, in the meeting that followed, we all agreed that further – more concrete – proof was needed before we put into action plans for quarantine and the evacuation of the forest population.'

'Couldn't my station at least have been informed?' demanded the police inspector.

Thornton regarded him coolly. 'I'm afraid not. I repeat: we had no definite proof of their existence, therefore we deemed it unnecessary to alert anyone at that time.'

'And is that your proof?' said the inspector, undaunted. 'The incident up at the churchyard?'

Once more, a babble of voices broke out in the lecture hall and Thornton's fountain-pen was tapped hard to bring order to the meeting.

'What does Inspector Reid mean?' asked a verderer above the other voices. 'What happened up at the church?' The question had more effect than the fountain-pen and all noise died down.

Thornton straightened in his chair and looked stiffly around the room. 'Firstly, let me say this meeting will be conducted in an orderly fashion. We need to progress rapidly if we are to implement immediate action. Further questions will have to be put at the end of this statement and the subsequent statements by any of my colleagues at this table. Now, Inspector Reid, I will answer your question. Yes, the churchyard incident does give us further reason to believe in the existence of the Black rat in the forest.'

'But it's still not definite proof,' said Whitney-Evans.

Thornton turned on him with barely disguised anger. 'Even you, Edward, can't close your eyes to that atrocity.'

'Would you please tell us what has happened?' It was the same voice from the back, obviously undeterred by Thornton's previous remark.

The private secretary's head snapped round. 'The remains of two humans were found in the churchyard this morning. One had been buried normally yesterday and the other . . . the other we believe to be the body of a Reverend Jonathan Matthews, vicar of the Church of the Holy Innocents.'

A loud gasp went round the lecture hall.

Thornton went on, his voice brisk and emotionless. 'Both bodies had been stripped of flesh. We believe the vicar discovered these creatures digging up the corpse and was killed by them. Indents on the bones and their fractured state indicate that sharp implements were used to tear off the flesh: sharp teeth in other words. What's left of the clothing is being examined to ascertain whether it was the vicar or not, but we fear there can be little doubt. Even more odd in this most bizarre of incidents, the skulls of both bodies were missing.'

Thornton did not allow the disquieting news to disrupt the meeting further. 'Although we still have only one actual sighting of these creatures, I think we can assume beyond all doubt that it is the Black rat behind these incidents. We know of no other creature in England that could cause such damage.

'Now, our plans to combat this menace. All homes in the immediate vicinity will be evacuated by midday tomorrow. The superintendent's men are at this very moment warning all householders to stay inside and keep their windows and doors firmly closed – even to erect barricades if necessary. Many will obviously prefer to leave their homes right away, even though they are quite safe for the moment.'

'How can they be safe with giant rats roaming the forest?' asked a councillor, leaning forward in his seat.

'The rats haven't broken into any houses yet,' said Thornton, now resigned to the interruptions. 'Besides, to our knowledge, they have only attacked one living person so far. It seems unlikely they would suddenly go on the rampage after being undetected for all this time.'

'But isn't it escalating?' the councillor insisted. 'I mean, at first just damage to property, then killing other animals. Now they're onto humans.'

Pender turned to stare at the man, realizing he was right. Considering the rats had not been seen in the forest before yesterday, there seemed to be a rapid and frightening increase in their activity.

'I think the vicar was attacked because he disturbed them,' replied Thornton. 'He may even have foolishly tried to chase them off. No, I'm sure people will be safe for the moment – as long as they stay indoors. If my colleagues agree, I think we should start a phased evacuation: the immediate area first, then moving out towards the surrounding woodlands. Major Cormack will organize the quarantining of the entire forest, working in conjunction with the Essex and London police forces.'

'How do you propose to keep the whole area out of bounds?' asked the director-general for the Forestry Commission. 'I mean, there's over 6,000 acres of woodland to cover.'

'We'll concentrate on the logical area – say within two or three miles of this spot.'

'It's still a hell of an area.'

'I agree. But there are plenty of broad roadways running through the forest; these can be marked out at various intervals. We'll also use helicopters for surveillance. I can't actually imagine anyone wanting to get into the forest once they know what's in there, can you?'

'I thought the idea was to keep in whatever's there,' the police commissioner commented drily.

'Quite. But we'll come to that later. The Ratkill people will move in at first light tomorrow morning and it will be their job to root these monsters out and destroy them. But I'll let Stephen Howard, the research director of Ratkill, explain his operation.' He looked encouragingly at Howard, who almost stood before he realized he was not addressing a public meeting.

'What we'll need,' he began, 'is full co-operation from everyone in the forest . . .' he smiled disarmingly '. . . and detailed maps of the whole woodland area. Most important will be plans of sewage works running beneath the forest, because you can be sure, that's where the rats will be. My crews will need army protection. Your Green Goddess fire engines, Major Cormack, will be invaluable; since they've been brought up to date with new, high-powered hoses, they'll prove ideal for protection – that's one thing we can thank the last firemen's strike for. Flame-throwers might come in handy, too, although I don't like the risk to the forest itself nor to my own men. They don't appreciate singed backsides.'

The remark barely raised a smile around the room.

'My crews will all be wearing protective clothing, similar to but more advanced than that used in the London Outbreak. A team of investigators will go in first and find the likely spots, then the destruction crews will move in. I'll let Mike Lehmann, our head biologist, explain exactly what will happen.'

Lehmann was uncomfortable under their gaze, but he struck out boldly. 'If it really is the new breed of giant rat in Epping Forest, then we're in serious trouble. And if these are the descendants of the Black rat from the London Outbreak – and all the evidence points in that direction – there are a couple of questions that need to be answered: how did they escape the annihilation of their species in the city; and how have they remained undetected for so long?'

'They could have found their way into the forest before the extermination took place,' the defence secretary suggested.

'It's possible, although the previous attacks suggested they were confined to certain areas of the city,' said Lehmann. 'The other possibility is that they were somehow unaffected by the ultrasonic sound waves we used to draw the rats from their nests into the gas enclosures, and fled afterwards when they realized the game was up. Nowadays the machines are used to drive the vermin away, not draw them in; but either way, our experiments with them at the Ratkill laboratories show that the ultrasonics become ineffectual eventually; the rats adapt, learn to ignore them.'

'I must point out here,' said Howard, 'that tests are still in progress with these machines. I think we can develop one that *will* be extremely effective once we find the correct wavelength – or indeed, wavelengths.'

'To do that, we'd need a mutant rat itself. Our own over-reaction killed them all off four years ago – apart from the few that obviously escaped. We'd have been wiser to have saved some for study.'

'Surely,' said the defence secretary, 'you can experiment on ordinary rats?'

'We've been doing just that,' the biologist replied. 'Unfortunately, the giant Black is no ordinary rodent: it's a mutation, its genes are different. They're not just bigger and stronger, they also have a high degree of intelligence. They'd need it, to have remained hidden these past few years. Of course, the fact that rats are nocturnal has helped; but what puzzles me is why there's been no evidence of them until now. Even more puzzling and, I may say, more ominous: *why* now?'

'My guess is that after the mass destruction of their breed, the survivors developed an even stronger fear of man, which was passed on to the following generations. We already know of their abnormal brain-power. I'd say this has advanced with the new generations, too. They've kept out of sight, foraged in places safe to them, left little evidence of their presence.'

'It could be that there is just a small number of them,' Whitney-Evans suggested hopefully.

'Yes,' agreed Major Cormack. 'A small group would be hard to detect in a forest full of wild animals.'

'It's unlikely,' said Lehmann. 'The life-span of a rat is from fifteen months to two-and-a-half years; the female can have five to eight litters a year with as many as twelve new-born in each litter. She's ready again for mating within hours of giving birth, and the young ones reach the reproductive stage after only three months. You can figure out for yourself just how many could be bred in the space of four years.'

Pender could almost hear the clicking of mental arithmetic going on around the hall.

'I think there's plenty of them,' Lehmann continued, 'but

they've gone literally underground. I believe they're in the sewer network beneath the forest; that's where we'll look for them. The perverse thing is that the normal Black rat, or Ship rat as it's sometimes known, is arboreal – it can climb trees, high buildings; the mutant has been forced to live below ground. It could explain why they dug up the corpse at the church: they've learned to be burrowers.'

'But that's impossible,' Milton began to say. 'It would take decades for them to evolve . . .'

'For any normal animal, yes,' the biologist cut in. 'We're dealing with the abnormal.'

Thornton spoke. 'So your recommendation is to tackle them at their source: the sewers.'

Lehmann nodded. 'If they're there. We'll pump gas into the network, using a proprietary powder that produces hydrogen cyanide gas when it comes into contact with damp soil or damp air. Our main problem – other than attack from the rats themselves – will be to block all holes leading from the sewers.'

'I'm afraid many of the sewers have overflowed into some of the streams,' said Whitney-Evans. 'We've complained to the local authorities often enough.'

'Those outlets will have to be plugged. We'll need the help of your forestry staff to locate them and any other outlets from the sewers.'

'Perhaps we can help too,' said Milton. 'My staff at the Centre know the forest like the backs of their hands.'

'Fine, the more, the merrier.'

'Why not use rodenticides?' the defence secretary asked.

'That could be our biggest problem, I'm afraid,' Lehmann said grimly. 'There are two main types we could use. One is of the single dose variety: sodium fluoroacetate and fluoroacetamide, which is normally used in sewers; zinc phosphide;

norbromide, which is harmless to most other animals; arseni-ous oxide, which is *dangerous* to most other animals; alpha-chloralose, normally used only against mice. The big disadvantage with these is that rats have a built-in instinct against anything strange to them. We call it *neophobia* – new object avoidance. It makes it difficult to get them to accept new bait. They might try it after a while, but only in small amounts. If they feel any ill-effects at all, they leave it alone completely. A single dose poison might just kill a few, but even that would serve as a warning to the others.'

'And the other type of poison?' the defence secretary asked.

'The others are anticoagulants. They kill by their reaction on the rodent's blood system: they interfere with a substance called prothrombin which causes the blood to clot when vessels are broken. The rat suffers a haemorrhage at the slightest damage to blood capillaries: a tiny scratch can kill it. Females having litters are obviously very susceptible.

'Three kinds are in current use: Warfarin, coumatetralyl and chlorophacinone. They're administered gradually, build-ing up to a lethal dosage. The rat gets used to the bait, feeds on it regularly, then suffers the effects.'

'And all this takes time,' said Whitney-Evans.

'Yes, but the process can be speeded up. However, that isn't our problem. Over the past few years, rodents in this country have been building up a resistance against anticoag-ulants. It began in a couple of countries on the Continent, now it's spreading over here. Luke Pender, there, has just returned from the North where he's been investigating the matter. Luke?'

'The resistance was first noted in Wales and the Midlands, but now it's spread as far up as Cheshire and down to the south-west coast,' Pender told them. We've bred Warfarin-resistant rats in our own laboratories, but these others have developed their own immunity. The point is this: the Outbreak rats had developed that same immunity before gas was used as the final solution. It seems likely that resistance will be inherent in those descended from the rats that escaped from London. That's why I agree with Mike: gas, providing we can trap them in the sewers, has to be the answer. If the machines can't be relied on to lure them out, we have to keep them in and destroy them there.'

'I think we're all agreed, then,' said Thornton. 'Gas it shall be. Gentlemen?' he asked the room at large. A murmur of assent was given.

A councillor raised his hand. 'What about disease from these rodents? How will we combat that?'

'I don't think we need worry ourselves about that problem at the moment,' Stephen Howard said smoothly. 'The disease caused by the vermin at the time of the Outbreak was a particularly hideous distortion of Leptospirosis or Spirochaetal Jaundice. Fever first, before jaundice set in. The victim became prostrate, blind, then all senses were lost. Coma, then the skin began to stretch and tear, and the victim died. The horrifying thing is that the whole process took only twenty-four hours. Fortunately, an anti-toxin was soon produced, so we needn't fear the disease any more. The other, more normal rodent diseases are too minor nowadays to worry about. No, the main danger it would seem is attack from the beast itself. Of course, everyone "out in the field" as it were will be wearing protective suits.' Howard reached behind his chair and drew out a large, mounted photograph of a dead mutant Black rat. 'At this stage, I think it might be an idea to remind ourselves just what our old enemy looks like.' He stood, resting the photograph's base against the tabletop so everyone could see.

Pender groaned inwardly. The research director was obviously enjoying throwing the fear of God into his captive audience. No doubt he felt it valuable to impress on them the dangers his company faced. It would make the company bill seem cheap. The move was effective. Pender could feel the shudders run round the room.

'Ugly brute, isn't he?' Howard said jovially. 'This is actual size. Over two feet in length – more than three, counting the tail; long, pointed head with deadly sharp teeth – the incisors are particularly large; ears pink, naked, pointed. The fur is actually dark brown, but mottled with specks of black that give it the appearance, from a distance, of being completely black. It's much like the normal Black rat apart from its size, the main difference being its large brain and strangely humped back – powerful hindquarters, you see. Its claws are lethal.'

One of the forest verderers had gone deathly white. 'My God, are they all like that?' he asked.

For a moment, Howard seemed flustered. 'What do you mean?' he said.

'Are they all that size? It's monstrous.'

'Yes. Afraid so. All that size.'

Pender hadn't missed the research director's reaction and he was puzzled by it. He could have imagined it, but Howard had almost looked shifty for a moment. As though he had been caught out. Now he seemed relieved that the question was only to do with size. Pender frowned.

'I have a question.' It was the police commissioner who spoke, a straight-backed, sombre looking man.

'Yes, Commissioner?' said Thornton as Howard swept the photograph from the table and placed it behind his chair.

'Earlier, Mr Lehmann was puzzled by the fact that the rats had remained hidden for so long. Someone else asked why their noticeable activities seemed to be on the increase. It all appears to be pointing to one thing, doesn't it?'

He left the question unanswered and there was silence around the room.

Pender cleared his throat. 'Er, I think I know what the Commissioner is getting at. There does seem to be an escalation in the rats' activities. Why have they been seen lately after all these years of hiding? What's given them their new boldness?'

'And your explanation, Mr Pender?' Thornton asked.

'One of two things; or perhaps a combination of both. At the time of the Outbreak the mutant rat was motivated by the desire for human flesh. The new breed may also have decided it would no longer be dominated by man, or fear him as it had in the past. It decided to strike back.

'They possessed a new brain-power and soon they had the essential ingredient which gives any army the confidence to become the aggressor: the power of numbers. Perhaps that was the real turning-point for them.'

'I see what you're getting at, Mr Pender,' the defence secretary said. 'You're suggesting the rats in Epping Forest have reached a sufficiently high number to bring out that aggressiveness.'

'As I said, it may be a combination of two factors. They have the strength now, although I doubt they've reproduced in the quantity Mike suggests – the forest would be overrun with them if that were the case. These are a mutant strain: their reproductive capabilities may be different to that of a normal rodent. We know from the few groups left after the Outbreak that their reproductive system had been impaired either by the ultrasonic soundwaves or their mutant genes, so it may well have become an inherent thing. The other factor is that the old bloodlust has returned. Their strength in numbers may have triggered it off, or the taste of fresh animal flesh may have awoken an old memory, a desire that's been lying dormant for years. And if that's the case, the attacks are going to get worse. Remember, they've now tasted living, human flesh.'

The statement caused a stir and once again Thornton was forced to use his fountain-pen as a gavel.

'I think it's time we got down to the details of the operation,' he said. 'I shall inform the Minister myself of what has happened and what action we shall take. There is no way we can keep this from the media, but I suggest that all statements are issued directly from my offices; perhaps then we can avoid alarmist reactions. Fortunately we have been alerted to the danger in good time; we are in a position to control the situation. There has been only one human killing so far – let's restrict it to that number.'

The next half-hour was spent discussing plans for the forthcoming operation, Pender and Lehmann putting forward their requirements for dealing with the vermin, the police commissioner and Major Cormack agreeing on the most effective ways in which to deploy their separate forces. Maps were brought in and ruled off into sections, phone calls were made, certain members left on various assignments, lists were drawn up. Things, Pender reflected with some satisfaction, were beginning to move.

He hardly noticed the Conservation Centre's secretary-cum-girl Friday when she nervously entered the lecture hall. She whispered something into Whitney-Evans' ear and he quickly left, his expression one of concern. He was back within seconds and brought an abrupt halt to the proceedings with a message that sent a chill through everyone present.

'I'm afraid I have some rather distressing news,' he began, his voice grave, devoid of its usual pomposity. 'One of my forest keepers has just returned. As you know, my men have been out warning the forest residents to stay indoors. He . . . he visited a smallholding not far from here, within a mile. The door to the farmhouse was open, but when he called out, nobody answered. So he went in. In the hallway he found two . . . bodies, presumably those of the owner and his wife, a Mr and Mrs Woollard. Identification was not possible because the bodies had been eaten; not much of them was left.'

11

Pender tapped lightly on the door. It was late, well past eleven, and there was nothing more anyone could do that night. The lecture hall was deserted now and only a few lights shone in the working area of the Centre itself. He had left the main building and walked over to the separate residential annexe. He knocked again, a little louder.

'Who's there?' he heard Jenny's voice say.

'It's me. Luke.'

The door opened and Jenny peered out at him.

'I'm sorry if I disturbed you, Jenny. I couldn't get away any sooner.'

'It's all right, Luke. I wasn't asleep. I'm glad you came.' She opened the door wide and motioned for him to enter.

The room was small, two beds occupying most of its space with a door presumably leading off to the bathroom. A lamp glowed in one corner, giving the room an intimate feeling, and glass-covered but frameless prints, together with delicately painted ornaments, bestowed some warmth upon the functional interior.

'Cosy,' he commented.

She smiled. 'I share it with Jan Wimbush. We've tried to put some life into it.'

'I've just left Jan. She told me where to find you.'

'Where is she?'

'In the kitchen, washing up. She's had a busy evening.'

Jenny looked angry with herself. 'I should have helped her out. I'm afraid today's events have disorientated me.'

'It's okay, Will has been helping her. They're doing fine. Are you still feeling bad?'

'No, I'm okay now. It was just the shock. The vicar's housekeeper came running round to the Centre, you see. The poor woman didn't know what to do when the groundsman told her what he'd found. I went there myself to check. It was so . . .' She quickly lowered her face, forcing back the tears; she'd cried enough that day.

Pender felt strangely awkward. He wanted to hold her as he had done earlier, but he was unsure of her mood. One moment she was cold, reserved, the next she seemed to be reaching out, seeking contact.

She lifted her head, pushing away her anxieties. 'Would you like some coffee? You must be dead beat.'

He grinned. 'I could do with something stronger, but coffee will do.'

'How about both? Jan and I always keep a bottle of scotch handy for our frequent mutual sob stories.'

'You're terrific,' he said.

'Sit down and relax while I get it.' She pointed to the only armchair and he sank back into it with relief, closing his eyes and resting his head back. The tutor disappeared with an electric kettle into the adjacent room and he heard the sound of running water. 'Have to be instant, I'm afraid,' she called out.

'Anything,' he answered.

Soon a heavy measure of scotch was in his hand and Jenny was feeding coffee and boiling water into two sturdy-looking mugs.

'Make it black, one sugar,' he told her. She placed the steaming mug at his feet, then sat on the single bed, facing him. He took a large swallow of whisky and studied her, wondering how good her legs were beneath the tight jeans. Pretty good, if outward appearance were anything to go by. The baggy, loose-fitting cardigan had been replaced by a tight-fitting man's shirt, her breasts swelling against the material in a very unmasculine way. It was her face that intrigued him, though: it was somehow both soft yet determined, her brown eyes liquid, but penetrating, as though she could see into his innermost thoughts.

'I'm sorry for yesterday, Luke,' she said.

'Yesterday?'

'At the meeting. I'm sorry if I seemed to blame you for what was happening. Or, I should say, what wasn't happening. I get so sick and tired of people who refuse to take on responsibilities, who are content to talk, talk, talk, and do nothing. I'm afraid I put you in with the rest.'

'What's changed your mind? If it is changed, that is.'

'Further thought. You did your best – they just wouldn't listen.'

'They're listening now.'

'Yes, and look what it took to make them.'

'It's the way things are, Jenny. You'll go mad with frustration if you don't acknowledge that. You don't have to accept it; just realize it's there. There are other ways to fight against it, whether you call it apathy, evasiveness, self-protection – I call it fear. The thing is not to let it get to you.'

'And you don't?'

He smiled. 'I try not to.'

She looked deep into his eyes. 'Luke, what's going to happen?'

For a moment he thought she meant between them, their growing interest in each other; then he realized the feelings could be entirely one-sided – from his side.

'You mean the rats?'

She nodded and, from his initial hesitation, he knew she had read his thoughts. He carefully explained to her the details of the operation which was to begin at first light the following day and which would continue till all the mutant rats had been exterminated.

'So we at the Centre will be involved?' she asked when he had finished.

'I'm afraid so. We'll need everyone who knows the forest. Don't worry, there'll be no danger to you.'

'I wasn't worried. I'd intended to stay and help in any way, even if it was only making tea for everybody. I can't stand the thought of them being in the forest, you see. Those monsters, feeding off the wildlife, destroying. They make the forest seem . . . unclean. I despise them, Luke.'

Pender sipped his coffee, the whisky having warmed the way for it. 'Why are you here at the Centre, Jenny? It seems a strange, almost lonely life.'

'It isn't. Not really. I love the work, it's as close to nature as you can get without kissing all civilization goodbye. The children I teach are fun. And the staff are marvellous; we all work together.'

'And Vic Whittaker?'

The old reserve came back into her eyes for a moment. 'What about him?'

'Oh, just a feeling. He seems to care about you.'

'He does, but he's foolish. He has a wife but they're separated. Kids too.' Her voice softened. 'He thinks he's in love with me, but half his mind is still on his family. Sometimes I think he accepted this job to prove he's independent of her, but, I think soon, he'll discover he isn't.'

'And you? How do you feel towards him?' He half-expected a rebuttal to his question, but she smiled sadly and looked down at her hands.

'I don't intend to be used in a situation like that. Not this time.'

And there, he thought, lay the answer. At some time or other she had been involved with someone who had let her down badly. It explained her reserve, the coldness that sometimes masked – and marred – her true nature. The Centre was her escape, a kind of nunnery without the harshness or the religion. Nor the total rejection of the outside world. He wondered how long it would take for her to adjust again.

'What about you, Luke?' she countered. 'Why aren't you married?'

'I love my work too much.'

'You hate your work.'

It startled him.

'Why do you do it, Luke? Why rats?'

'I told you yesterday: the money's good.'

She shook her head. 'No, that's not it. There's some other reason.'

He drained the last of the coffee and placed the mug on the floor.

'I think I'd better make a move. It's an early start tomorrow . . .' he glanced at his watch '. . . I mean today.'

She rose with him. 'I'm sorry if I was probing.' She moved closer. 'Really.'

He smiled down at her. 'I started it. I got what I deserved.'

'Will I see you tomorrow?'

'Of course. I'll be pretty busy, but as of now, Jenny, you're part of the operation, so we'll be working together.' And then he wanted to kiss her, but foolishly – ridiculously – he was afraid to. He hadn't felt that heart-shaking fear since he'd been fifteen, on his first date. It was crazy, but irrefutable: he was afraid his advance would be rejected. He stood there like a naïve fool, too nervous to take a forward step. So she kissed him.

It was a light touch, and on the cheek; but a pleasurable shock ran through him dispersing his uncharacteristic timidity.

'Jenny . . .'

'It *is* late, Luke. Walk me over to the main building so I can help Jan clear up. Then you go and get some rest; it sounds like you're going to need it.'

He relaxed, no longer the schoolboy. 'Okay. I'm staying at the hotel in Buckhurst Hill. It shouldn't take me much more than ten minutes to get there, and only two minutes more to be sound asleep. It's been a long day.'

But it wasn't over for him yet.

Jan Wimbush wiped the steam from her spectacles with the end of her sweater. All the cups and saucers were washed now, the ashtrays emptied and clean, the big table in the lecture hall wiped of all stains. Tomorrow would be a busy day but, thank God, there would be no classes and all the Centre staff would be helping.

Alex Milton had spoken to the staff earlier that evening, explaining the rat problem to them and how the Centre was to be the operational headquarters. If any of his members wanted to leave, they could do so – he wouldn't blame them in the least. But their help was needed by the men who were coming to destroy the vermin. He had been assured by Ratkill's research director that there would be no real danger to the staff, providing they did exactly as they were told and wore the protective clothing that would be issued when outside the confines of the building itself. Everybody volunteered to stay, of course, most looking forward to the drama. The fact that the local vicar had apparently been eaten alive by the monsters seemed hardly real to those who hadn't visited the graveyard, although the warden did try to stress the deadly seriousness of it all.

The three classrooms had been cleared, the desks in each room pushed together to make two big tables. The laboratory itself was to be used as a storeroom for the gas tanks and rodenticides the Ratkill people would be bringing. The protective suits would also be kept there. The lecture hall would be used as the main operations room, while the library would be reserved for smaller, more select meetings by the inner committee.

Jan put her spectacles back on and tried to look out into the night through the large, single-frame window; all she saw was her own reflection. She didn't much fancy walking over to the residential wing by herself. Anything could be out there in the dark. Most of the staff had retired for the night, but Will Aycott had stayed to help her finish up. He was around somewhere checking that all the windows and doors were secure; he also had the keys to the main door.

Jan turned from the window, not too keen on her own reflected features, and switched off the kitchen light. Will would see her back to her room – he'd tried to get into it often enough. Luckily, Jenny Hanmer was a good chaperone to have around – in fact, they were useful chaperones to each other at times. Not that she disliked Will. Sometimes she wished she had her own room.

She wondered if Jenny was feeling any better. She'd had a terrible shock up at the churchyard; Jan wondered what had possessed her to go up there in the first place. *She* wouldn't have had the nerve. Still, Jenny was different. She had guts. She stood up for herself.

'Will, where are you?' Jan called along the darkened corridor. There was no reply so she walked its length, peering into doorways as she went. The lights in the end classroom were still on, throwing a rectangle of brightness across the corridor. She marched towards it, assuming he would be there and hadn't heard her call.

'Will, are you in there?' She peered round the door and saw that the classroom was empty. He must be at the other end of the building, near the library.

Jan glanced around the room, checking that it was in order and the sliding windows closed. The large windows ran the length of the building without a break on that side, compensating for the lack of glass at the front. Satisfied all was in order, she reached for the light switch, then groaned silently when she noticed the lone coffee cup resting on the worktop beneath the windows. Will must have missed it.

She crossed the room and stared disgustedly down into the cup. Someone had dropped a cigarette end into it. Sighing, she looked up at her reflection in the black glass again, brooding on her physical inadequacies. Too thin, neck too long, chin a little too firm. No breasts to speak of. Her hair was too straight and always lank two days after washing. And the glasses. No matter how well she groomed herself for a special occasion, no matter what make-up she used, what perfume, how beautiful the dress, she always had to detract at least twenty per cent of the overall effect by donning the glasses. It was unfair. Still, Will seemed to find her attractive; maybe she was being too hard on herself.

Jan suddenly had an uneasy feeling. It must have been the total, obscuring blackness outside, the lightless forest – something to which she had never quite adapted. But now it worried her more than ever before. Obviously, the fact that there were monster rats roaming around out there had a lot to do with it; for her, Epping Forest had rapidly lost all its charm. She shivered. Silly, but it was almost as though the creatures were out there watching her. She leaned forward, pushing her face close to the window and shielding the light from behind with her hand. She stared out into the night through the shadow her own form had created. Then the window exploded into her face.

Pender and Jenny were just entering the main building when they heard the crash of glass and the shrill scream that accompanied it. They looked at each other in shocked surprise, then rushed into the reception area, almost colliding with Will Aycott as he emerged from the corridor.

'Where did it come from?' Pender asked, grabbing the young tutor's arm to steady him.

'The other end. One of the classrooms.'

'Come on.' Pender ran down the corridor, Jenny and Will hard at his heels. They made for the lighted room at the end, further screams and scrabbling sounds urging them on.

'It's Jan!' Jenny shouted, fearing the worst.

Pender stopped at the doorway, his eyes widening and the skin at his scalp tautening. The two tutors crowded in behind and he held them back, preventing them from entering the room. Jenny screamed at the sight before them.

Jan Wimbush was dragging herself along the floor towards the door, her spectacles gone, her face a bloody mess, glass slivers projecting from her cheeks and forehead glinting like silver shards in the overhead light. Rivulets of blood ran down her arms and her chest was stained red. She raised a quivering hand towards them as though beseeching help, strange gurgling sounds coming from her throat.

Clinging to her back, weighing down her frail body, was a

huge, evil-looking black creature. Its head was buried beneath the hair at the back of her neck, its shoulders jerking spasmodically as it drank in her blood.

'Oh, God, help her, Luke!' Jenny implored and she saw the ratcatcher's face was a mask of sheer hate.

'Get help, Jenny,' he told her, his voice tight. 'Don't go outside the building. Use the phone.'

She stood there, mesmerized by the awful scene, and he had to shove her hard. 'Move!' he shouted.

Pender held on to Will, feeling the younger man's fear, but knowing he was courageous enough to run forward and help the girl.

'For Christ's sake, we've got to save her!' the tutor shouted.

Pender motioned towards the window with his head. 'Look,' he said.

Perched on the worktop before the shattered window squatted another huge rat, its body hunched, hindquarters quivering. It stared at them through evil, dark eyes. It was suddenly joined by another.

Jan's screams had died into a low, heart-rending wailing, and she still pulled herself forward, the pain in her neck pushing her on, her eyes imploring the two blurred figures to help her. She tried to reach behind her with one hand in an effort to drag the deadly weight off, but the creature ignored her feeble struggles.

'We've got to get rid of those two first,' Pender said grimly, shutting the girl's cries from his mind.

'But Jan . . .'

'The other two will attack while we're helping her. Come on, we'll have to move fast. We've got to prevent more getting in.'

Pender pulled the young tutor forward towards the

arranged desks in the middle of the room. 'Quickly. Grab two legs – we'll use the desk as a battering-ram.'

As they snatched up the flat-topped desk, Pender glanced towards the broken window. There were now three rats perched on the sill.

He knew they would attack at any moment, for their hindquarters were bunched and trembling, building up pressure.

'Now!' The two men ran towards the window, the desk held before them, its top a strong, flat shield. They hit the vermin with all the force they had, sending them scurrying back, through the broken window, out into the night. But one managed to slither clear; it scrambled off the worktop and disappeared beneath, scuttling into a dark corner.

'Hold the desk against the window-frame, Will. Don't let them get back in. I'm going to help the girl.'

The tutor could only watch as Pender dashed away. He felt a blow against the wooden surface and the desk shifted back a few inches. His muscles stretched taut as he pushed it further against the frame.

Pender already knew the weapon he was going to use against the rat; he had seen it from the doorway when he had forced himself to think clearly and not be panicked by the situation. His loathing of the creatures had helped override his natural fear. He reached up for one of the metal skewers used for soil-testing mounted on the far wall of the classroom. They were between three and four feet in length, having a single-bar crossing handle at one end and tapering into a corkscrew point at the other, resembling an oversized wine bottle opener.

He ran back to the girl. She was still crawling, almost at the door now, but her movements were weak, her wail diminished to a dull moan. The black creature clung to her, oblivious to the two men. Jan suddenly rested her head on the floor, as though she'd given up, the effort too much. Pender prayed he wasn't too late.

He stood above the mutant, his legs astride the girl's recumbent body, and raised the skewer high, one hand halfway down its shaft, the other over and around the handle. He plunged down, using a slight sideways movement for fear of impaling the girl. The rat emitted a high-pitched squeal as the sharp point struck into its flank. Its pointed head arched upwards, its mouth wide, revealing blood-soaked teeth, red liquid spurting from its throat as it choked.

Pender used all his weight, pushing hard, sinking the skewer deep, dislodging the squirming creature from its perch. It fell against the floor, claws tearing at the wood surface and causing long scars. Pender began to twist at the handle, the corkscrew point churning into the rat's intestines, bursting through its stomach, sinking into the floor itself.

The mutant rat struggled, its squeals almost pitiful, child-like; but Pender did not relent until the skewer was imbedded into the floor, pinning the black creature there, its struggles becoming weaker until they became just a nerve-twitching reaction. He left the improvised weapon standing rigidly upright and bent down towards the girl. He winced at the sight of her mutilated face when he turned her over. Her eyes were closed, but he was relieved when a low sob escaped her.

'It's all right now, Jan,' he softly told her. 'You're safe.'

Pender knew he had to stem the flow of blood from the back of her neck if she were to survive her ordeal. He turned her over again and parted the blood-clotted hair to examine the damage. He almost retched when he saw the open wound. The top of her spine was exposed but, fortunately, the rat had burrowed beside it and not into it. She would have been permanently paralysed, if not killed, if it had. He reached for a handkerchief and placed it over the wound, pressing it against the flow of blood.

'Luke, help me, help me!'

The ratcatcher whirled at the sound of Will's voice and saw a rat biting into the young tutor's calf. Will's arms were still pushing at the upturned desk and Pender could see the claws and pointed snout of a mutant on the outside as it balanced on the window-sill trying to push its way through the narrow gap between table and frame on that side. The tutor was kicking his leg out, afraid to let go of the desk; the rat refused to be shaken off.

Pender quickly looked around for another weapon and his eyes rested upon the red and white surveyor's stakes propped up in one corner. They were at least five feet long and about two inches in diameter; these, too, had pointed ends for sinking into the ground. He hurried over and grabbed one, the others clattering to the floor as he disturbed them.

Holding the stake before him like a lance, the ratcatcher ran at the rodent clinging to Will's calf and struck. The point slid off the rat's back, cutting a red groove beneath the bristling, black fur. It lost its hold on the tutor and turned to face its aggressor, long front teeth baring in a ferocious snarl, one front paw raised, claws outstretched.

Pender poked at it with the stake, aiming for the eyes, trying to blind it. The rat tried to duck beneath the point, but Pender immediately lowered it, keeping the creature at bay. He stabbed again, striking at the head, hoping to pierce the skull, but once again, the blow glanced off. It caused the rat to stagger back though, and Pender pressed his advantage, stepping forward, pushing, stabbing.

The mutant reared up and it was frightening to see its full length. Pender aimed for the stomach, but the rat fell backwards, turning over and scrambling round to face its assailant again. It clawed at the tormenting stake, its jaws open wide, hissing a stream of pink-flecked saliva. Pender lunged, the point disappearing into the creature's mouth and cutting into the throat.

Once more, the rapid, high-pitched squealing as the rat scuttled backwards, trying desperately to escape the choking weapon. Pender went with it, not allowing the rat room to break free, but it suddenly shook its body violently, twisting and turning until it was loose. Pender struck again and this time the point cut into the creature's hindquarters, penetrating, but not deeply. The rat broke away and scuttled for the open doorway, passing between the impaled rat and the limp body of the girl.

'Luke, I can't hold them off much longer,' came Will's desperate cry.

Pender hurried over to the young tutor who was ignoring his leg wound and keeping his arms taut against the desk, his hips resting against the work-top unit. Pender struck out at the lethal-looking claw curling around the wood and when it disappeared, helped Will to shift the desk along, filling the gap.

'Will, can you get to Jan? Drag her out into the corridor?'

'What are you going to do? You can't hold them off forever.'

'Pretty soon they're going to have the sense to break through the other windows. That's how they got in in the first place. When they do we'll have no chance – this room will be swarming with them.'

He gasped as a body thudded against the other side, the desk-top juddering and moving back an inch. They pushed it back.

'Get the girl out, Will, then stand by the door. I'll be

coming through fast and you'll have to get it closed behind me.'

'Okay. Ready? I'm going to let it go now.'

Pender redoubled his efforts as the bodies thudded against the wood. He could hear claws scrabbling at the surface as they ran up its length. 'Hurry, Will, for Christ's sake hurry.'

The young tutor limped towards the prone body, his teeth clenched against the pain, his face deathly pale. He almost wept when he turned Jan over and saw the damage the broken glass had done, but he knew there was no time for grief. He grabbed her beneath the shoulders and, in a half-crouched position, began to drag her through the doorway.

'Look out for the rat that got into the corridor,' Pender warned him.

The pressure against the table was becoming too much, the thumps against it increasing in frequency. He propped the bright-coloured stake against the wood, hoping it would hold the desk in position long enough for him to make it to the door. Then the indescribable happened.

The long windows on either side all shattered at once. The noise of falling glass was deafening and the sight of the black, furry bodies hurtling through, squealing their fury, skidding off the worktop onto the floor, was almost enough to make his heart stop beating.

Pender ran.

The rats were too stunned and confused to attack at once, and Pender gave them no second chance. He dived when he was still feet from the door, rolling into the corridor and crashing against the wall opposite.

'Shut it!' he screamed, and Will lost no time in doing so.

The door rattled in its frame as the vermin threw themselves against it. They could hear the scratching sounds, the splintering as the creatures gnawed at the wood.

Pender shook his head to clear his senses.

'Are you okay?' the tutor asked anxiously, holding on to the door-handle as if to keep it closed.

'Yes. I knocked my head, that's all.' He got to one knee and crouched beside Jan and felt her pulse. It was weak. 'We've got to get her to a hospital. I don't think she'll make it, otherwise.' He looked up at Will. 'You can let go of the door – I don't think they're *that* clever.'

Will sheepishly dropped his hand. 'My God, listen to them. It won't take them long to gnaw their way through.'

'No, and we'd better be out of here before they do.'

'Luke, I've called the police.' It was Jenny, standing at the end of the darkened corridor, by the reception area. 'I've also called the Warden, on the internal phone and warned him to keep everybody inside the living quarters until the police get here.'

'Good girl. Stay where you are, we'll bring Jan . . .' His voice broke off when he noticed something dark moving along the corridor, something low, crouched close to the wall. It was making towards Jenny.

'Jenny, run! Get away from there!' He was on his feet, running down the corridor. Jenny stood transfixed, her eyes wide with terror.

The rat moved with incredible speed, Pender's shouts and footsteps galvanizing it into action. It broke free from the shadows. Jenny could only step back as it sped past her, its stiffened fur actually brushing her legs. It scuttled madly around in the wider reception area, looking for an opening, a crazed look in its eyes. Jenny leaned back against the far wall and watched in fascinated horror. Pender reached her and shielded her body when he saw the rat's frantic actions.

A full-length window stood by the glass door, giving half the reception area a glass wall appearance. The rat ran at the lower pane and bounced off its rigid surface. It tried again, throwing itself at the glass with desperate strength. Pender was conscious of a police siren in the distance, the unmistakable wail growing louder with each second.

The rat scrambled away from the glass and made towards them. Pender got ready to kick out at it, but the creature turned before it reached them and hurtled itself at the window once more. This time, the glass shattered and it was through, disappearing into the shadows outside, leaving scraped-off hair and blood on the remaining window fragments.

'Oh, God, Luke. It's vile. It's so vile.' Jenny leaned against Pender's back; he was too afraid to take his eyes off the broken pane in case the rats came swarming through.

'Luke. Come here, quickly.' It was Will calling from the gloomy end of the corridor.

Pender grabbed Jenny's arm and took her with him.

'What is it?' he asked when he reached the crouched figure.

'Listen!'

Pender heard nothing. Then he realized what the young tutor was getting at. 'The rats,' he said. 'They're gone.'

12

It was the dogs who aroused the slumbering Police Training Camp on Lippits Hill. For the cadets and training officers who survived, it was to be a night they would never forget, a horrific memory that would fill their dreams for years to come.

They staggered from their barrack huts, half-dressed, half-asleep, cursing the animals for the terrible noise, cursing the handlers for not keeping them quiet. Yet they knew from the sound that the dogs had been disturbed by more than just a prowler; their frenzied barks had merged into a fearful howling ululation that pierced the bitter night and sent shudders down the spines of all who heard.

'What the fuck's got into them?' one young cadet asked as the men gathered in groups outside the huts.

'Where the bloody hell's their handlers?' another cursed.

They began to move in the direction of the pens, but a sergeant, hastily donning a heavy coat, brought them to a halt.

'Listen!' he commanded, and those nearest to him held their breath. The word spread back to those at the rear, and the excited voices died; they stood shivering in the dark, each man's senses keened to the night.

'What is it?' one finally asked, mystified and a little afraid.

'It's screaming,' another answered. 'I'm sure it's screaming.

If someone could get the bloody dogs quiet we could tell for sure.'

'No, no, it's not screaming,' someone else said. 'It's the ducks. The noise is coming from the duck farm. They sound like human voices from a distance.'

They all listened again, while the dog-handlers hurried towards the pens, anxious to calm the agitated dogs. Not far from the training centre, a quarter of a mile at the most, in a remote but mainly unwooded area, a large, wire-fenced pound had been erected. Inside, various breeds of duck were raised, some for their meat, most for their eggs. It was a specialist enterprise and held hundreds of birds within its boundaries. Now the policemen and trainees had something to relate the sound to, they began to agree: it wasn't human screams but the cries of disturbed fowl.

The camp supervisor joined them and they could not see how drawn his face looked in the darkness. He had received a phone call from his superior earlier that evening, and the news had been bad.

The supervisor quickly gathered the senior officers and instructors around him and explained just what his fears were, and within ten minutes firearms had been issued to the officers and most capable trainees. They set off in force from the camp towards the duck farm, trudging over the fields behind the training centre, the route being more direct than the long detour by road. Beams of light from powerful torches struck into the night; the dogs, eager to confront an age-old enemy, pulled at their leashes, snarling and yelping in their desire for combat. A token force was left to guard the grounds, the camp supervisor remaining with them, trying to make contact with the deputy assistant commissioner, who would inform the assistant commissioner, who would inform the commissioner. The order for all officers and cadets to remain within the confines of the camp came too late; by then, the policemen were approaching the duck pound itself.

'Hold it! Hold it!' No one was sure who was giving the order, but they all came to a halt and looked uneasily around.

'Keep those bloody dogs quiet!' came the voice again and the burly figure of the sergeant in charge of firearms came striding forward from the rear. 'Just listen, everyone.'

The handlers tried to muzzle their dogs with their hands, but the animals were too restless. They pulled away from their masters, deep growls coming from their throats. The ducks were frantic: the men could hear the flurry of wings above the squealing clamour. But other sounds began to come through and it slowly dawned on the policemen that they were human voices. Human screams.

'It's coming from the mobile home site!' the sergeant shouted. 'It's not just the ducks. It's on the other side of the pound!'

He ran forward and the men followed, skirting the high, wire fence, running downhill to the small track that led to the secluded estate. Lights were on in the large private house that stood near the entrance to the mobile home site and they could see figures at the upstairs windows, waving. One window opened and a man began shouting down at them, but his words were lost in the overall clamour.

There were thirty houses in all, constructed of timber and glass, resting on concrete bases. They were called mobile homes because they had been brought fully built to the site on wheels and planted in position like giant dolls' houses, ready for occupation. Most of the inhabitants were young couples who could not afford the high price of more permanent, brick-built homes, or retired couples who sought small accommodation in peaceful surroundings. They all enjoyed the community spirit in the tiny, one-street estate, and agreed that the timber houses were as solid and permanent as any built of brick. That night they discovered just how vulnerable they were.

The policemen were suddenly aware of the dark shapes running through the grass around them, streaming from the site, meeting them and scurrying through their midsts. The lead dogs went wild, attacking the black creatures, while the men stood perplexed. The torchbeams probed the long grass and the cry went up: 'Rats! They're the Black rats!'

The policemen kicked out, sickened and frightened. Those with weapons began firing at the vermin, cautious of hitting their companions, but anxious not to be touched by the creatures. The officers tried to bring some order into the chaos, but they themselves were near to panic. A young cadet went down, a bullet in his leg. As two of his companions pulled him up, they found two rats clinging to his body. They tried to tear the tenacious beasts from him, but soon found they had to defend themselves from similar attacks. The wounded cadet fell again and his scream was added to the others.

The officers ordered the men on, urging them not to attack the vermin, but to press on to the mobile home site. It was too much for some of the young cadets; they ran off into the night, seeking refuge from the nightmare. Unfortunately for them, their fleeing figures attracted the attention of the rats more than those who had stayed to fight, and they were followed. From different points in the darkness came their solitary cries as the rats sought them out and attacked.

The main body of men found themselves on the estate, the vermin sifting through them as they ran on. Each policeman had tried to avoid the scurrying black shapes beneath his feet, unwilling to provoke attack, anxious to get to the people at the site. The handlers stayed with their dogs who were in a mad frenzy, snapping at the vermin, lifting them into the air, shaking them furiously like rag dolls. The dogs, fierce and brave as they were, had no chance against the swarming vermin, the razor teeth cutting into their flesh like sharp knives, their bodies brought down by the sheer weight of the leaping creatures. The handlers tried to help but they, too, were engulfed by the rats, and they cried for help as they fell. Several armed policemen turned back and fired into the scrabbling heaps, no longer caring who or what they hit.

The two lamps that lit the street dividing the facing row of houses revealed a carnage that stopped the policemen in their tracks. Gaping holes in the wooden structures showed where the rats had torn their way through to reach the people inside; broken windows gave evidence of the other means of entry. There were black, bristling-bodied creatures swarming all over the houses, scuttling in and out of buildings, over the rooftops, through the tiny gardens. The policemen saw groups of them fighting among themselves over bloodsoaked objects – objects they realized were dismembered parts of human bodies – tugging, ripping apart. An old man, his naked body thin and wasted, crashed through a glass door, falling into the tiny garden area, twisting over and over in the flower-bed, one rat clinging to his shoulder, another at his buttock. A woman appeared shrieking at a window, trying to tear away a rat entangled in her hair. She slumped forward, and jagged shards of glass jutting from the window-frame cut into her ribs, piercing her lungs, stilling her cries. A man stood fully-clothed on the roof of his house, a small bundle that must have been a baby cradled in his arms, kicking out at the rats as they scurried up the walls in an effort to reach him. In the garden below lay the crumpled figure of a woman, the rats feeding off her body while their companions tried ceaselessly to gain purchase on the roof-top. An elderly couple, both clad in dressing-gowns, marched defiantly down the centre street, the man striking out with a heavy-looking walking-stick, the woman wielding a metal dustbin lid, using it as a shield. When the man went down, she tried to cover him with her own body, the lid protecting their heads; but the rats found other, more vulnerable, parts. A man wearing only a pyjama jacket sat on the steps to his house and stared down disbelievingly at the dozen or so rats eating away at his legs. A boy, barely fourteen, hacked away at the mangled body of a rat with a carving knife. He knelt on the ground, the creature between his knees, while three of its companions nipped away the flesh from his back. An obese woman, her voluminous pink nightie patterned with red stains, wildly smashed a black creature against a wall, both hands wrapped around its neck, cursing the vermin, screaming in hate rather than fear.

One of the houses was ablaze, the flames creating dancing shadows, the scene a madman's dream. A figure – impossible to tell if it was a man or woman – appeared in the doorway and ran screeching into the turmoil outside, body aflame, lungs already seared by the heat. Black creatures followed, their stiff fur on fire, squealing and dashing to and fro in their own terror.

And above it all was the screaming, the wailing, the moaning, the crackle of flames, the squealing of the vermin themselves. The cries for help. The crash of wrecked furniture. The thuds of makeshift weapons. The overturned radio, volume accidentally turned up full, blaring out sentimental ballads linked by the silky voice of the late-night DJ.

Wherever the stunned policemen looked was a new horror, and finally their minds refused to accept any more, everything becoming a confused blur. They attacked, using guns, firing indiscriminately, hardly needing to select targets for the rats were everywhere, merged almost into one struggling heap before them. Hundreds, hundreds, hundreds. The men without weapons used anything they could lay their hands on, tearing off strips of low fencing, porch support, anything they could use as a club. They tried to work in large groups for self-protection, but so many went down under the vast numbers of rats that they found themselves battling in smaller pockets. Smaller and smaller.

The mutants left not because their acute hearing could pick up the sirens approaching in the distance, but because their hunger was satiated, their bellies glutted. They fled almost as one, many carrying awkward loads they had patiently severed from lifeless bodies. Across the fields they went, heading for the forest areas, the scuttling thuds of their many feet the only sound they made. The other woodland creatures froze, too terrified to move as the vast black river passed over them. Soon the forest was silent again. Only the sound of low-pitched moaning rolled over the fields and this was soon drowned by the blaring sirens.

Lair

The rat, a peculiar white scar running the length of its skull, threaded its way through the rubble, its load hardly hindering the journey. Others followed behind, a few bearing similar burdens to that of the leader, while still more carried dismembered limbs and meat chunks. Their own bellies were full; the food was for their masters. The main force had returned to their dark sanctums beneath the forest, the excitement of killing still with them, their bodies tired but still trembling from their recent onslaught.

The leader had broken away from them, its squeals commanding certain others to follow, for they still had a duty to perform. They came with their burdens, submissive to their leader, who in turn was submissive to others.

There was little light when they began to descend, the moon-beams finding only small openings to penetrate, casting silvery pools of reflection in scattered patches. But the creatures were used to the darkness, and those below had little use for the sun. The leader was aware of the stirring all around as it dropped from the last incline and landed in the lower level. The burden dropped from its jaws and the rat hissed menacingly as others scudded towards it. It retrieved the sticky, dripping thing and padded forward, making for the far corner where its master lay. The underground room was alive with rustling and spasmodic movements, filled with excited mewling sounds.

The rat was challenged by others of its kind as it approached the bloated thing in the corner, but it hissed back, dropping its burden and baring its teeth. They backed away and crouched low, ready to spring forward at the slightest provocation. Further, more strident hissing came from the blackness in the corner, and the creature there shuffled around in its bed of straw and damp earth, impatient, hungry for the food the Black rat had brought.

The rat lifted the heavy object once more and moved closer to the obese creature, fearful yet fascinated, almost mesmerized. It vaguely remembered a time before when the dominant rat had been more powerful, its claws sharp enough to have caused the searing injury to its head, subduing it, making it obey. The creature still held that terror for the Black rat. It dropped the food into the straw and the thing shuffled its fleshy bulk forward, its two heads weaving to and fro in the air, snouts twitching, the teeth curled back, tusk-like from the lack of gnawing. The two mouths plunged at the bloody object, seeking the natural openings, sucking noisily at them.

The rat edged forward, wanting to share in the prize, afraid of its master, but arrogant enough to express its own leadership. The thing screeched in rage, sending the rat scuttling back, the guards following and lashing out with their claws. The scuffle was brief, the rat breaking away and rolling over, exposing its neck in the submissive gesture, bleating for mercy.

The guards returned to their crouched positions and the rat heard the sucking, gurgling noises as the creature in the corner resumed eating. The others in the underground chamber, those like the dominant mutant, bloated, hairless, began to attack the food brought to them, tearing it away from the black vermin, hissing and squealing in their lust.

The big rat turned and padded away towards the incline leading from the chamber. It stopped just once and glared around at the dim, gorging shapes. Then it scuttled up the slope, its companions following.

13

Two days after the massacre at the mobile home site in which sixty-three residents and forty-eight policemen and trainees had been killed, the task of locating and blocking all sewer openings in Epping Forest was still in hand. Although no one had been foolhardy enough to enter the sewers, the operatives knew the vermin were in there: they could be heard. The main exits had already been sealed with concrete and small apertures were left to take the tubes through which cyanide powder would be pumped. The search was now on for the smaller holes that would be used as escape exits by the rodents when the underground tunnels were filled with the killer gas. Groups of men wearing protective clothing and guarded by armed soldiers scouted the woodland, looking for rat 'runs', the paths made from constant use by vermin, tracing them back to their source. Each group carried detailed plans of the sewer network with accurate positioning guides related to the ground above. It was painstaking work, but necessary if the operation were to be successful.

The idea was to create a vast underground tomb for the vermin. The gas would be poured in through thick tubes from machines bearing no resemblance to the old-fashioned hand-pumps that had once been used. The machines, which looked like huge vacuum cleaners, had been hastily developed after the London Outbreak, and were powered by their own generators. Their air-blast enabled the cyanide powder to penetrate the deepest sewers without risking the lives of the operatives, as long as all the openings were tightly sealed. Should they accidentally come in contact with the toxic fumes because of a leakage, each man carried amyl nitrate capsules to counteract the gas.

It was realized that not all outlets could be found in the dense undergrowth of the forest, but it was hoped the channels would be so heavily impregnated with the gas that the rats would have little time to break out. The few that did could be dealt with in the following days. The purge would be relentless, with no thought to other woodland wildlife – the consequences if any of the mutants escaped would be too serious. The Prime Minister himself had promised the country that the whole of Epping Forest would be razed to the ground if necessary. Encouraged by this statement, certain members of the public had been discovered starting their own forest fires, and had been promptly arrested.

The outcry against this second rodent invasion within five years had, of course, been enormous. The government – true, it had been a different government at that time – had promised that a catastrophe such as the London Outbreak would never happen again. So much for the 'official' word. Members of the ruling body shuddered as they anticipated the recriminations to follow, while the Opposition rubbed their hands in vengeful glee, remembering the humiliating beating they had taken from the public years before. The principal department involved, the Ministry of Agriculture, was already busy preparing documents to prove there had been no negligence on its part. The Ratkill board of directors gloated with satisfaction while their executives revelled in the sudden storm of activity. It had been a Ratkill investigator who had confirmed the infestation and who had recommended instant action, only to be overruled by the private secretary for the Ministry of Agriculture, who had wanted matters to progress more cautiously. Of course, that 'delay' would not be denounced publicly by Ratkill – unless a later inquiry brought it out in the open. No, it would be a matter between themselves and Antony Thornton; it might prove useful to have the gratitude – unspoken, of course – of such an influential man.

Epping Forest itself was now devoid, apart from those involved in the eradication itself, of all human life. It was decided after the massacre that not just a confined area would be cleared of residents, but Epping Forest's entire population. The more nervous considered the whole green belt area to be in danger, but were assured that this was not the case. There were very clear indications as to the extent of the vermin's penetration, and this was well within the forest itself; there would be no danger to those living in the surrounding areas.

The evacuated area was ringed by a human chain – troops spread as wide as possible without breaking visual contact, armoured vehicles constantly patrolling the perimeters. Their numbers were strengthened by the metropolitan and county police forces and even local fire stations stood by in readiness. Gazelle helicopters swooped low over the treetops and scanned the ground below. Chieftain tanks stood immobile and menacing, facing into the forest, ready to rumble into action at the first command.

The only occupied area within the guarded boundary was the Conservation Centre, its small car park and front lawn crowded with military, police and Ratkill vehicles, the main building itself buzzing with activity. No one was allowed to enter the restricted area without an army escort, and the same applied when leaving the Centre. Eight Green Goddess fire-engines stood along the road cresting High Beach, glaring down into the valley like mechanical predators. Army scout cars, their personnel feeling secure and protected inside the rough metal carriages, raced carelessly along hoggin paths, keeping a sharp lookout for misguided or just plain stupid civilians who had ignored the warnings and slipped through the cordon. Why anyone should do so, knowing full well the dangers, was beyond the soldiers' comprehension, but they had learned from past experience never to underestimate the imbecility of certain individuals on occasions like these.

More atrocities had been discovered in the two days following the mass attack: the tattered remains of a tent in a remote corner of a field, the inside splattered with dried blood, the floor littered with the remains of twelve missing Barnardo boys and their supervisor; bones of what had obviously been a courting couple in a small clearing not far from the roadside, the couple's fawn-coloured car nearby; an empty rowing boat drifting an one of the few lakes where fishing was allowed, the missing occupant's rod and sandwiches still lying in the bottom of the dinghy; an empty lorry, the driver's door wide open as though he had jumped down to clear the winding forest road of some obstacle or animal – cattle often wandered across the roadways; an abandoned but sparkling new bicycle; a saddled, riderless horse; a house, close to several others, but empty and bloodstained.

It had been impossible for the warnings to reach everyone despite the frequent radio broadcasts, the patrols with loudspeakers, the knocking on doors – there was always someone whom the news did not reach. Most of the residents had fled without further prompting, but there were several surly old farmers who had to be forcibly 'persuaded', and a few of the wealthier residents who considered themselves above the attention of mere rats, who had to be ordered out. But finally, the woodland had been cleared and the mass execution of the vermin was underway.

The forest was quieter than it had ever been, the wildlife nervous. The sun shone bright but impotently on the verdant acres, the autumn chill dissipating its warmth. The country held its breath.

Pender spoon-fed the powder into the hole, ensuring there was no breeze to blow the substance back into his face. The fumes could easily enter the grille in the strong, plastic visor, part of the protective suit he wore against rodent attack. The group around him were also dressed in the silver-grey suits, the material a combination of tough fabric and fine strands of close-knitted, flexible steel. The helmets, with their plastic face coverings, gave the men a sinister, alien appearance, but each was confident that no sharp teeth could penetrate their armour.

Pender cursed the clumsiness of the heavy gloves, but felt no inclination to remove them. For all he knew there could be a mutant rat lurking only feet away in the passage he was preparing to block, ready to snap off his fingers. The hole looked hardly big enough to contain a giant rat, but he knew from the map Whittaker was holding that there was a sewer below, so he was taking no chances. There was a definite run leading from the tunnel which showed it was in constant use. He shook the long-handled spoon free of the deadly powder and withdrew it, wiping the surface against the soil as he did so, then pulled up a clod of earth from the ground nearby and plugged the hole, turning the grass roots so they faced outwards. That way the powder would not be covered with loose earth.

Pender stood. 'Okay, Joe, block it,' he said.

Joe Apercello, another Ratkill operative, stepped forward, bringing a large tin of ready-mixed, quick drying cement with him. He struggled with the tightly sealed lid for a few seconds, then began to remove a glove for better purchase.

'Leave it on, Joe!' Pender snapped, and the man shrugged, pulling the glove back.

'It's bloody awkward,' he complained.

'It's more bloody awkward without fingers,' Pender told him.

The lid came away with a sucking sound and Apercello dug in with a trowel, thickly spreading the compound over the hole. Sealing every opening with concrete was an added precaution: generally, earth would have been sufficient, the powder itself acting as a death-dealing sentry, but it had been agreed that extreme measures would be taken – the mutant rats would never be underestimated again.

Vic Whittaker had the network map spread out on the ground before him and was marking the position of the now-plugged exit with a felt-tipped pen.

'That's the fifth this morning,' he said with some satisfaction 'The channel runs dead ahead . . .' he extended his arm in the direction he meant '. . . north-east.' He looked up and added, 'The undergrowth has certainly covered the area since the sewer was dug. We'll have a hard job locating any openings.'

'We're bound to miss more than a few,' Pender said, 'but that's not the point. Once the machines start pumping the gas into the main exits, the rats will have little chance of escape. They'll be finished before they know what's hit them. The object of this exercise is to stack *all* the cards in our favour.'

Whittaker nodded, the movement barely noticeable inside the helmet. He stood, folding the map so only the next relevant section showed.

'Do you think we'll be ready by tomorrow?' he asked.

'We've got to be. We can't . . .' Pender frowned. 'Captain,

tell your man to get his bloody helmet back on.' He pointed towards a soldier who was wiping his forehead with his sleeve.

The captain flushed behind his plastic screen. 'You, get it back on immediately!'

The startled soldier hastily began to don his hood. 'Sorry, sir, it's so bleedin' hot in here,' he said lamely.

Captain Mather glared at the small squad which formed a protective semi-circle around Pender, Whittaker and Apercello. An army truck stood waiting in a clearing nearby, its engine idling, ready to move at the slightest hint of trouble.

'You all know the danger,' the captain said, 'so let's not have any more silliness. Clear?' He neither expected nor received an answer as he turned back to the ratcatcher. 'Sorry, Mr Pender, it won't happen again.'

'That should do it, Luke,' came Apercello's muffled voice as he patted down the fast drying cement. 'No bugger'll get out of there.'

'Right,' Pender said, picking up the container of cyanide powder. 'Let's move on.'

The senior tutor fell in beside him as they trampled down foliage with heavy boots, helmets bent in constant examination of the ground before them, searching for signs. The soldiers fanned out on either side, also searching the ground but keeping a wider alert for any impending danger.

'You were saying we have to be ready by tomorrow...?' Whittaker prompted.

'We can't risk holding them inside any longer,' Pender continued. 'We drilled probes with microphones attached, so we know they're there. I listened in myself – it was bedlam. They seem to know they're trapped and they're panicking.'

'But we know these mutants can burrow – why don't they dig their way out?'

'Oh, they will. That's why we have to move fast. At the moment hysteria is preventing them from using whatever sense they possess. Pretty soon, though, they're going to get the notion to tunnel their way out. Fortunately, these sewers have been firmly constructed – they'll hold the rats for a while.'

'And these holes we're sealing? Why haven't they come pouring through?'

'Don't tempt providence: they could do just that. My guess is that the rats are afraid. Remember, their ancestors were virtually wiped out in London. Call it race-memory, or sheer instinct, but they know they're under attack from their worst enemy: man. They're just plain terrified at the moment, too scared to come out and show themselves. How long they'll remain in that state is anybody's guess.'

They trudged on, both men lost in their own thoughts. It was Whittaker who finally broke the silence.

'I don't understand why the other animals haven't been slaughtered by the vermin. I mean, if they're so ferocious and there are so many of them, why haven't they overrun the forest?'

'Firstly, we don't know exactly how many there are. My guess is that there are a thousand or so – they haven't reproduced like the normal rodent. It would still be enough to make them aggressive.'

'A thousand? My God, that's terrible.'

'Not really, not in an area this size.'

'What makes you so sure? There could be several thousand.'

Pender shook his head. 'I'm *not* sure, but I don't think so. If there were, they'd have been seen sooner. They would almost certainly have begun slaughtering the other wildlife. I'm sure their build-up has been gradual. Remember, compared to the normal rodent they're giants, and Mother Nature isn't keen on allowing her bigger creatures to have large litters.'

'They're no bigger than dogs. Even pigs . . .'

'In the vermin kingdom, the mutants are as big as elephants. Anyway there's the other side of the argument: these are freaks, mutants – their genes have been altered in some way. Maybe the ultrasonics used on their ancestors did it, maybe not, but their difference could easily have changed their reproductive cycle.'

'But there were many thousands in London!'

'They were mating with the normal species of Black rat. It's all theory on my part, but here, I think, we have the pure strain. I'll bet they're even stronger and more cunning than the first. They've been clever enough to keep out of sight – until now.'

'It makes you wonder if we really are going to beat them.'

'We will.' Whittaker could not see the grim determination on the ratcatcher's face.

'All right, if there really are as you say just a thousand or so, it still doesn't explain why they haven't attacked the local wildlife before now.'

'Rats can survive on practically anything. You can be sure they've killed other animals, but on an unnoticeable scale. Their main supply of food has obviously been scavenged from other sources: houses, farms, allotments, the countryside itself. I bet if we were to check now, we'd have reports of all sorts of vermin trouble that in the past has just been put down to rare and isolated cases. It's frightening to consider, but I wouldn't be surprised if these mutants have deliberately been keeping a low profile regarding their raids.'

'It's a little hard to believe.'

'What's happening now is a little hard to believe. One thing we do know for sure: their restraint has gone. They're out to kill anyone or anything.'

Apercello, who was some distance ahead, turned and waved at them. His words through the plastic grille were hard to catch, but he began pointing towards the ground quite near his feet.

'Looks like Joe's found another opening,' said Pender, hurrying forward.

The hole the ratcatcher's colleague was standing over was much larger than the one they had just plugged. Its sides were smooth, as though used by many bodies.

'Christ, that's one all right,' Pender muttered, bending low and examining the hole. 'It's the right size. Captain, let me have the torch, will you?'

Captain Mather passed the square-shaped torch over to the ratcatcher who shone its powerful beam into the tunnel.

'Nothing there,' Pender said, straightening. 'Let's get some powder down fast. The sooner it's plugged, the happier I'll be.'

They went through the process of laying the cyanide and sealing the exit again, Pender helping Apercello pack the cement.

'Okay. Number six done. Mark it . . .' He didn't know what had made him look up into the trees at that moment, but Pender suddenly felt even more uneasy than before. Had he seen something move? The other men regarded him curiously.

'What is it, Mr Pender?' Captain Mather enquired.

Pender studied the nearby trees for a few seconds longer before replying. 'Nothing. I thought I saw . . . heard something, that's all.'

The officer looked around nervously. 'Perhaps we should be moving . . .'

'There's something up there!' It was Apercello's voice. 'I saw it move. It was darting along a branch.'

The soldiers who were nearer to the trees began to back away apprehensively, their firearms pointing into the foliage overhead.

'There's another!' shouted Vic Whittaker pointing to a different tree.

All eyes swivelled. They saw a swaying branch, but nothing else.

A sudden rustle to their right had everybody spinning in that direction. A flurry of dead leaves fluttered to the ground, but the tree's branches were still too full of brown foliage for the men to see what had caused the downfall.

'Keep still, everyone,' Pender ordered. Now scan the trees around us. If you see any movement, don't shout, just point.'

Their heads turned slowly as they studied the treetops, each man scarcely daring to breathe. Pender kept an eye on the men, occasionally, irresistibly, glancing upwards. His eyes riveted on a soldier who suddenly began gesticulating towards an overhead branch.

'Captain,' Pender said quietly. 'One of your men has spotted something.' He nodded towards the pointing man. The others became aware of their companion's excitement.

'There it is!' someone shouted. 'Creeping along that branch! It's one of 'em, one of the rats! Jesus, there's another!'

It became too much for the soldier. He raised his rifle and aimed into the tree, his gloved finger pushing its way awkwardly though the trigger guard.

The explosion and consequent high-pitched squeal seemed to act as the signal for the rats to attack. They fell from the trees almost as one, dropping through the air on to the men below, the forest suddenly alive with their screeching squeals and flying black bodies.

14

Pender rushed forward, crashing through the brittle under-growth, making towards a fallen soldier who was desperately trying to push away a rat clawing at his chest. All around, the soldiers were struggling with vermin that had landed on their shoulders and heads, several of the men on their knees, others running wildly in circles, completely unnerved by the attack.

The ratcatcher pulled at the creature on the fallen man's chest, grasping its twisting neck and tugging and squeezing at the same time. A sudden weight on his back sent him tumbling forward over the soldier. He kept rolling, hoping to crush the creature, but it clung tenaciously. The pain was excruciating as the rat bit into the tough material of the protective suit, the teeth not piercing but pinching the skin together. As he tried to roll his body free, Pender realized there was not just one, but two rats attacking him. He lay on his back, endeavouring to still their movements with his own weight, reaching behind to grab at their scrabbling legs. He was conscious of the screams around him, the sharp reports of gunfire, the thrashing of bodies both human and animal. More black shapes were dropping from the trees, leaping from the branches, running down the rough bark, filling the forest glade with their numbers.

He tried to rise, but a rat landed on his chest and for a

brief moment he found himself staring through the plastic screen into the monster's slanted eyes. It was almost as if the rat were studying him, looking deep into his mind, a cold hate stabbing its way through. The creature's jaws opened and Pender stared in fascinated horror at the cruel, yellow teeth, the deformed and over-large incisors honed razor-sharp from constant gnawing. Spittle smeared the plastic visor as the mutant hissed at its prey. The pointed head snapped forward and Pender jerked his head back in a reflex action. The teeth skidded across the plastic, leaving deep grooves and a trail of saliva. The ratcatcher forgot about the struggling bodies beneath him and began to pummel the creature on top with his fists. The rat staggered sideways but recovered, the blows driving it to a new fury. Its powerful jaws locked around one of Pender's wrists and he screamed at the intense pain, the thickness of the gauntlet gloves saving him from serious injury.

He managed to pull the arm free, but the rat's head was poised above him, ready to strike again, this time at his throat. Even the steel-lined clothing could not save him if those teeth locked onto his windpipe. Pender tried to turn his body, but the two rats beneath him held him back. The rat's head plunged.

And then exploded in a cloud of blood and tissue. The gunshot ringing in his ears and his visor splattered red, Pender pushed the slumped body away from him. He quickly cleared his vision with a gloved hand, wiping away the running blood and clots of bubbling substance. Captain Mather towered over him, a revolver still smoking in his hand.

'Over. Quick!' came the command, and Pender felt his body turned with a rough kick. He waited for what seemed an eternity, knowing the captain was taking careful aim, ensuring the bullets would not pass through the vermin into his body, and shuddered when the sharp reports came and the paw grips on his back were released.

Mather helped him to his feet and once more Pender was allowed a clear view of the frantic struggle taking place. The rats seemed to be everywhere, swamping the soldiers with their numbers, pulling and tearing at the terrified men. Automatic gunfire stopped the soldiers from being completely smothered, and the armoured suits prevented them from being torn to pieces. Nevertheless, for the soldiers it was a losing battle. The pain inflicted by the clamping jaws was evident from the screams that rang out, and it could not be endured for much longer. The rats were dying in large numbers, their bodies leaping into the air in shock as bullets struck, a strange shriek, like a hurt child's, bursting from them as they died.

Pender looked around for Whittaker and Apercello, but it was impossible to recognize anyone in the bizarre uniforms. They didn't carry guns, but then there were so many now who had dropped their weapons and were using their hands to ward off the vermin.

Captain Mather dropped to his knees beside him, a rat perched precariously on his shoulders, another biting into the material at his stomach. Pender grabbed the rodent that had its teeth sinking into the top of the officer's helmet and pulled it free in one swift, sharp movement, tossing it as far away as possible; Mather carefully shot the one at his stomach, ignoring the pain, refusing to succumb to panic. The rat that Pender had thrown came scurrying back, leaping at its attacker without breaking stride. Pender kicked out and was lucky enough to make contact. The rat's long body jack-knifed in the air and fell into the undergrowth. The ratcatcher dashed forward and brought his heavy boot crashing down on its head, crushing the skull.

He turned back to the army officer who was trying to shake his arms free of two more mutants that were weighing him down, making it impossible for him to use the revolver. Three others were scrambling up his body and his knees were beginning to sag with the load.

Pender ran to him and began tugging at the bristling bodies, ignoring another creature that had attached itself to his leg. He pulled and the thing he had been dreading happened: as the rat came away, its teeth firmly clamped into the suit, the material tore. It was a small rent, but it proved the suits could be penetrated. Under the onslaught all the suits would soon be in tatters. He grabbed the rodent's snout, avoiding the teeth, and twisted with all his strength. The neck broke and he dropped the twitching body. Then he grabbed the gun from the officer's hand, hoping there were still enough bullets in the chamber. He had never handled a gun before, but pulling a trigger seemed an uncomplicated operation. Regardless of the two rats that were now nipping at his legs, he carefully took aim and shot the relentless vermin clinging to the soldier. He groaned aloud when he turned the weapon on his own aggressors and found that now it was empty. Instead he used it as a club, beating down on their exposed heads until they dropped away senseless.

He almost went under the wheels of the heavy army truck as it ploughed its way through the bracken and juddered to a halt beside him. It was Captain Mather who pulled him aside in time. From the window above came automatic fire, the driver and his mate firing into the mêlée.

'Into the truck, Pender!' he heard Captain Mather command.

'We've got to help the others,' he gasped, but a hard shove sent him reeling towards the back of the truck.

'We'll see to them! Grab a rifle if you can and get onto the tailboard. You can use it from there!'

Pender scrambled along the side of the vehicle, kicking out at vermin as they threw themselves at him. With each blow they would stagger back, then advance on him again. Someone fell at his feet, his body almost invisible beneath the covering of bristling vermin. His cries were terrible to hear and Pender saw the red gushing liquid that sprayed over the backs of the frenzied rats. The man's suit had given and now the vermin were driven on by the smell of blood. He knew the man was beyond help, his mind cold to the fact, and he staggered around the struggling heap, the rats now bypassing him for more easy prey.

Pender saw the weapon lying only yards away from the truck, its black-metal surface soiled with mud. He lumbered towards it, clumsy in his suit, for the moment ignored by the vermin. He went down on one knee to retrieve the fallen weapon. Just in time he saw a rat launch itself into the air at him and he rose to meet it, grabbing the automatic by the barrel and swinging it like a club. The butt met the leaping animal in mid-air with a sickening crunch and the rat fell limply to the ground.

Without further thought, Pender reversed the weapon and began pumping a spray of bullets into the nearest vermin, avoiding the figures of his companions but well aware of his lack of marksmanship. He began to back away towards the rear of the truck, staggering under the impact of the rats that managed to escape the hail of bullets, but determinedly keeping his feet. His back bumped something solid and he was surprised when he felt himself rising, two hands gripped under his shoulders. Two soldiers pulled him into the truck, while three others fired down into the glade. One of the two who had lifted him quickly and efficiently dealt with a rat that had refused to let go of its quarry, using the edge of a bayonet to slice the mutant's throat. He kicked the body down among its thronging companions.

Pender pulled himself to his feet, realizing these men had been lucky enough to make it to the truck, and were now using it as a fort from which to strike back. The two that had rescued him were guarding the entrance, hitting out with bayonets at the vermin trying to scramble up into the cavernous interior, while the other three killed as many as possible with gunfire. Captain Mather suddenly appeared below, extending a hand to be pulled up. Miraculously, he was free of clinging rats as Pender reached down and grabbed his wrist. The ratcatcher heaved and Mather came up into the interior.

'Help's on the way!' the officer shouted over the din. 'The men in the truck radioed HQ as soon as they saw us in trouble.'

'We've got to help the others,' Pender shouted back. 'Those suits won't hold out much longer. The rats are too strong!'

'Right! We'll get them! I've told the driver to reverse slowly. He'll stop and start at my signal.' Captain Mather suddenly thumped his hand against the side of the truck and it began to trundle slowly backwards, bumping over sudden rises, jolting down into small dips. The army officer banged twice again as they neared two struggling figures slightly to the right. The truck stopped.

'You and you!' He patted two soldiers on the back. 'Get them up here, help one at a time! The rest of you use concentrated covering fire! Go!'

Without hesitation, the two assigned soldiers leapt from the tailboard, bayonets grasped in their fists. They launched themselves at the first man, mercilessly using their weapons against the vermin, the soldiers in the truck keeping them reasonably protected with well-aimed fire-power. The relieved man was hauled back to the vehicle where others dragged him into shelter. The two soldiers dashed back to the other man and the process was repeated, again successfully. Captain Mather struck the side of the truck again as the two soldiers clambered up, their bayonets thick with blood.

'You two next!' Mather ordered, slapping the backs of two different soldiers as another figure was reached, this one rolling over and over on the ground. They disappeared over the side, but this time yet another soldier had to be sent out as a rescuer and was almost overcome by black bodies. They made it back to the truck and virtually threw their companion into it, quickly climbing up behind him.

Mather ran deeper into the interior and, lifting his visor, shouted at the soldiers in the cab. 'Bring your wheel down hard left! There's a group of men about ten yards in that direction.'

The vehicle lurched forward, the wheels churning up mud, bouncing over the prostrate forms of dead or wounded vermin. Mather banged the side again as they approached a figure lying ominously still in the undergrowth. Pender turned his head away in shock.

The man's helmet had either been knocked accidentally or pulled from his head. Five rats squatted around the exposed face and gorged themselves. Others systematically tore at his suit, gnawing at the material, wearing it thin.

In a rage the soldiers began firing into them, regardless of the human body, knowing the man was dead.

'Leave them!' Captain Mather ordered dispassionately. 'We can't help the poor sod now, and at least his body is keeping them occupied!' He kicked at the side of the truck and it drove on.

Pender was horrified at the officer's cold logic, but he knew Mather was right. The living had to be their main concern. He leaned against the side of the truck, grasping an iron support to keep balanced. It wasn't the scratching sound that attracted his attention, for the noise of the rifle fire was deafening: it was the furious indents that were appearing all over the thick canvas covering.

'Mather!' he yelled. 'They're trying to get through the roof.'

Mather glanced up. 'Shit,' he said. Then 'Forget them. If we shoot through the canvas we'll only make holes that the others can use to their advantage. We'll keep an eye on them and shoot only when it's necessary.' With that, he turned his attention back to the action below.

Pender raised the automatic rifle to his shoulder, spotted a rat wriggling its way into the vehicle at one corner, kicked out with venom, sending it toppling back, then began firing at random. It felt good to kill.

The next man to be hauled in was Vic Whittaker. He lay on his back on the floor of the truck, his chest heaving with exhaustion. His suit had held, but Pender could see several places where the material had begun to give. The tutor had been rescued just in time.

Pender knelt beside him for a moment. 'Are you okay?' he yelled.

Whittaker reached for his visor, intending to push it up, and Pender grabbed a wrist.

'I can't breathe,' Whittaker moaned. 'I must have air.'

'Just for a moment, then!' Pender shouted, lifting the plastic face-mask with his gloved fingers. The tutor gratefully sucked in air.

'Where was Apercello?' Pender asked. 'Did you see him?'

Whittaker shook his head from side to side. 'No . . . no . . .

he went down . . . then I lost sight of . . . him. I think . . . his helmet . . . came off as he . . . fell.'

Pender rose, his face white and drawn. He now knew whose face it was the vermin had been eating. He began firing into the scuttling bodies again.

They managed to rescue one more man before the first rat broke through the canvas roof. There were at least a dozen men inside, seven including Pender, crowded into the opening, firing down at the rats. The others, those that had been rescued, lay on the floor groaning, clutching their bruised and, for some, torn flesh. It was these the rat dropped down onto.

Pender and Mather wheeled round at the sudden outburst of cries and saw the injured man kicking out at the Black rat which ran among them, confused and frightened.

'The roof!' Mather shouted as another black shape dropped through the gaping hole. 'Quickly! Shoot them!' He shot the second rat as it fell, its body jerking in mid-air.

Pender and another soldier began spraying the canvas ceiling with bullets, tearing it to shreds, but instantly killing the rats that were clawing their way through. The bodies plummeted into the truck and the men drew themselves away, not sure if the creatures were dead.

The interior was suddenly bright as daylight broke through the tattered roof and Pender saw one of the injured men struggling in the far corner with what presumably had been the first mutant to gain access. The man's visor was up and Pender saw it was Whittaker.

The ratcatcher scooped up a bloodied bayonet which lay at the feet of a soldier now using his automatic rifle, and stumbled over the recumbent figures and dead vermin towards Whittaker, knowing it would be too dangerous to use the rifle in the confined space.

There was a nasty gash in the tutor's cheek where the giant rat had slashed him either with teeth or claws. He was desperately trying to hold the rat's gnashing teeth away from his face, his hands around the creature's neck. The rat's eyes bulged as Whittaker squeezed and its hind legs raked the tutor's body in a demented motion.

Pender fell to his knees before the struggling tutor, locked an arm beneath the rat's lower jaw and began pulling it away from Whittaker's exposed face. He raised the bayonet and carefully, deliberately, slid the tip to a point beneath the rat's ribcage. Then he struck deep, twisting the blade and drawing it down.

Dark blood poured from the creature's abdomen, flooding over the tutor, soaking him. The rat twitched spasmodically, trying to turn its head and strike at the man who had inflicted the mortal injury. But it was no use; Pender held it tight until the twitching had stopped and life had gone.

'Oh my God, oh my God,' was all Whittaker could say.

Pender looked up as a shadow was cast over him. Captain Mather banged three times on the back of the driver's cabin and the vehicle suddenly lurched to a halt. It then began to move forward, gathering speed as it went.

Mather turned towards Pender. 'That was the signal to get us out of here,' he explained. 'There's nothing we can do for the others without all of us being killed. It's regrettable, but that's how it is.'

Pender felt the shock again. Leaving men to die in that way.

'As far as I could ascertain,' the officer said apologetically, 'there were only two men still alive, and they looked pretty much done in. There was blood on them. These useless bloody suits . . .' he left the sentence unfinished. 'I'm sure the others were dead.'

He rose and made his way to the rear of the truck where the soldiers, relieved to retreat, were firing back at the creatures in the forest glade. Pender joined them and saw the vermin were making no attempt to pursue but, for the briefest of seconds, he found himself staring directly into the eyes of a mutant which stood apart from the others, a curious white streak running the length of its head. He was thrown to one side as the vehicle jolted into a dip and when he looked again, the rat was gone. He closed his eyes and breathed a silent prayer.

Soon the soldiers stopped firing, for their targets were out of sight. None felt like cheering as the truck jolted its way back to the road, not even when other army vehicles came racing towards them. They were too exhausted. And they felt too defeated.

15

He found Stephen Howard in the lecture hall, a large map of Epping Forest before him, with Mike Lehmann and Antony Thornton seated on either side. There were others present at the long table, but Pender strode briskly towards the research director without looking at their faces. The Centre itself was alive with activity which increased considerably on the arrival of the recently besieged men. The injured had been able to walk, albeit painfully, to the classroom set up as a makeshift medical room, although one or two had to be half-supported. All their companions wanted to do was to calm their jangled nerves with a quiet smoke.

Howard looked up as Pender approached the table.

'Luke. The radio message said you were under attack . . .'

'We were.' Pender began to remove the heavy gloves, his plastic-visored helmet already discarded and lying somewhere in the reception area. 'There were rats on the outside, in the trees.'

'But we thought they were all in the sewers,' said Lehmann.

'They've either got an exit we haven't discovered yet, or . . . they were outside all the time.'

'Our patrols would have spotted them.'

Pender turned to regard Major Cormack who was seated at the table, his back to the ratcatcher. 'I don't think so.

195

They've remained hidden for a long time now. Besides, who would think of looking up into the trees?' He turned his attention back to the research director. 'We've got to use the gas immediately, while we've got the majority trapped.'

'But we don't know that all the exits have been blocked yet,' said Thornton.

'We have to take that chance; we can't waste any more time. If they suddenly make up their minds that they want out, nothing will stop them.'

'I agree with Luke,' said Lehmann. 'It appears to be too dangerous to send out small groups to seal the holes anyway.'

'How many of these groups are out at the moment?' asked Thornton.

'Seven,' Howard answered promptly. 'Roughly in these areas.' His fingers stabbed seven times at the map before him.

'Call them in,' said Thornton, firmly. 'No point in risking further lives. We'll do as Mr Pender requests: use the gas immediately.'

'But if they should break free? If they can't be contained . . . ?' Pender recognized the voice and turned towards Edward Whitney-Evans.

'The cyanide gas will work within seconds and the pumps are powerful enough to penetrate deeply. They shouldn't have a chance to escape.'

Major Cormack tapped the map thoughtfully. I think we have enough men to cover any area above the sewers we think particularly vulnerable. We could cover the whole blessed network if necessary, although that would mean thinning our perimeter considerably. Flame-throwers and machine-gun fire should take care of any beggars breaking loose, provided we keep a sharp lookout.'

Stephen Howard leaned forward. You realize we can't

provide your men with protective suits. There just aren't enough.'

Pender smiled grimly. 'I'm afraid the suits don't give enough protection. We left six or seven men back there in the forest who would testify to that – if they were still alive.'

There was an uncomfortable silence for a few moments, which was eventually broken by Thornton. 'How many rats attacked you? Have you any idea?'

Pender shook his head. 'It seemed like thousands – they were everywhere – but in reality I don't think there were more than a couple of hundred.'

'Good God, that many? We imagined they were a small isolated group.'

'Hopefully, there's even less now. We ran into your reinforcements on the way up. They should have destroyed quite a few.'

'I'm afraid not.' Captain Mather had appeared at the ratcatcher's side. 'We've just had word by radio. When the troops got to the area, there were no rats in evidence. Plenty of dead ones – those we killed – but no living rats. Apart from what was left of our men, and the vermin corpses, the area was deserted.'

Pender made his way towards the improvised medical room at the end of the corridor – the same room where Jan Wimbush had been attacked only two nights before. He glanced into a classroom to his right as he passed, surprised at its dramatic transformation. It now had the total appearance of a military operations room, banks of radio equipment stretched along one wall, blocking out half the light from the picture windows, an enlarged, mounted map displaying numerous coloured pointers spread out on the joined tables in the centre of the room, and machinery – some looking like television monitoring sets, others like radar scanners – that Pender could not hope to recognize. A constant hubbub came from the room and he wondered how anyone could *think*, let alone direct operations from there. Mingling with the brown uniforms of the military were the dark blue uniforms of the police. A joint operation. He hoped they wouldn't get in each other's way.

He passed on and entered the last classroom where the injured soldiers were being treated. It wasn't meant to cope with any serious crisis, for there were enough proper hospitals in the surrounding suburban areas; it was only a place to attend to minor injuries, cuts and bruises. The Warden's wife, Tessa Milton, was busy organizing tea and coffee for the soldiers who were good-humouredly asking for whisky and gin, while the medical officers were dabbing at their wounds with treated pads. He saw Vic Whittaker near a window, Jenny clearing the blood from the gash in his face, and he headed towards them.

Tessa Milton caught him lightly by the arm as he passed. 'Oh, Mr Pender. Is there any news of the other groups?'

'They're being called back in,' the ratcatcher told her, realizing she was concerned about her husband who was with one of the search-parties. 'They haven't run into any trouble yet – they'd have radioed in if they had. We were just unlucky, that's all.'

She smiled up at him, the anxiety still in her eyes. 'I'm sure you're right. Did you get hurt?'

'A few flesh pinches, bruises. No cuts.' He was suddenly aware of just how painful those 'pinches' were.

'Jolly good,' she said brightly. 'Would you like some tea? Or coffee?'

'No thanks. I've got to get back out there. We're going to gas the sewers.'

Tessa frowned and was about to ask another question, but Pender excused himself and walked over to Jenny and Whittaker.

Jenny's smile was radiant when she saw him. 'Are you okay, Luke? I've been so worried about you . . . all.'

'I'm fine,' he assured her. He looked down at Whittaker and studied the deep wound on his face. 'You'll have a handsome scar there,' he told him.

'It's the rest of my body that really hurts,' said Whittaker. 'I feel as though every inch of skin has been bitten.'

'We had a lucky escape. If it hadn't been for Captain Mather keeping a cool head, we'd have been finished.'

Whittaker looked down and studied his hand which was red and raw with teeth marks. 'I want to thank you for helping me back there, Pend . . . Luke. I don't think I could have held that bastard away from my face much longer.'

Pender said nothing.

'You're going to need stitches, Vic,' said Jenny, 'so I'll let the experts take care of that. Let's have your shirt off and I'll treat the bruises.'

As the senior tutor peeled off his shirt Jenny turned to Pender, concern in her eyes.

'Are you sure you're all right, Luke? Let me have a look at you.'

Pender grinned. 'Jenny, I've got bruises in places you wouldn't believe; but I haven't got time to let you examine them.'

'You're not going out there? There's nothing more you . . .'

'We're going to gas the sewers a little earlier than planned.'

'But they don't need you for that.'

'I'm going to be there.' Any warmth had left his face and she knew it was pointless to argue.

'What if they get out?' Whittaker said and both Jenny and Pender winced as they saw the red patches and teeth indents all over his torso. Large areas of skin were already turning a yellowish purple. By tomorrow, he would hardly be able to move.

'The troops are moving in,' said Pender. 'It's something we should have done in the first place. Instead of sealing any exits with cement, they'll keep them blocked with fire and bullets.'

'And the rats that are already outside – those that attacked us?'

'Disappeared. When the other soldiers got there, the rats had all gone. Hopefully, they found their way back into the sewers.'

'And if there are others running free?'

'We'll deal with them later. Our first concern is to eliminate the main force – and they're in the sewers. The rest should be just a tidying-up exercise.'

'I hope you're right.'

Pender pulled the sleeve of his protective suit up, tugging at the elasticated wristband to examine his watch. 'The soldiers should be in position within the hour. In the meantime, I'll do a quick tour of the main pumping sites to make sure they're ready. I'll see you both later.' He turned and headed for the door.

'Luke?' Jenny's voice made him pause, and he was surprised at her hurt tone. 'I'll come with you to your car,' she said, catching up with him.

They walked out into the busy corridor leaving the senior tutor staring after them.

'I won't be using my car, Jenny,' Pender said, 'I'll be under armed escort. There's no way I'm going back into the forest on my own.'

'Then I'll walk you to your escort,' she replied. 'Luke, do you really have to go? Haven't you done enough for one day?'

He stopped and placed his hands on her shoulders, looking intently into her face. 'Jenny, I won't stop until those bastards have been wiped from the face of the earth.'

The venom in his words frightened her and she dropped her eyes from his. His grip slackened and his hands fell away. Jenny kept up with him as he strode towards the reception area.

Once there he stooped to retrieve his fallen helmet, then pulled the tutor to one side, away from the figures that bustled to and fro. He smiled down at her, the old warmth returning.

'Stop worrying. Everything will be under control after we've used the cyanide, you'll see.' He leaned forward and kissed her cheek.

Jenny responded by clasping a hand around his waist, but drew it back hastily when he winced.

'Luke, you really are hurt.' She looked anxiously down at his side.

He drew in a deep breath, smiling. 'That doesn't help.'

'Please, let the medical officer look at you.'

Pender shook his head. 'It's nothing serious. Just bruises. Hey, you didn't tell me how Jan Wimbush and Will are doing.'

'Jan is still under sedation. Oh, Luke, her injuries are terrible. Her face ... The wound at the back of her neck is the one the doctors are really worried about. Fortunately, the spine was undamaged, but the wound beside it is so deep. It was touch-and-go for the first twenty-four hours. They think she'll pull through, though.'

The coldness had crept back into Pender's features. 'And Will?' he asked.

'He should be out tomorrow. He's got a nasty wound in his leg where the rat bit him, but no muscles or tendons were torn. They're only keeping him in to make sure there isn't any infection. Or disease. He's terribly upset about poor Jan . . .'

'Ready, Mr Pender?' Captain Mather stood two yards from them, Mike Lehmann at his side.

'You're going back for more, Captain?' said Pender, surprised.

'Why not?' came the reply. Then, with a grin, 'They're only rats.'

Mike Lehmann rolled his eyes heavenwards, but seemed in good humour now that the gassing was underway.

'Okay, Luke. Check the north first, then the southern outlets. There's no way the vermin can get into the surrounding sewer networks – every connection is sealed tight. So we won't be getting any complaints from the local authorities saying we've driven monsters on to their patch. We've got 'em boxed in, Luke, no way out.'

'Okay. I'll report back to you from each base. I'll stay with the last one until they've completed pumping.'

'Right. Good luck.'

Pender looked down at Jenny. 'I'll see you later,' he said.

'Be sure you do.'

Then he was gone, tramping down the path in his awkward suit, Captain Mather striding briskly by his side. They headed for a scout car, two lounging soldiers snapping to attention as they approached.

'Why did he have to go this time?' Jenny said aloud. 'He's done his job.'

'His job?' Lehmann had joined her at the reception area's

long window. 'It's more than just a job to Luke, miss, er . . . Jenny, isn't it?'

She nodded, turning towards Ratkill's head biologist. 'What do you mean, more than just a job?' she asked curiously.

'With Luke, it's more of a vendetta. He despises the rats.'

'But why?'

'You didn't know? I thought . . .' Lehmann left the sentence unfinished, and turned his gaze back to the window, his face expressionless.

'Please tell me,' Jenny persisted.

Lehmann let out a deep breath. 'Luke's parents and younger brother were killed by Black rats in the London Outbreak, four years ago. He was living in the North at the time because of his work.'

Jenny closed her eyes. She had *known*, sensed instinctively, that there was an underlying seriousness behind Luke's flippant remarks regarding his job.

'It was months after the incident that Luke contacted Ratkill. I suppose it took that long to get himself together. Stephen Howard was an old friend of his. He knew the full story and discussed it with me before he decided to take him on. I must say, I was against the idea, even though we needed as many men as we could get at that time: I didn't want any of my staff taking unnecessary risks, you see. Anyway, Howard overruled me, said Luke was a professional, whatever his motives. When I got to know Luke, I had to agree.'

Jenny shook her head. 'I didn't realize.'

'I'm sorry. I assumed he'd told you. From what I've seen over the last couple of days, you two seem, er . . . close? It's not something Luke talks about much, although I think it would be better for him if he did. It might get it out of his system. Maybe he'll tell you in his own time. I wouldn't mention that I . . .'

Jenny shook her head again. 'I won't. At least now I know why he does this godawful job. I'm sorry, I didn't mean . . .'

'It's all right,' Lehmann said, chuckling. 'You're right: it *is* a godawful job. But thank God some of us are inclined to do it. Now I've got to get back next door and synchronize the gas pumping. We want all the machines to be used at the same time so there's nowhere for the vermin to run to.'

Lehmann smiled at the tutor. 'Don't worry about Luke, Jenny. This'll be good for him. It'll help purge some of the hate that's been building up inside him for all these years. You can be sure of one thing though, he won't be happy until every last one of them is dead.'

They pumped the cyanide into the underground tunnels and prayed. There was no reason why the deadly fumes should not eliminate the vermin completely, for they were trapped, sealed in their own tomb; yet every man felt uneasy, as though they were dealing with more than just animals, but something unknown, something alien to their world. They listened to the sounds from below through earphones, the microphones sunk deep into the earth, penetrating the dark chambers, and heard the cries of the dying creatures, their panic as they fought to free themselves, the frantic scraping against solid walls, their terrified squeals as they scrambled over each others' backs to get clear of the destructive, seeping gas.

Some, just a few, managed to scrabble their way through an undetected opening, close to where Pender's group had been attacked earlier, but the soldiers were waiting for them. The first through were burnt to black ash by the flame-throwers, and those immediately behind had their lungs seared with the heat. Their corpses blocked the narrow passageway as effectively as the cement, for although their companions tried to gnaw their way through the bodies, the creeping fumes stole over them and they quivered in final, painful death-throes.

The men above the ground could not see the carnage that was taking place below, but they could feel the death in the air, they could envisage the desperate struggle inside the black catacombs. Even the forest itself seemed to maintain a respectful silence.

On the faces of the men who listened into the receivers was a mixture of disgust and pity. The cries in their ears seemed to belong to hundreds upon hundreds of children, screaming their panic, wailing as they died. It did not take long for the gas to penetrate every dark hole of the sewer network and soon the radio men at their different points began removing the headphones, feeling no gloating victory, just an ebbing of their spirit. They looked up at the silent men around them and nodded. The rats were dead.

16

'Luke, you look done in. Come and join us in the Warden's office, we'd like to discuss something with you.'

Pender wearily tossed the helmet into the corner of the reception area and stared into Stephen Howard's smiling face.

'If it's all the same to you, I'd like to get back to my hotel and take a long, hot bath. Can't we meet later?'

'Afraid not. I promise you, it won't take long.' The research director turned on his heels, still smiling pleasantly, and strode from the reception area, taking the corridor leading to Alex Milton's office. Pender followed, his limbs stiff from the bruising he'd received earlier that day.

The only people in the small room were Mike Lehmann and Antony Thornton. The research director immediately walked over to a cabinet on one side of the office on which stood an assortment of drinks.

'The Warden sent these over from his private stock,' Howard explained, his smile now beginning to irritate Pender. 'Still Scotch, no ice, no water?'

Pender nodded and sank into a straight-backed chair beneath the room's only window. He pulled off the thick gloves and dropped them on the floor, flexing his fingers and examining the red marks on them. Howard handed him the Scotch, his expression one of sympathy.

'I'm sure you must be rather sore in places after that

dreadful attack today. Thank God we had these suits reinforced after the Outbreak.'

Pender took a long swallow of his drink, momentarily closing his eyes at the liquid warmth. 'As I said earlier, they'll need to be made even tougher. They didn't stand up well enough.'

'Of course. Now the danger is over, we'll have time to improve them.'

Thornton, seated at the Warden's desk, raised his own glass. 'I think congratulations are in order, Stephen. Once again your company has provided an invaluable service to the country. God knows where we'd have been without your expertise.'

'It's not all over yet,' said Mike Lehmann staring down into his glass. 'There may still be others running free on the outside. Those that attacked Luke, for instance.'

'I quite agree,' said Howard, his smile gone. He sat in a seat facing Thornton and reached for his own drink that had been perched near the edge of the desk. 'We have to be pessimistic, Antony. You may think us over-cautious, but we can take no chances whatsoever. It *is* possible the rats that attacked Luke and his group returned to their companions in the sewers – after all, the one unblocked exit that was discovered when the gassing started was quite near the spot where the attack took place. But we cannot assume that is the case: the forest has to be searched thoroughly before we can give the all-clear.'

'Yes, yes, of course. But the point is, the *main* force has been dealt with,' said Thornton. 'The rest is surely a "mopping-up" exercise.'

'We hope so, Antony,' said Howard, 'we certainly hope so. However, it will be weeks before we can be absolutely sure. First, we have . . .'

'I think it's time we put Luke fully in the picture.'

Pender's eyes shot towards Mike Lehmann who had just spoken. There was silence in the room for a few moments and the ratcatcher's gaze shifted to Stephen Howard, who looked distinctly uncomfortable.

'Yes,' the research director said, 'it is time.' He looked first at the private secretary, then at Pender. 'I'm sorry I've never spoken of this to you before, Luke, but it was decided at the time – that time being immediately after the London Outbreak – that it should be a matter of secrecy. The less who knew of it, the better.'

Pender leaned forward, resting his elbows on his knees, the Scotch held in both hands. His eyes never left Howard's.

'As you know, we discovered the source of the mutant Black rat when London had been cleared of people and the vermin had been successfully gassed. Their original breeding-ground had been in an old disused lock-keeper's house on a canal near the docks in East London. You know how the zoologist Schiller had smuggled a mutant rat into the country from the radiation-affected islands around New Guinea. He mated his mutant with the normal Black rat – the area in which he lived, of course, was infested with them. The result – the terrifying result – was the giant Black rat, a new strain, stronger, more cunning than any other rodent. They dominated the indigenous Black rat and utilized their strength of numbers.'

Lehmann had become impatient. 'We thought we had killed them all off,' he said, 'but we hadn't. We didn't discover their nest, you see. We didn't know about the canal-house, the lair of the original mutant.'

'It was discovered by a man named Harris, a teacher who knew the area well, and who was helping us at the time.' Howard placed his glass back on the desk and swung round to face Pender. 'In the cellar of the house, he came upon a monster. From the description he gave, you could hardly call it an animal, let alone a rodent.'

'Wait a minute,' Pender said evenly. 'Why haven't you told me about this before? Do any of the Ratkill investigators know?'

This time Thornton interrupted. 'Your company has been acting under strict government instructions, Mr Pender. We saw no reason to panic the public any more than it had been. The slightest leak ...' He spread his hands, leaving the sentence unfinished.

'So what happened to this ... monster?' Pender asked impatiently.

Howard exhaled a short, dissatisfied breath. 'I'm afraid Harris destroyed it. Chopped it to pieces with an axe.'

Pender almost grinned. To Howard and his colleagues, it must have seemed like the vandalization of a valuable work of art.

Lehmann sensed the ratcatcher's inner amusement. 'We could have learned a lot from the animal's genetic structure, Luke,' he said seriously.

'But you must have had thousands of corpses to study.'

'Not like this one.'

We know what the creature looked like,' said Howard, 'from the description Harris gave us. Also there were many drawings of it in the zoologist's study. The body itself was too mutilated to piece together; it was almost as if it had literally exploded.'

'Exploded?' Pender sat straight in his chair.

'Yes. The body, you see, was not like that of the mutant rats. It was almost hairless, bloated, pinkish in colour. The skin was so taut the veins could be seen through it. It was like a huge, fat slug, crippled by its own obesity. And the most ghastly thing of all . . .' He paused, made nervous by his own description. 'It had two heads.'

Pender stared at him in disbelief.

'It's true, Luke,' Lehmann said quietly. 'I've seen the drawings myself. And what was left of the animal. According to Harris, it was blind and too heavy to move itself; totally defenceless. It really was a pity he hacked it to bits.'

'I don't blame him,' said Pender. 'I'd have done the same.'

Lehmann came straight back at him. 'No you wouldn't have. You know the value of such a freak animal. We could have studied it, discovered what had caused the mutation . . .'

'Bred your own mutant . . .'

'Yes, even that. That way we might have stood a chance of controlling them in the future. If we knew more about them . . .'

Howard held up a hand. 'All right, Mike. I think Luke takes your point.' He stood, then leaned back against the desk, looking down at the ratcatcher. 'We need to know if that particular strain has come through again. After a generation, it's quite possible.'

'You mean there might be two kinds of mutant rat.'

Howard nodded. 'Just that. If there are, we still consider it best that it be kept secret. The giant Black rat on its own is terrifying enough.'

A suspicion began to creep into Pender's mind. 'So?' he asked warily.

'We've taken you into our confidence, Mr Pender, because you have been involved in this particular operation from the start,' said Thornton. 'Indeed, your contribution has been remarkable.'

'And, as one of the few people who know of the original mutant's existence, there is something we would like you to do,' said Howard.

Pender's eyes widened and he felt his back stiffen as he listened.

He drove with Jenny to his hotel where they ate a dismal meal, mostly in silence. Pender was too fatigued and his body too sore to make light conversation. And his thoughts dwelt too much on the task he was to perform in two or three days' time.

Jenny sensed his mood and she, too, found it difficult to talk of trivial things. She drank her wine, then ran a finger around the rim of the glass.

'Luke,' she said, breaking the silence between them. 'I don't want to go back to the Centre tonight.'

He looked at her in surprise. 'It's perfectly safe there, Jenny. The whole area's floodlit, it's surrounded by troops. There's no possible danger.'

'It's not that. I am afraid, yes, but I know it's safe. I haven't slept too well the last couple of nights, knowing the forest has been infested. It'll never be the same for me again.'

'It's over now, Jenny. They're gone.'

'Are they? Can we be sure?'

'We will be in a couple of weeks' time. That's all it will take to search the area. Then you can go back to your work without any fears.'

'I don't think so. The forest used to be a wonderfully pure place to me, somewhere I escaped to; now it's different. It's tainted.'

He sighed. 'I'm sorry it's been spoiled for you.'

She took her eyes away from the glass and looked directly at Pender. 'I want to stay with you tonight, Luke,' she said.

A strange sensation ran through him: a thrill, but not of the triumphant kind. He realized he was deeply touched.

'Jenny, I . . .' he began to say.

'Please, Luke.'

He reached for her hand. 'Jenny, you don't have to say please to me. I should be hopping up and down with lecherous glee, but . . .'

'. . . but you're not. I know that, Luke. I know your feelings towards me.' Her eyes went back to the glass again. 'At least, I think I do,' she added.

He gripped her hand tightly and smiled. 'My feelings are confused just at this moment, Jenny. There's so much going on and I have to admit my nerves are a little frazzled. But one thing's for sure: there's no way I'll let you leave me tonight.'

Her eyes lifted and she smiled back at him. His depression evaporated and he felt he could sink into that smile. Her hand trembled in his, just slightly, and he knew she, too, experienced the same confusion of emotions.

'Vic Whittaker, Jenny?' he forced himself to ask.

Her face became serious, her eyes almost earnest. 'There's been nothing between us, please believe me. Some understanding, some mutual sympathy, but nothing beyond that. If Vic felt there was more, then it was in his own mind.'

'And us? Is it just an understanding?'

'No, it's not just that. We're both aware there's more to it. Just how much is something we have to find out.'

'Okay,' he said. 'Let's not try to analyse it. Let's just see what happens.'

Now it was her turn to grip his hand tightly. 'One thing, Luke,' she said. 'No games. I'm not playing games.'

'Jenny,' he replied, and her name felt good to say. 'I couldn't be more serious.'

They left the dining-room and Pender felt his weariness begin to disappear. They climbed the stairs and he let her into his room, thankful that, at Ratkill's expense, he always booked himself a double room when on field trips. Jenny placed her shoulder-bag on the floor and stood in the centre of the room waiting for him to close the door and switch on the light. Then she was in his arms, looking up at him, examining his face as though for the first time. His lips reached down for hers, but the movement was slow, almost tentative, both of them giving the moment its full meaning. When their lips joined, the kiss was soft, moist. Then it became firm and they felt themselves swimming into each other, seeking but becoming lost, plunging until their probing was done and they had found each other. All in a simple kiss, and Pender was almost afraid of it. Never had he felt so vulnerable.

He was suddenly aware of the crushing tightness with which he held her and the pain in his bruised back told him her grip was just as tight. She felt the sudden flinching of his muscles and realized she was hurting him.

'I'm sorry, Luke,' she said, relaxing her hold.

But he was smiling at her and she wasn't surprised to see the mistiness in his eyes, for she looked at him through her own blurred vision. She rested her head against his chest, conscious of his heartbeat, feeling small in his arms. He kissed her hair and ran a hand beneath it, touching her neck, caressing the skin behind her ears. Her arms encircled his waist and this time he cried out as she squeezed him.

'Oh, Luke, Luke, I'm so sorry.'

He laughed and held her away from him. 'Me too, Jenny. It looks like I'm going to be a disappointment to you.'

'We'll see,' she said, smiling wickedly. 'Let's try and do something about your wounds first, shall we?' She reached down into her bag. 'Take off your jacket and shirt and let's have a look at you. I brought some ointment from the medical supplies that should do your bruises some good.'

Pender winced as he shed his jacket, slowing the operation down to cause the least movement in his sore limbs. She watched him struggle, concern on her face.

'Here, let me help you.' She eased the jacket from his shoulders and laid it over one of the room's two armchairs. Then she began to unbutton his shirt.

'Oh God, Luke. They really did get at you.'

His shoulders and back were covered in small, red weals where the rats' teeth had sunk into the material of the protective clothing and pinched his skin together. Still in evidence, but to a lesser degree, were the long undefined scratch marks where the creatures' claws had raked him. Much of the skin around his shoulders and upper arms was turning a sickly purplish yellow and there were clear indents made by sharp teeth on either side of his wrist.

'Why didn't you say it was this bad?' Jenny said. 'You must have been in agony.'

'I didn't realize myself. It's only now it's really beginning to hurt.'

'I'm going to run a bath for you. That should stop some of the bruising.' She made for the bathroom. 'Get out of the rest of your things. I'll rub the ointment in after you've bathed.'

'I'll look forward to it,' he said, grinning.

He heard the sound of running taps and looked down at himself sheepishly. He shrugged, then whipped off his shoes and trousers. His underpants barely disguised his feelings. Sitting on the bed, he stripped off his socks, then sat there, feeling a little awkward. A towel came sailing from the bathroom.

'Use this if you're feeling bashful,' Jenny's voice called out.

He pulled the towel from his head where it had landed and stood, tugging briskly at the last garment as he did so. The towel was round his waist within seconds. Pender looked up to see Jenny smiling at him from the doorway, steam from the hot water billowing over her shoulders.

'My, my, such modesty,' she said.

She came towards him and her expression changed to one of concern once again.

'Your poor legs. Lucky you were wearing the protective clothing – you'd have been eaten alive if you hadn't.'

Jenny touched his shoulders, his arms, his chest, her fingers gentle. He pulled her close and she said, 'Careful, Luke,' but her words were smothered under his kiss. When their lips parted, she was breathing sharply, an urgency in her eyes. Her hand reached up to his cheek and he could feel himself pressing into her, the rough towel threatening to loosen and fall at any moment. His lips sought hers again.

She pulled away. 'No. Not just yet. Let's see to your wounds first.'

Pender drew in a deep breath and tightened the towel at his waist. 'You're the boss – for now,' he said.

She kissed his chest, quickly and lightly. 'Into the bath with you. I'll be there in a minute.'

The splash of water and his muffled groans told her he had immersed himself as she picked up his clothes, folding them and placing them neatly over the arm of the chair. She walked towards the bathroom, unbuttoning the sleeves of her blouse as she went.

Jenny looked down at his naked form in the bath, the still-running water rippling over his body and distorting it. Leaning forward, she turned off the taps, then stirred the water into swirling eddies with her hand, mixing the hot with the cold. When the currents settled down she examined his body, for the moment ignoring the injuries to study his shape. She smiled approvingly.

Jenny began unbuttoning her blouse. She slipped the silk

from her shoulders in a fluid movement and hung the garment on a hook behind the bathroom door. She was bra-less and Pender gazed at her breasts, the twin points risen and pink.

She knelt beside the bath and rested her arms on its edge, looking into his face and loving what she saw. He stretched his neck forward and they kissed once, twice, three times. He opened his mouth to speak, but she pressed a finger to his lips, then reached for the flannel and wiped the moisture from his face.

Pender closed his eyes and let Jenny bathe him, her hands soft and caressing, smoothing the soap over his limbs, spending more care and attention than necessary on his aroused penis, leaning over the bath to gently kiss it. He groaned, but in pleasure this time, reaching for her, cupping a breast in his hand. Then he leaned forward, his upper body clear of the water, one arm encircling her naked back, his head bending low, lips seeking a thrusting nipple. He caressed it with his tongue, leaving a trail of moisture across her chest as he sought the other.

Jenny moaned and closed her eyes, wanting him badly now, the muscles in her thighs becoming taut. She pushed him back, gently but firmly, determined to ease his pain first. She sponged the soap from his body in silence, relishing his touch, his fingers running smoothly over her breasts, the insides of her arms, along her neck. Then she drew him from the water, and gently patted him dry, pulling the towel over his aroused organ, then beneath it, squeezing his testicles without force but nevertheless causing him to draw in his breath. Once more she kissed him there, allowing his penis to enter her mouth, drawing the first drops of sticky fluid from it, holding his hips as he moved slowly.

Then he was pulling her up, knowing he was losing control

and wanting her fully. He held her against him, pressing her nakedness into his, their kisses no longer tentative, but hard and thrusting, their tongues meeting and tasting each other's sweetness. His hand fell to her waist and he pulled at the zip fastener, the skirt falling away from his grasp. Her tights came next, her shoes already gone, and as he drew the nylon down her thighs, he kissed her stomach causing it to contract as though stung, her hands closing over the back of his head. He allowed his lips to linger, drawing them down to the silky material of her panties, feeling the soft resistance of hair beneath them, pressing into it with his tongue.

He rose and she moved closer into him, saying his name softly. His hand, trembling and nervous, touched the outside of her thigh, then stole inwards, reaching into her panties, smoothing its way through her hair, sinking low and reaching the moist entrance to her body, his fingers piercing gently. She shuddered and leaned her head against his chest.

She reached for him, pressing herself against his hand, wanting more of him.

'Jenny,' he said, knowing neither could hold back much longer, and she paid heed, relaxing her grip, desperate now to have him inside her, filling her body with his own, wanting every inch, every nerve-end pressed against his skin.

He led her from the bathroom and laid her on the bed, drawing off the last piece of clothing, standing over her, gazing down at her body, the long, long legs, the smooth flatness of her stomach, the breasts so full, hardly losing their shape now she was lying on her back. She raised a hand towards him and he sank down on to her, finding her lips, and kissing them with a tenderness that overrode desire. Her arms clasped around his shoulders and she pulled him tight, forgetting his bruises. His legs were between hers, her knees raised just slightly on either side, and his penis pressed against her stomach, a thin trickle of fluid leaving a narrow, silver trail as he lowered himself. He reached down and guided himself into her, wanting to be gentle, resisting the screaming desire to thrust himself forward. Her head turned to one side as he entered and her hips rose to meet him, urging him on, demanding him there, deep, penetrating, wanting his whole length, her hands reaching down to his lower back, pulling him in.

Her soft moans turned to a whimper and he paused, raising his head so he could look into her face. She turned her head back to him and her eyes shone, her smile strained, her expression pleading. Then he could hold back no longer: he pulled away and thrust forward again, hard, rigid as iron, but as soft as velvet. She thrust with him, her excitement rising with his, her eyes half-closed, her knees striving to press together, gripping him, silently calling for more, more, more.

His teeth bit into her neck, making her cry out and he couldn't be sure if it was from pleasure or pain. Or both. He felt her limbs stiffening, felt her breath held, felt her silent scream, felt his muscles becoming taut, the liquid beginning to flow, seeming to draw itself from every part of his body, stretching every nerve until he thought they would tear, then the sweet ascending, the bursting through, the tightness of her inner muscles, the relaxing of nerves, the floating fall, the sighs that told him their pleasure had been shared, the sinking against her and the draining contentment.

They held each other for a long, silent time, she softly stroking his back, he with his head tucked into her hair that flowed across the pillow.

'You weren't,' she said finally.

He raised his head slightly. 'Huh?' he murmured.

'A disappointment.'

He grinned and allowed his head to slump back into her hair. Twisting his body, Pender withdrew from her and slid an arm beneath her neck. He pulled her close, kissing her cheek, then her lips. Both felt at peace, the traumas of the last few days laid aside for the moment.

After a while, Jenny said, 'I wish we never had to go back.'

'It will be all over soon.'

'It never will be for me. Not now. I thought I'd find something here – some respite. It's been shattered in a way I never dreamed of.'

'Respite from what?'

She turned her head away from him and became quiet. Pender touched her chin with his hand and drew her face back towards him.

'Tell me, Jenny.'

She searched his eyes for several moments before speaking. 'Coming to the Centre was a kind of retreat for me. I suppose I wanted to get away from life for a while. I thought living there, working with children, helping them understand the simple way of nature would uncomplicate my own life. It hasn't really worked.'

'What were you running away from?'

'The obvious; I think you can guess. The ironic part is that I promised myself I'd never get involved with a married man. My father left us years ago under those circumstances. We never even knew he was unhappy until the day he told us he was leaving. I'd always taken his love, his *being* there, for granted; I think my mother had too. To have that security taken away so suddenly and irrevocably was shattering. I watched what it did to my mother, how it changed her, the bitterness it left in her, and it frightened me. Sixteen years of marriage wiped out as though it had been a trivial affair.

'I still saw my father, I still loved him. But the change was in him. It was as though his guilt was tearing him up inside – and the full realization of that guilt was when he was with me. I suppose in the end it made us both uncomfortable. We don't see too much of each other now.'

Jenny's voice had become distant and Pender turned on his side, pulling her even closer. He was surprised to see there was no emotion in her eyes, just a dull flatness, as though emotions had long since been cried out.

'At fifteen I vowed I would never be like the woman that had caused such grief. God, how I hated that bitch. And then, five years later, I was that woman. Can you explain it, Luke? How can you become the very thing you loathe?'

She looked at him as though he really might provide her with an answer, but he shook his head. 'Things just happen, Jenny. You can't always control them.'

'I tried, oh, how I tried; but he meant too much to me. I just couldn't stop myself, Luke, even though I hated what I was doing. Please try to understand.'

Her body trembled as she closed her eyes, and he could see the moistness creeping through the lashes.

'Jenny, Jenny, you don't have to explain anything. That was in your past; it had nothing to do with me.' But it hurt, just the same.

'I want you to know, Luke. Like I said, no games between us.' She kissed him, her eyes opening, allowing tiny rivulets to run from each corner. 'He was the one that ended it and I guess I didn't put up too much of a struggle. I wanted him more than I could ever say, but I couldn't let myself beg; I couldn't fully become the woman I detested. I'm over him now, Luke, please believe that. I still … respect him; I still even like him. But the love has gone.' She stared at the ceiling for a few moments. 'I just drifted for a while after we broke up, then, when the opportunity came to join the Con-

servation Centre, I jumped at it. It seemed better than joining
a convent.'

He smiled at her attempt to make light of it. 'And then you
met Vic Whittaker,' he said.

'I told you, there's nothing between us. He's a nice man,
and interesting, but I only ever wanted to share the work with
him, nothing else.'

'I'm glad, Jenny.'

Her head buried itself into his chest, her arms encircling
him. 'And I'm glad you came to the Centre. It's another irony
– that something so horrible should bring you there – but I'm
almost pleased the rats invaded the forest. Luke, don't get me
wrong, I'm not putting any responsibility on you; but I feel
alive again. The past may not be dead, but it's faded into
another time. All I ask is that you be honest with me.'

He pressed against her, his leg going between her thighs,
and they held on to each other, the touch of their bodies an
assurance in itself.

'It would be easy for me to say so much to you now,' he
whispered, 'but give me a little time. Let me finish this job
first. I have to be sure they're really gone.'

'You really hate them that much, Luke?'

'So much, I thought at one time I'd never have room for
any other true feelings. You're breaking it down, Jenny, and I
can't let you. Not until it's over.' And then he told her why he
despised the vermin, how his mother and father, his younger
brother, had been slaughtered by them four years before,
their bodies devoured, leaving hardly enough to bury. How
he had pleaded with Howard to give him a job so he could
fight all vermin – not just the mutants – to ensure that a
disaster of that nature could never happen again.

Jenny cried as he spoke, feeling pity for him and a sad joy
that he was speaking to her of things he had kept buried for

such a long time. When he had finished, she held him till his body had lost its rigidity, had become relaxed, the tenseness gone. And he knew he loved her then, yet he could not allow himself to say it, fearing that with no barrier left between them, he would not have the courage to face what was still left to be done, knowing she would try to stop him.

It was only later, when he lay stretched out on the bed and she knelt next to him applying ointment to his injuries that he told her of the task he had been asked to perform within the next few days. Her hand stopped its soothing motion and she looked down at him in dismay.

'But surely there's no need?' she said 'Surely they can just clear out the sewers with machinery? Why, Luke? Why do you have to go in there first?'

'They want me to look for something ... I can't tell you what. I have to search the sewers before anyone else is allowed in. I won't be alone – Captain Mather will be with me – and there shouldn't be any more danger.'

'How can you be sure? How can anyone be sure of anything with these monsters?'

It was a question he had asked himself many times that evening.

They entered the sewers wearing breathing apparatus, the stench of the rotting corpses wafting up from the opened manhole cover and sending their unmasked helpers reeling back. Pender and Captain Mather climbed down the metal ladder into the darkness below, both men fighting against their natural fear, expecting to hear the scurrying of clawed feet and squealing shrieks at any moment. They had waited three days before the final decision to go in was made; three days of pumping in more cyanide, listening for sounds through their receivers, praying it really was the end of the vermin menace. No signs of the creatures had been found above ground, but the soldiers and the operatives were still wary, their eyes continually looking around, searching the trees, the undergrowth, never venturing into the forest alone or unprotected. Those gathered near that particular sewer entrance on the third day after the initial gassing did not envy the two men now descending into the infested labyrinth. The residue of lingering gas had been suctioned clear by the very machines that had pumped it in, but the thought of wading through the piled-up, decomposing bodies sent shudders through them. The soldiers were relieved that only two men were going down on the first mission, none of them keen to be part of a spearhead.

Both Pender's and Captain Mather's limbs were still stiff from the bruising their bodies had taken in the rat attack and they found their descent awkward, the protective suits and oxygen cylinders on their backs impeding their movements even further. Pender stood at the bottom of the ladder and swung the powerful torch he was carrying in a wide arc. A feeling of revulsion swept over him when he saw the heaped bodies, many with bloated stomachs, the result of a build-up of internal gases, others with jaws wide in silent agony, their legs extended stiffly into the air, their skin flaking and rotting. Mather joined him and regarded the nightmare scene with equal disdain, sweeping his torchlight into both directions of the tunnel.

He shone the torch on the boldly drawn map of the sewer network and a gloved finger pointed to their location. He then indicated the direction they had already agreed upon and Pender gave an exaggerated nod. The ratcatcher moved off, Mather following close behind.

Two hours passed, then three. The men gathered around

the point of entry began to grow anxious. They knew the two men had a wide circuit to cover, their route eventually leading them back to the starting point, but it was nerve-wracking to stand by completely inactive. Mike Lehmann and Stephen Howard eyed each other nervously. Antony Thornton was, at that moment, reporting personally to the Prime Minister and his Inner Cabinet, assuring them in soothing tones that all was well in Epping Forest, and the situation was under complete control. Jenny Hanmer sat alone in her room at the Conservation Centre and stared at the window. The curtains were drawn together.

Another hour passed.

Mike Lehmann tucked his wristwatch back inside his sleeve and pulled the thick glove back on. He turned to the research director. 'I want to go down there with some men,' he said firmly.

'Not just yet, Mike,' Howard replied. 'Give them time. They've got a lot of ground to cover.'

'They've had time enough. I'm going.' He reached for the helmet lying at his feet.

'You know you can't take any soldiers down there just yet!' Howard snapped. 'We agreed with Thornton.'

'To hell with Thornton! Luke may be in trouble.'

'Keep your voice down, Mike. Listen, if he . . .'

'They're coming up!'

Both men wheeled around at the sound of the soldier's voice and looked towards the opening to the sewer. The soldier who had called out, his mouth and nose now covered with a handkerchief, was reaching down with one hand into the hole. An arm appeared over the edge of the opening, then a helmet and shoulders. The figure clambered through followed by another and a cheer rang out among the relieved soldiers. The first figure stood erect and the hands pulled at his helmet, then pulled away the oxygen mask. The only expression on Pender's face was one of weariness.

He spotted Lehmann and Howard and began walking towards them, his strides heavy, awkward. They saw his face was shining with perspiration and steam from his mouth escaped into the cold air in swirling billows. He stopped before them, dropping the torch and helmet onto the grass, and looked at each man in turn.

He shook his head. 'Nothing,' he said.

17

Charles Denison smiled to himself as he steered the Land-Rover along the rutted track. It was over. His forest was free.

He looked out at the bright sky. Even the weather seemed to acknowledge that all was well. The sun had shone brightly, like an omen, since the sewers had been cleared of dead vermin two weeks before. There was a clean dryness in the air, the brown-gold leaves crisp and brittle on the ground, shattering underfoot into flaky powder, ready to replenish the soil. The animals were more in evidence now, venturing forth from their habitats, still cautious, but becoming bolder by the day. The troop activity had probably frightened them more than anything else, the heavy tanks and army vehicles lumbering through their domain like great metal prehistoric monsters. The constant drone of helicopters searching overhead had not helped, either. The main force was gone now, leaving behind a sufficient number to patrol the woodland, but not enough to intrude unpleasantly on the life there. The residents would be allowed to return soon – perhaps in two or three weeks' time when every building, every cellar, had been thoroughly scoured. It had been a mammoth job, for there were more homes and deserted buildings on the vast woodland estate than people realized, but it had been carried out with typical military efficiency. Just a few more and the task would be complete.

Of course, anyone entering the forest still had to wear the damned uncomfortable protective suits, but everyone knew they were now just an unnecessary precaution. The soldiers had complained at first because they had not been kitted out with the silvery clothing – there simply had not been enough to go round – but now they laughed at their companions in house-searching parties who had to wear them. Everyone had relaxed. Except Whitney-Evans. His concern was now of a different nature.

It looked as if Epping Forest might lose its financial independence. The extermination exercise had cost more than the City coffers could afford at that time and the Greater London Council had rubbed their hands in glee at the prospect of becoming joint owners of the green belt area. The battle was on: Whitney-Evans and his City friends were endeavouring to sue the government of the day for the disaster. The local authorities who each owned a slice of the greenlands around Epping Forest were screaming for tighter controls in the area, demanding that the government itself should take total responsibility for the woodland's upkeep, and the GLC were claiming that the forest was a natural extension of London itself, therefore it should come under their jurisdiction. The clamour from the public over the scare they had received – and, of course, the many deaths that had occurred – was being nicely stirred by the main opposing political party, with the smaller antagonists jumping up and biting the government's ankles with furious relish. The media had had a field day, dreaming up a new title for the circulation-stimulating event, their elected title following aptly on the heels of 'The Outbreak': they called it 'The Outrage'.

Denison slowed the Land-Rover as a squirrel hopped on to the track ahead, cocked its head at his approach, and darted back into cover.

'You're one vermin I don't mind any more!' Denison called out, chuckling to himself. The vehicle gathered speed and the head keeper began to hum a tune to himself, happy to be carrying out his normal duties in the almost deserted forest. It would be a long time before the day-trippers returned and the thought made him even happier. It also warmed him a little to think of the insufferably pompous Whitney-Evans squirming under the sudden pressures inflicted upon him. The man undoubtedly loved the Epping Forest, but he had a tendency to regard it as his own domain, his own back garden, and all those employed in its care as his personal gardeners. Denison hoped fervently that the City would retain control of the woodland, but had to smile at the upset now taking place.

He brought the Land-Rover to a halt before a large gate, the entrance to a six-acre enclosure in which the forest deer were kept. They had been herded together and brought here for their own protection years before, because their numbers had depleted rapidly through cars and lorries knocking them down when they wandered across the many roads running through the woodland. Dogs had also been a menace to them, chasing them, savaging their young. They had sustained injuries on fencings, cut themselves on broken glass and choked on plastic bags left by tourists. The occasional poacher had left his mark, too. It was decided that if the deer population were to survive, it could only do so in the safety of a reserve. One of Denison's biggest fears during the rodent invasion was that the deer would be attacked. He had begged for a guard, or at least a patrol, to cover the perimeter, and the army had complied with his wishes until the threat was over. Of all the forest wildlife, he loved these gentle, skittish creatures most.

He pulled the gate open wide, climbed back into the Land-

Rover, and drove through. He left the engine idling while he closed the gate again. There were no deer immediately in evidence, but that wasn't unusual: they were shy creatures. He drove around the perimeter, checking for breaks in the fencing, ensuring there were no deer strung halfway over the boundary, their efforts to wander free foiled by their inability to clear the wire.

He sensed the presence of the bodies before he saw them. They were scattered over a wide area as though their panic had made them flee in different directions. They lay motionless in the grass, bloody, half-eaten carcasses. He jumped from the Land-Rover, leaving behind the two-way radio that had now become standard equipment, and stumbled towards them, shaking his head as he went, his cheeks glistening wetly. Five, six, seven, more. Nine in all. Oh God, no. Another, a hundred yards away. One by the fence, another ... He stared at the slumped form, unsure, too much blood to be certain, but the unstained areas light in colour ...

He moved closer to the particular animal, his grief making him oblivious to any danger that might still be lurking in the vicinity. As he drew nearer, he became more certain. And as he stood above the ravaged body, a raw, gaping hole in its skull beneath the antlers, the blood still viscous as though death had been recent, he knew from what was left untouched of the light, fawn-covered coating, that the rats had slaughtered the white deer.

Whittaker swung the rusted iron gates wide and Pender drove the Audi through. He waited for the senior tutor to close the gates again and stared through his windscreen at the long, straight road ahead, the forest of pine trees providing a high, green wall on either side. In the distance he could just make out the sombre, square shape of Seymour Hall, its chimney stacks a dark silhouette against the clear sky.

The passenger door opened and Whittaker climbed in. The car moved forward at a slow speed, both men looking keenly into the trees, searching for any scarred barks, any sudden movement.

'What do you think?' Whittaker asked, his eyes still scanning the forest. 'We haven't seen any signs for two weeks now, not since the gassing.'

Pender shook his head. 'I don't know. I'd like to think we got them all, but I still feel uneasy.'

'Why? Nearly every inch of the forest has been covered and there's only a few buildings left to search. Even the one ahead has been cleared by the helicopter reconnaissance – the pigs running loose up there all seemed healthy enough.'

'I still won't be happy until every building has been crossed off our list.'

'Maybe you're right. I'll certainly feel relieved when the whole area has been given a clean bill of health. Even then I think I'll be a little scared of the forest for a few years to come.'

Pender brought the car to a halt before the rough wooden gate and cattle-grid that barred the entrance into the rising field leading up to the desolate mansion.

'You won't get the car up there,' Whittaker said. 'It's hard down here, but the pigs have churned the track into a muddy swamp at the other end.'

'Okay, we'll walk.' Pender quickly ran his eyes over the surrounding fields, studying the wooded fringes. He was glad to be clear of the pine forest, the memory of the mutant rats leaping from the trees still all too vivid. Ahead, to his right, he saw the small round copse that had made him feel uneasy on his last visit to this place. It would have to be searched later. He reached for the two-way radio lying on the back seat and informed the Operations Room at the Centre of their precise location, a strictly adhered-to procedure for any of the search parties in the forest. Then he strapped a gun holster around his waist.

'Okay,' he said when he had finished, 'let's take a look.'

Whittaker pushed open the door and clambered out, the sun reflecting sparkles of light in his silver-grey protective suit.

'Hey! Helmet,' Pender said reaching down into the front floor-space where the tutor had carelessly thrown the headgear.

'Oh, Christ. Is it still necessary?' Whittaker complained.

'Carry it. You never know.'

Whittaker took the plastic-visored helmet and tucked it under his arm. He gazed around him, fingers scratching his beard.

'It's so bloody peaceful,' he said. 'It seems impossible that it all happened such a short time ago.'

Pender closed the car door, and smiled grimly. 'Let's hope it stays this way,' he said.

They walked towards the gate, carefully negotiating their way across the metal cattle-grid. Pender released the catch and swung the gate open a few feet, lifting it clear of the rutted earth at its base. The tutor passed through and Pender made sure the entrance was closed properly before catching up with him. They trudged along in silence, the track becoming muddier as they went. The ratcatcher examined the rough soil on either side.

'The pigs don't leave much, do they,' he commented.

'No, they eat anything and everything. That's what makes them so cheap to keep. These free-rangers virtually look after themselves.'

'I don't see any,' said Pender, craning his head round.

'They'll be up at the house – in the shelter there. We can look in on them to set your mind at rest.'

The mud began to pull at their boots now, making walking awkward.

'I'm surprised this hasn't dried up,' Pender said, 'with all the bright weather we've been having.'

'It's become too water-logged over the years. It'll never dry up now. It gets worse further on.'

Once more there was a silence between them as they plodded through the oozing mud, and Pender felt the tutor's resentment towards him. He'd been conscious of it before, on the other days he and Whittaker had teamed up as a search-party, and had ignored it. The tutor hadn't actually said anything antagonistic towards him, nor indicated his feelings over Jenny and Pender's relationship – it was more an under-lying animosity tempered by the fact that Pender had pulled the rat from him during the attack, possibly saving his life, or at least saving him from serious injury. But it was coming, and Pender could sense it.

He almost smiled when Whittaker said, 'Look, Luke, about Jenny . . .'

Pender kept walking, his eyes searching the empty windows of the building ahead. 'What about her?' he said.

'You know she's in a confused state at the moment. This business with the rats has upset her terribly.'

Pender remained silent.

'What I'm trying to say is, she's very vulnerable right now . . . I don't think she knows her own mind.'

'I don't agree. She seems to me to be very clear-minded.'

Whittaker reached out a hand and brought the ratcatcher to a halt. 'Look, what I mean is, I'd hate to see her taken advantage of when she's in this state.'

Pender faced him. 'Listen,' he said through tight lips. 'I understand your problem, but it *is* your problem. It's nothing to do with Jenny and me. Jenny's neither confused nor being taken advantage of. I could explain to you how we feel about each other, but *that* has nothing to do with you.'

There was a flush to Whittaker's face. 'Before you came along . . .'

'Before I came along nothing! Jenny told me you were good friends, but that was all. Anything else was what you assumed yourself.'

The tutor wheeled away, his boots making sucking noises as he stomped towards the house. Pender hurried after him.

'Hey, Vic, I didn't mean . . .'

But Whittaker marched on, ignoring Pender's words, and the ratcatcher fell silent once more. When the tutor's foot slipped and he went down on one knee in the mud, Pender reached out for him and, suppressing a grin, helped him to his feet.

Whittaker looked at him sullenly. 'Okay, maybe I did imagine much of it. But I do care about her, even though I've got my own . . . responsibilities. I don't want to see her hurt.'

'I understand, Vic, believe me, I understand. I've no intention of hurting Jenny; I'm in too deep for that. I'm sorry you're the loser, but try to see: you were never really in the race.'

Whittaker shrugged slowly. 'Perhaps you're right. I don't know. She'll make up her own mind.'

You poor idiot, Pender thought. She already had. And strangely, right at that moment, so had he. When he left the forest, his work done, Jenny would be leaving with him.

'Come on,' he said, 'let's look at the house.'

They continued their journey, boots squelching noisily as they sank deeper into the mud. A low, barbed-wire fence appeared on their left, presumably to keep the pigs from the lush vegetation on the other side.

'That was part of the gardens,' Whittaker explained, not looking at Pender, his voice low. 'They stretch right back and around the house itself. It's like a jungle round there.'

By now they were close to the gutted manor house and Pender was surprised at its true size. He had only had a side-view as they approached along the track but now, as the rough-hewn road swept on past the entrance, he could see the whole frontage. The large ground-floor windows and arch-shaped door were barricaded with corrugated iron, decorated with mindless, sprayed-on graffiti. Rubble was heaped against its walls as though, year by year, more and more brickwork had dislodged itself from the upper floors and formed a defensive barrier around the perimeter. The first- and second-floor windows were no longer black and ominous, for he could see the sky through them, as most of the building's roof was completely demolished. The many chimney stacks were perched precariously on inner walls, rising above the main shell like solemn sentinels. A balustrade ran round the roof-top, joined at the centre by a triangle of grey stonework that stood above the projecting wall of the main frontage. From where they stood, the whole structure seemed to dominate the surrounding countryside.

'It must have been some place in its day,' Pender said.

Whittaker made no comment, but turned off the main track, taking an even muddier path that ran alongside the building.

'There are old stables around the side here,' he called back. 'They've been converted into pig-pens.'

Pender followed, treading warily through the mire, clutching his protective helmet in one hand. He concentrated on one foot at a time, choosing the firmer patches of mud and avoiding the water-filled troughs. When he looked up, the tutor had disappeared round the corner of a wall jutting out from the side of the main building which obviously formed the outer wall of the stables. As he rounded the corner, he saw Whittaker with his back to him, looking into the gloomy interiors of two facing stable blocks. The floors of both sections were covered with deep layers of straw and, as Pender narrowed his eyes to pierce the shadows, he saw bulky, pink shapes lying amongst it, their bodies half-concealed. He almost choked on the nauseous smell and wondered how even an animal could live with such a stench.

Whittaker turned his head towards him. 'There they are,' he said. 'Sleeping like babies.'

'What a lovely life,' said Pender, moving past Whittaker for a closer look.

'If you like muck and dirt,' the tutor said. He saw Pender suddenly stiffen. 'What's wrong? What is it?'

Pender's voice was low, almost a whisper. 'Take a closer look.'

Whittaker frowned and peered into the gloom. 'I can't see . . .'

'Closer. Look, just over there. That one.' Pender was pointing at a nearby recumbent form. The tutor edged forward until Pender grabbed his arm. 'No further. Can't you see from here?'

This time it was Whittaker who stiffened. 'Oh God,' he said. 'It looks like blood.'

'Look at the others. There's no movement, no breathing. And listen – there's no noise at all.'

Whittaker slowly shook his head. 'They're dead.'

The ratcatcher moved forward, his senses alert, eyes searching for dark-haired shapes among rough bedding. He knelt down and pulled at the straw, clearing an area around one of the still bodies. The pig had been torn to pieces, its neck ripped, the head almost severed from its body. There were only stumps where its legs had once been and the stomach was punctured with large holes from which its insides had been dragged through, presumably to be devoured. Pender now realized that the terrible stench had come from corrupted flesh. The pigs had been dead for a long time.

Whittaker was uncovering another decomposing body and as Pender stood, his eyes becoming accustomed to the gloomy interior, he saw they were littered all around the stable, a carnage of destroyed animals. Most of the bodies were shrivelled, bearing little resemblance to the creatures they once were, the flesh of their underbellies gone.

'The rats must have attacked them at night while they were sleeping,' Pender said. 'They had no chance at all. Not even to get out into the open.'

'But they're only half-eaten. Some of them . . .'

'The rats have probably been feeding off them since they were killed.' He paused, then added wryly, 'Their own private supply. Jesus.' He surveyed the area in disgust. 'Come on, I think we'd better get out of here.'

But Whittaker's eyes were transfixed on something ahead of him. 'Pender, one of them is breathing. It's still alive.'

'That can't be.' Pender looked in the direction of the tutor's gaze and saw that the body, unlike most of the others, was still grossly swollen. And there was a slight movement from it.

'We can't help it now,' he said. 'Let's go.'

'Wait, wait. We can at least put it out of its misery. Let me have the gun.'

'No. The sound would arouse anything else that might be lurking around here. Leave it be.'

But Whittaker was insistent. 'Please, I can't leave it like this.'

Pender reluctantly undid the flap of the holster and handed Whittaker the Browning. 'Push it into its neck – try to muffle the sound. And make it quick.'

He watched anxiously as the tutor removed his glove and curled his finger through the trigger guard, making towards the unfortunate animal. The mystery was how the pig had managed to survive all this time.

'Pender, look at this.' Whittaker was crouched over the pink, bloodstained body. The ratcatcher quickly joined him, eager to be away from the place. He frowned when he saw the long, gaping tear in the bloated belly.

'It's dead. Nothing could survive that,' he said.

'But look, the lungs are moving. It's breathing.'

Pender bent forward. The skin *was* undulating, yet the rest of the body was stiff with rigor mortis.

He realized what the movement was just before the sleek, black head pushed its way through the jagged slit in the pig's stomach.

Whittaker screamed as the rat scrabbled its whole body through the opening, leaping at the tutor as he fell back into the straw. Pender, too, fell back in surprise and for a moment could only watch the struggling bodies in frozen horror. Then he was on his knees shouting at Whittaker, trying to be heard over the man's screams.

'The gun! Use the gun!'

But the weapon was no longer in the tutor's hand; it was hidden somewhere in the straw, released in shock. Pender quickly searched for it, but it was no use, the gun had disappeared.

Whittaker had a hand clamped inside the rat's mouth, his fingers curled round the lower jaw, and blood was flowing down his wrist as the creature's teeth sank in. Claws were frantically raking his chest, scoring the suit's material, threatening to penetrate at any moment.

Pender crouched, then leapt forward, grabbing the giant rat at the back of the neck with one hand, the other going beneath its jaw. He pulled back with one mighty heave, trying to snap its neck, but the mutant twisted, spoiling the leverage. It momentarily released Whittaker's hand and the tutor pulled it clear, his head swimming with the pain.

Pender lifted the rat, keeping his arms outstretched, using all his strength, holding the squirming body with its lethal teeth and claws away from him. He lost his balance, the struggling weight too much for him. He crashed down into the muddy yard between the facing stables, falling on top of the rat, crushing it with his own weight. He clung desperately to the thrashing creature's neck, pushing the head down into the ooze in an attempt to suffocate it. The wet earth flew furiously in all directions as the rat panicked and Pender knew he did not have the strength to hold it there for long.

'Find the gun!' he yelled at the tutor who still lay in the straw moaning in pain. 'Shoot the bloody thing!'

Whittaker scrambled around on hands and knees, but could find no sign of the weapon.

'It's not here! I can't find it!' he screamed.

The mud was making Pender's gloved hands slippery and he could feel the creature forcing its way loose, pushing its haunches down and pulling its neck up. Pender squeezed, trying to choke the rat to death.

Then Whittaker was slivering in the mud next to him, something held in his uninjured hand.

'Hold its head out, Pender! Hold it where I can reach it!'

Pender allowed the creature to raise its head from the well

it had created in the mud, and Whittaker struck down hard with the brick he had found, bringing it down on the small, pointed skull. The rat squealed but continued struggling, almost breaking free of Pender's grasp.

'Again!' Pender shouted. 'Again!'

Once more the brick descended, but the mutant's struggling became even more frantic.

'Again!' Pender was almost screaming now. The heavy weight struck.

'Again!'

The rat stiffened momentarily.

'Again!'

They heard the crunching of bone. Yet still it moved.

Pender leapt to his feet, dragging the limp body with him and, without pause, swung the rat by the neck against a stout wooden beam supporting the stable roof. He felt the snap in the creature's neck and let it fall to the ground, its body twitching in death throes.

Pender collapsed on to one knee and drew in deep gasps of air. His face and body were caked in mud, but that was the least of his concerns. Whittaker sat hunched in the slime, clutching his injured hand in his lap.

'Are you okay?' Pender asked.

'I can't . . . move . . . my fingers. I think all the tendons . . . are gone.' His face was screwed up in agony, tears running freely down his face into his beard.

Pender staggered to his feet and put a hand beneath the tutor's shoulder. 'Come on,' he said, pulling him up. 'We'd better move fast. No telling how many others are around here.'

The two men stumbled from the stable yard, helmets forgotten, fear giving them impetus, the mud making them slip and hold on to each other for support. They rounded the corner and made for the track leading from the house to the car on the other side of the field. As they reached the front of the building, Pender now half-supporting the injured man, they bolted down the gentle slope leading away from the house towards the open fields. And something made Pender pause to take in the peculiar circular tree copse in the middle of the nearest field.

The trees seemed to be quivering with hidden life, the branches moving, shedding leaves, trembling as though shaken by a swirling wind. It seemed to be almost thrumming. A coldness gripped him as he saw the hundreds of black shapes pour from the copse and come streaming up the slope towards them.

18

'Run! Get moving!' Pender shouted as Whittaker stood mesmerized by the advancing horde. The tutor stumbled forward, intending to run towards the parked car, but Pender caught his arm and swung him round.

'No! Towards the house! We'll never make it to the car – they'll cut us off.'

He pushed Whittaker towards the old building, giving one last look at the black vermin streaking across the field. The two men soon reached the piled bricks and rubble which sloped up the side of the house, and they clambered over it, the ratcatcher slipping and rolling back down, the heavy clothing preventing any severe damage. He clawed his way up to the top again and saw Whittaker pushing against the iron sheeting that covered one of the large ground-floor windows. The ratcatcher added his weight, using his shoulder to push against one corner of the corrugated iron.

He turned to see the black shapes darting beneath the two-strand wire fence that bordered the field, their bristling bodies momentarily lost in the undergrowth, then bursting forth, racing across the widened track that formed the frontage to the ruin. He stooped and picked up a brick, throwing it at the leading rodent, which swerved to avoid the missile.

Then it seemed as though every square foot of the frontage area was covered in black bodies, the air filled with their high-pitched squeals. Pender began using his boot on the metal barrier just as the first rat reached the bottom of the slope.

Whittaker saw the creature and managed to lift a fair-sized portion of brickwork from the rubble, hurling it down at the rat as it began climbing. The rat was crushed, killed instantly, but its companions were now at the base of the rough slope.

The corrugated sheet began to give and Pender redoubled his efforts. It came away from the top with a grinding tear and he squeezed an arm through, creating a triangular gap big enough to allow them entry.

'Get inside!' he yelled at Whittaker, pulling him roughly. The tutor complied without hesitation, squeezing his frame through the gap, grunting with the effort. Pender turned in time to give a rat that was only inches away a hefty kick, sending it hurtling back down to its companions. He wasted no time in pushing his way into the building's interior, gasping in pain as he felt strong teeth bite into his calf, one leg still on the other side of the barrier.

Whittaker was already pushing at the metal sheet, trying to close the gap in an effort to keep the attacking vermin out. Pender dragged his leg through, the rat still clinging to it. He pushed his foot down towards the floor once it was inside, the rat's shoulders becoming trapped at the narrow end of the triangle between wall and metal sheet. Whittaker had managed to close the gap at the top and was pressing against it with his shoulder. Pender forced his leg down even further, the edge of the metal sheet pressing into the rat's neck, choking it. The suit material tore under the strain and suddenly Pender's leg was free. He turned and brought his boot crunching down on the rodent's skull, forcing its neck further into the wedge shape. It struggled to pull back, the metal edge now cutting into its throat and Pender, in a furious, hate-filled madness, rained kicks upon the trembling head. At last the eyes became glazed and the head slumped, but Pender could not be sure it was really dead.

He could see other mutants through the small opening left above the rat's body, climbing on its back trying to push their way through, and he joined Whittaker, his back pushing against the corrugated iron. They could hear the vermin leaping at the barricade, their claws scrabbling at the surface. They winced at every thud, the metal shaking with each blow.

Pender looked around the interior of the ruin, seeking a means of escape. Many of the inside walls had caved in and he could see through to the rear of the building, the windows there also covered in metal sheets. He wondered what chance they would have if they made a break for it and tried to get out the back way, but realized that by the time they had forced an opening, the vermin would be through on this side and swarming all over them. He looked upwards to see if there was a way to reach the upper levels. The blueness of the peaceful sky seemed to mock him, for there were no floors above; the upper levels had been completely gutted. Even the staircases had gone. There was one way of getting above ground level, though. It was dangerous, but their only chance. And what he saw next told him there was no choice anyway.

Not far from where they stood, through the half-collapsed wall to the hallway, he could see a black body perched on top of a metal barrier. It was the section blocking the main entrance, a curved gap left between the doorway arc and the corrugated iron barrier. The rat waved its pointed head in the air, its nose twitching.

'It's no good,' Pender cried out. 'They've found another way in!'

Whittaker followed his gaze and drew in his breath.

Pender nudged him and pointed to a jagged rise of brickwork, the remains of a wall which had once divided that room from the next.

'If we can get up there, we may have a chance!' he yelled over the clamour of squealing rats and thudding sounds. 'There's just a small corner section of flooring up there. If we can get to it we may be able to hold them off until help comes!'

'Help? What help?' came the frantic reply.

'They know our location at the Centre. They'll send someone out when we don't return.'

'But that will be bloody hours, man! We'll never last that long!'

'It's all we have! So move. Get up there!'

Pender could see the gap above the door was now empty; the rat had dropped down, was among the debris. Two more shadows appeared in the opening, then these, too, disappeared from view.

'They're in here, Whittaker! Climb up or, by Christ, I'll leave *you* to hold the barrier!'

Whittaker ran across the rotted floor, avoiding a large hole near its centre, leaping over debris, a trail of blood streaming from his injured hand. He began to climb, brickwork crumbling away under his touch as he pulled himself upwards, using hands, feet, knees. The broken wall was irregular in shape, sometimes steep, sometimes a more manageable slope. Pender gave him a chance to reach a good height, knowing the tutor would only block his own path if he broke too soon. The appearance of three rats scurrying around the wreckage of the next room made him decide it was now or never. He sprang away from the barricade and sprinted towards the makeshift stairway to the upper level, hearing the sound of tearing metal behind, knowing the rats were pouring through.

He leapt over the gaping, black hole in the centre of the floor and when he landed on the other side, the rotted boards cracked and gave under his foot. His impetus carried him forward and he was fortunate not to fall into the cellar below. He scrambled to his feet and ran on, praying he wouldn't trip on all the loose rubble. The mutants in the next room were scurrying towards him, leaping over obstacles in their way, skirting round the larger objects. Behind him the rats were swarming through the ever-widening gap in the metal barrier.

He reached the foot of the broken brick wall a second or two before the lead rat approaching from the opposite direction, and leapt onto the first easy step, immediately moving upwards, pulling away loose bricks as he went, blindly throwing them down in the hope they would deter the vermin from following. The lead rat went with him, scurrying up his back, making for his exposed neck. Pender twisted his body, almost falling from the precarious perch, bringing his elbow around sharply to hit the rat's side. The mutant had no firm grip on Pender's clothing and the blow sent it tumbling down into the rubble again.

Pender climbed and when he looked up saw that the tutor had reached the next floor level. He was sitting astride an even outcrop of wall, a large chunk of masonry held above his head, ready to be thrown down. He was staring at Pender and their eyes locked.

For one dreadful moment, Pender thought the tutor was about to hurl the brickwork down into his face, his jealousy over Jenny erupting into violence. His fears were unfounded; Whittaker's arms heaved forward and the heavy weight sailed over Pender's head to land squarely on the back of a climbing rat. Within seconds he was beneath the tutor's feet.

He turned to look down at the swarming rats and kicked one away from his heels. It slid back, then fell, taking a companion with it. Pender was relieved to see only one rat at a time could advance up the incline, and its steepness in parts made their ascent difficult. The floor below seemed alive with the creatures, those at the base of the wall on their haunches, stretching their bodies upwards, leaping and tumbling back when their claws could not gain purchase. The sounds of their strident screeching echoed around the immense, stone cavern, rebounding off the walls, magnifying the noise. He saw others had found another source of entry near the back of the house and were filing through, joining the throng on the floor below. It seemed they were no strangers to the deserted ruin.

He was thankful that the ceilings of the old house had been high, for the further away he was from those slashing teeth and claws, the safer he felt.

'Where have they come from, Pender?' Whittaker yelled down at him. 'They should be dead!'

'It looks like they weren't all in the sewers,' Pender replied, aiming a swift kick at the twitching snout of an advancing rat. 'Get onto that ledge over there. There should be room enough for both of us.'

The tutor eased himself up slowly then stepped over to the outcrop, the corner remains of the first-floor level. He tested its strength before resting all his weight on it and when satisfied left his crumbling perch completely. Pender scooted up after him.

'Will it hold us both?' he asked before stepping across.

'I think so. It seems strong enough,' came the reply.

There wasn't much room on the small platform and both men clung to the wall it jutted from for support.

'I can reach any rat that gets to the top of the wall with my boot from here,' Pender said. 'They'll find it difficult to get over that last stretch anyway; it leans out at an angle.'

As if to prove his claim, a rat tried to scramble over the projection, easy enough for a man to do, but difficult for a smaller animal. Some of the brickwork crumbled and the rat went crashing down to the floor below. It rolled over and came to its feet again, shaking its body as if stunned.

'We should be safe here,' Pender said.

'For how long? What happens when it gets dark?'

'The Centre will send out a search party before then. We'll be okay.' Pender wished he could put some confidence behind the statement. 'How's your hand?' he enquired to change the subject.

Whittaker brought the injured hand away from the wall and Pender frowned when he saw the deep rent above the knuckles.

'I still can't move it! God, it hurts!'

Pender's worry was that the tutor might faint with the pain. A fall into the vermin below would be fatal.

'Try to hang on,' he said, feeling helpless. 'They know where we are; they'll get us out.'

He eased his body round on the platform so his back was against the wall, giving him a better all-round view.

'How many of them down there, Pender?' said Whittaker, his teeth clenched against the pain.

'Maybe a couple of hundred. They've stopped coming in now; I don't think there are any more.'

'That's enough to kill us, isn't it?' There was a note of hysteria in Whittaker's voice.

'Just keep calm and we'll be all right. They can't reach us here.'

But he was wrong. Even as he spoke, some of the black vermin were breaking away from the mass and climbing sections of other broken walls. Pender watched in horror, guessing their intention. If they climbed well enough, they could reach the next level above their precarious perch, then skim down the wall on that side to reach them. With astonishment, he noticed one of the climbing rats had a white marking on its pointed head; could it be the same rat he'd seen in the forest two weeks before among the group that had attacked his search party? Perhaps that was the reason these were still alive: they hadn't returned to the sewers, they had fled into the forest instead.

'Vic,' he said, trying to keep his voice calm. 'They're coming up the walls around us.' He felt the tutor's body stop trembling, as though shocked rigid. 'You'll have to turn around. We may be able to dislodge them before they get above us by throwing whatever we can break off the walls.'

'Can't we climb up further?' Whittaker said, closing his eyes and pressing his face against the rough brickwork.

'No, the broken wall we came up runs out just above my head. The rest is smooth to the top. Come on, turn, it's our only chance.'

Whittaker numbly did as he was told, his body beginning to shake again when he looked down at the bristling bodies below and the creeping black shapes on the walls around them. Some of the flooring beneath his feet crumbled and he cried out as he pressed himself back into the wall. The falling remnants of flooring seemed to excite the vermin even more and their squealing took on a new pitch.

Pender pulled a brick free from the wall they had climbed and aimed it at the lead rat, the one with the scar, which was patiently working its way up the opposite corner section of the same wall. More by luck than judgement, it struck the rat on one shoulder, causing it to lose its grip and tumble down. It scurried off and Pender lost sight of it in the shadows.

He aimed more pieces of masonry and Whittaker joined him, but they managed to strike only a few of the climbing vermin. Every so often, Pender had to kick out with his boot at the pointed snouts that appeared over the overhang in the wall by his side.

'It's no good, Pender! We'll never stop them!'

He saw that the tutor was right. There were just too many, and the missiles were becoming more difficult to pull from the wall, the looser ones used up now.

'Okay. We'll have to climb,' he said.

'But you said we couldn't! The walls are too smooth!'

'We'll have to try! We'll have to dig out handholds as we go – the walls might be soft with damp.'

Whittaker looked at him as though he was mad. 'That's impossible! We can't claw our way to the top!'

'There's no bloody choice! We can't stay here. Look, I'll have to go first; you won't be able to use that hand much. Try and keep close behind me – I'll help where I can.'

Pender clambered onto the brickwork that jutted out at right angles from the wall they were leaning on and began his ascent, testing every grip on the crumbling stone. He was relieved to see Whittaker following his example.

He soon reached the highest limit of the climbing wall and he stood erect, keeping his hands flat against the facing surface. Kicking into the brickwork, careful not to overbalance, he created a small foothold. Then he undid the empty gun-belt and used the metal buckle to dig into the wall's surface. The outer layer crumbled like powder, but the going became tougher when he reached the stone underneath. There was just the slightest chance the idea might work, though. If he could just create enough holds for their hands and feet, they might . . .

He saw there was no chance at all. Above, on the top of the building's inner wall, a pointed, black shape appeared, looking over the edge, nose twisting and waving in the air.

The rat opened its jaws wide and gave out a snarling hiss as it saw its quarry below, revealing its enormous, yellowed incisors. It was joined by other black shapes and Pender saw still more running along the wall's length. They had found another way up.

Whittaker clutched at his leg. 'What is it, Pender? Why have you stopped?'

The tutor saw the vermin above and screamed aloud. The next moment, the rats were stretching their bodies over the edge, digging their powerful claws into the brickwork, then letting themselves go, hurtling towards the heads of the men below.

19

Pender managed to throw his arm up in front of his face before the first giant rat landed on him, but the sudden force knocked him from his perch, sending him crashing downwards, taking Whittaker with him, other black bodies following their descent. It seemed ages to Pender before the impact came, as though his body had floated down in slow motion. His muscles tensed for the blow, but he barely felt it when it happened. The squirming bodies of the vermin cushioned the initial impact and the rotted floorboards beneath them gave way with a dry, cracking shriek, breaking the fall even further. They fell headlong into the dark cellar beneath the house, squealing vermin toppling in after them.

Pender's breath was knocked from him and everything was a mad blur of swirling dust and black, leaping shapes. Bodies were landing on top of him, claws slashing at his face and hands as he tried to protect himself. But the rats were too confused and startled to attack. They scrambled around in the underground chamber, snarling and clawing at each other in their panic, trying to climb the walls of the cellar as though this was a place in which they had no desire to be.

Pender wiped the grit from his eyes and looked up at the gaping hole above, the sunlight shining down through the old mansion's shell, flooding the basement with shafts of dust-filled light. Their fall had caused at least half the floor above to cave in and the rats were spilling over the jagged edges.

'Pender!'

He turned his body to see Whittaker crawling in the rubble, free of any clinging rats, blind terror driving him forward. Pender tried to reach him, but he had not yet recovered his breath. He started to call his name but only sharp gasps came from his throat. The tutor was crawling away from him, trying to get from beneath the vermin still tumbling down. One landed on his back and crouched there, its claws digging in, sending the tutor into an even wilder frenzy. His screams filled the cellar with their shrill sound, rising above the squeals of the vermin, and he staggered forward, still on hands and knees, heading into the darkness beyond the shafts of sunlight.

Pender managed to raise himself on one elbow and tried to call out to the tutor, but was still unable to do so. A terrible, cloying stench filled his nostrils, making breathing even more difficult. A falling rat knocked him back amongst the rubble and he pushed the creature away in a frantic movement. It nipped at his hand and darted away; mercifully, Pender was still wearing the tough gloves. He gained his knees and rose up from the sea of bristling fur. He could see Whittaker's figure just beyond the area of light, now standing, the black shape gone from his back, others scurrying around his ankles. His figure was still as though shocked rigid, and he seemed to be gazing at something in the corner of the cellar.

Abruptly, as though a signal had been given, all movement in the underground chamber stopped. Only the disturbed dust swirled and eddied, trickles of earth running down from the broken floor above. For a brief second, Pender felt a curious ringing in his ears, but he couldn't be sure if it wasn't just the sudden silence playing tricks. He looked down at the vermin around his feet and saw they were all crouched, their bodies quivering, eyes staring, slightly bulged. Their ears were stiffened as though they were picking up a sound too high in pitch for him to hear. Something white caught his eye. Something lying in the dust close by.

The light from the sun above shone through the skull's empty eye sockets, entering through a large hole in the cranium. Pender felt his body sway as a dizziness hit him. The skull was human. And beyond it was another. Beyond that, yet another. He desperately tried to keep upright, not wanting to fall among the vermin. There were more white objects around him, gleaming bones of severed limbs. But mostly there were the skulls, some in shattered pieces, others like the first with just their craniums cracked open. He slowly began to back away from the area of light, careful not to step on the crouching rats, afraid that one wrong move would set off the whole demented bedlam again. He moved towards the wall that should be somewhere behind him, hoping there would be a way up from the cellar there, wanting to call out to the tutor, but too afraid. If he found a way out, then he could guide Whittaker towards it without wasting time. A rat let out a sharp squeal as he trod on its claw. He froze, but the rat merely shifted its position and crouched low. Nothing else moved.

Soon he found his back brushing against the rough surface of the cellar wall and he quickly looked from left to right in search of an exit. The staircase, what was left of it, was to his right. He groaned inwardly when he saw the top was blocked with boards and rubble. He looked around for another way out.

The cellar was much larger than Pender had first thought; it stretched to the back of the house, most of it still in shadows. As he peered into the murky greyness he saw things moving against the gloom. Shapes that were light in colour, animals that were larger than the rats around them.

Whittaker's cry made Pender quickly turn his attention back to the figure standing on the other side of the patch of light. The tutor was moving backwards, his eyes still on some object before him, his body moving stiffly as though automated. His mouth opened and closed and whimpering sounds came from it. Sunlight burst onto his head and shoulders as he passed into the light. He stumbled over a crouching rat and the creature scampered away. Whittaker regained his balance and then emitted a swift-rising scream as a black shape scudded from the shadows and launched itself at him.

To Pender it looked huge, bigger than the other giant rats; another, equally big, joined in the attack.

Whittaker went down, holding the first creature off with his hands and kicking out at the other with his feet. Miraculously, almost as if panic had lent him strength, he caught hold of the first rat's head with one hand and snapped it backwards, breaking its neck. He tossed the twitching body away from him and struck out at the rat now nestled in his lap and trying to burrow a hole through the protective clothing into his stomach. Another Black rat of the same size ran from the shadows and leapt at Whittaker's exposed face. It seemed to be the signal for every rodent in the cellar to throw themselves at the struggling man.

Pender could only watch in horror as Whittaker's body was engulfed in black, bristling bodies, the tutor's screams becoming a blood-choked gurgle. Pender was about to rush forward, knowing it would mean his own death, but unable to stand by while the tutor was killed in such a terrible way, when a great explosion of blood spurted into the air from the undulating heap, telling him it was already too late. The rats, as though incensed by the fresh smell, went into a new paroxysm, scrabbling over each other's backs, snapping and scratching out at their companions in a demented effort to get to the man's body. Incredibly, a form began to rise from the heap, a figure so covered in blood, so mutilated, it was almost inhuman. Whittaker's face had been torn away, his eyes gleaming whitely amongst a mass of red, glutinous substance. His exposed, blood-stained teeth, no lips or beard to cover them, opened wide in a silent scream, red fluid gushing from his throat to splash onto the backs of the clinging vermin. The protective suit hung in tatters and the rats had their incisors clamped onto his chest and arms. A black body shot upwards and Pender saw it was one of the larger giant rats; it bit into the deranged man's throat and his body went over backwards, falling stiffly like a stone statue.

Pender closed his eyes as the slumped form was once more covered by the jostling vermin and when he opened them all he could see of the tutor was a hand, the fingers missing, twitching in the air above the gorging bodies. The tutor was dead – of that there could be no doubt – and the macabre action was caused by the elbow tendons being gnawed.

Pender felt vomit rising and suddenly he was leaning forward, the sickness pouring from him. Something strange had taken place when he had wiped his eyes with his sleeve and straightened, his back pressed against the wall. The larger rats were driving the other mutants back, away from the mangled corpse, snarling and hissing at their fellow-creatures, their sharp claws lashing out. The smaller vermin seemed afraid even though they could easily have swamped the two larger beasts with their numbers. They backed off, many dragging strips of flesh with them. One, more bold than the others, ran forward again and bit into Whittaker's mutilated body, but the larger rat pounced, teeth sinking into its neck. The imprudent creature squealed, then died, the wind-pipe severed. The big rat shook itself free of its victim and turned to face the others. They pushed away, heads low, haunches high and trembling. It was then the huge, bloated creatures shuffled forward into the light.

Pender felt nauseous again, hardly able to believe what he saw. The creatures were from a nightmare, deformed monsters, freaks from hell! They were almost hairless, just a few white wisps clinging sparsely to their obese, grey-pink bodies. Their long pointed heads and thick, scaled tails gave them some identification with the vermin they were derived from, but there the resemblance ended. Their swollen bodies, almost too heavy for their legs to carry, were covered in a network of blue, throbbing veins. Some were hunch-backed, their spines twisted upwards to a high peak, descending towards their haunches in a sharp swoop. Several had long, curling tusks; incisors deformed from lack of use. Two or three had shrivelled limbs projecting from various parts of their bodies, hanging uselessly, a few with twisted claws attached.

Pender suddenly understood what they were, why they were here in this dark cellar. These were the extreme mutants, their rodent bodies genetically corrupted into these obscene shapes. These were of the same kind Stephen Howard had spoken of, descendants of the creature that had been destroyed in the canal-house! These were the monsters who governed the more numerous black-furred mutants, controlling them, using them as hunters.

And this was their lair. This was where they hid their ugly, distorted bodies from the world, this underground chamber so like the dark underworld their precursors had once fled from.

That day he had looked up at the ruined house from the

field beyond and seen what he and Denison had thought to be a pig – it had been one of these creatures! The house had been left alone because the arsenals seen from a distance wandering in the ground were thought to have been pigs, and it was assumed that pigs would have been slaughtered by the Black rats if they were in the vicinity! But the pigs were already dead, killed earlier by the rats and used as a food supply, the cold weather preventing the corpses from rotting completely. How had it started? The main force, the hunters, living in the sewers, existing on anything they could find, killing small animals, bringing the corpses into the cellar, down to their masters? The sudden awakened yearning for fresh blood, warm flesh? The slaughter of the pigs they had been cunning enough to leave alone until then, bloodlust overpowering their caution? The growing need for human flesh, the desire to strike back at their mortal enemy? The growth and strength in their own numbers the catalyst that drove them forth? The questions tumbled through Pender's mind.

He became aware of the cold silence in the cellar once more. He could see the dark trembling shapes, the basement floor littered with the creatures, and the bigger, pinkish mutants gathered around the still form of Whittaker, blood bubbling from his stripped body, filling the air with its sickly heavy odour. He could hear the shuffling, dragging sounds coming from the dark place Whittaker had backed away from only minutes before.

The beast emerged from the shadows into the glaring sunlight, two of its eyes flinching in the brightness, the two on its other head white and sightless.

Pender felt his knees beginning to give, his back sliding down the rough wall. He steadied himself, his hands pressing into the brickwork behind.

The creature dragged itself forward, its two heads waving in the air, separate noses twitching. One head had long descending tusks sprouting from the upper jaw, keeping the mouth permanently open; the other, sightless, head had normal incisors and these were bared in a furious snarl. A peculiar rasping came from both throats.

It seemed to be sniffing the air, relishing the fresh blood smell. The other mutants backed away, allowing it to drag its gross form towards the dead human. It paused when it reached the body, its head wavering over it, quick, snuffling sounds escaping from its nostrils. One of the larger Black rats crept forward, its body crouched low as if in obeyance to the master. What happened next made Pender's senses reel.

The giant Black rat moved around to the tutor's head and opened its jaw wide. It lunged forward, clamping its razor-sharp teeth down in the top of the dead man's skull, the sickening crunching sound of shattered bone rebounding off the cellar walls. Pender could only watch in mesmeric fear as the gnawing sounds continued.

The rat finally withdrew its head, the snout covered in a sticky redness. Something dark bulged against the gaping hole left in Whittaker's skull. The two-headed beast shuffled forward and the head without the tusks plunged into the open wound, digging deep, then withdrawing, dragging out the meaty, veined substance with its teeth, blood and watery slime oozing from the emptied shell. The monster dropped its prize onto the dirt, then both heads attacked the brain at once, ripping it apart and swallowing the meat and tissue.

Pender's legs finally gave way completely and he slid to the floor. He knew he would be next.

20

Pender looked up at the open ceiling, desperately wondering how he could reach it. He cast his eyes around, trying to ignore the terrible sucking sounds coming from the centre of the cellar. In the gloom to his left he could just make out a bulky, square-shaped object, its surface rusted dark red. He'd noticed it before, but then he had been looking for a staircase so had paid it little attention. It looked like the remains of a large water-tank or at least something of that nature. Whatever it had been used for didn't matter; if he could move it, he might just be able to use it as a platform to reach the opening above. The question was: how to shift the object – if that was possible – without arousing the rats?

The other gross-shaped mutants were now crawling over the body, gorging themselves, while the dominant creature hunched over its particular spoil. The lesser, black-furred creatures were becoming agitated, their own desire for the human flesh unquenched. They edged forward, but the two larger of their species warned them off, haunches high in the air and shoulders low to the ground. Pender realized that these two, and the one Whittaker had killed, were probably guards to the dominant mutant. They had attacked Whittaker when he had unwittingly approached their leader. A Black rat darted forward and pushed its way through the grey-pink bodies to get at the corpse. Another Black joined it and the guards set on them, leaping onto their backs and dragging them away.

The movement was almost too fast for Pender to see as a rat dashed forward and sank its teeth into one of the guards' neck. A furious struggle ensued and the mutant with the two heads turned its obese body towards the aggressors, emitting a high-pitched mewling sound. But the fight had gone too far, the two rats tearing at each other with a fury that carried them into the shadows. Pender could hear their thrashing bodies, then came one strident scream followed by a hushed silence. The victor appeared again in the area of light, its jaws red, fur scuffed with dirt and scratch marks. Pender saw the now familiar scar running the length of its long, pointed head. Suddenly, the whole cellar seemed to erupt into movement as every rat converged on the ground around the dead human. They leapt on the grey-pink mutants, swamping them, covering the gross bodies with their own. Pender saw the remaining guard rat leap into the air, three smaller creatures clinging to it, each with deadly grips that would kill or maim. The bloated animals were helpless under the onslaught, hardly able to move beneath the crush, screaming like human babies, their fragile bodies bursting open, dark liquid gushing from them.

The Black rat with the scar scrambled over the mass of bodies, making for the dominant mutant which was, as yet, untouched, the other rats still afraid to go near. They glared at each other, only inches separating them, the mutant's two heads weaving in the air in agitation. The Black rat lunged, ignoring the harmless tusked head, striking for the throat of the blind head, dodging beneath the sharp incisors. It bit deep and the two heads screeched their agony. And fear.

Others joined the Black rat, pouncing on the obese hairless body and tearing into it. It seemed to Pender to shrink in size, almost like a punctured balloon, but he realized the mutant was sinking to the ground, blood pouring from the ripped veins. Its piteous mewling increased and the head that was blind suddenly slumped sideways, its neck almost severed by the Black rat.

The tusked head tried to pull away, rising in the air, but unable to move far because of its collapsed body. The Black rat bit out an eye before turning its attention towards the throat.

Pender felt no pity for the beast as it wailed in agony. Its remaining eye became glazed as the scarred Black rat tugged at its throat, and the head began to tremble, finally slumping to the ground. The monster died, helpless in its own obesity, no longer able to dominate its lesser subjects. Bloodlust was the instigating traitor in their ranks. They had served the creature, brought it food, protected its lair; but now they were beaten and the desire that had exploded within them could no longer be quenched. They turned on their leader in rage and its obscene body became their food.

The floor was a dark, seething mass as the rats devoured the creatures that were of the same mutant strain, yet had developed into bizarre monsters. Pender knew he had to act now or he would have no chance at all of surviving. He pushed himself to his feet and stood for a few moments with his back to the cellar wall. Then he inched his way along the uneven floor, keeping in the shadows, trying to move soundlessly. When he reached a point opposite the square, tank-like object, he allowed his breath to escape. So far, so good; the vermin had ignored him, too intent on their own activity. He stepped away from the wall, carefully avoiding fallen rubble. His head sank down onto the rough surface when he reached his goal and he tried to control his breathing, certain the short gasps would remind the vermin of his presence.

The tank reached chest height and he prayed it would be tall enough for him to grasp the collapsed ceiling. He gave it an exploratory push; it didn't budge. Oh God, don't let it be fixed to the floor. He pushed again, this time harder, and clenched his teeth at the sudden grinding noise it made as it shifted.

Pender crouched behind the metal tank, holding his breath and waiting for the vermin to come pouring round from the other side. Nothing happened. The sound of their eating and squealing relish continued. He rose and pushed against the tank again. It moved with a heavy rumbling noise and this time he did not stop, deciding speed was now his only ally. He stopped pushing when the tank was directly beneath the edge of the opening, afraid to move it any further because it would infringe on the area covered by the rats. He gazed upwards and saw the shell of the house stretching into the clear blue sky above; he felt like a condemned man being given his last glance at the outside world.

Pulling himself onto the improvised platform, he froze as the rusted metal gave out a loud crack, the surface buckling. It held, though, and he was on his feet stretching towards the jagged edge over his head, reaching for a hold, grabbing for life itself.

Pender managed to grip a broken beam and then he jumped, using it as a lever, trying to throw the other arm over onto the floor above. His legs were swinging in space, his elbow crooked over the rotting boards; and he was rising, his head drawing level with the floor above, his arms shaking with the strain.

And then he was falling, the flooring giving way, tumbling back down into the rat-infested basement.

The tank broke his fall and he rolled off its surface, wood and rubble crashing down with him. He landed on the vermin and they scattered in surprise, giving him a brief respite.

Pender wasted no time on examining any injuries he might have sustained. He was on his feet, staggering, tripping, going down on hands and knees, sheer instinct driving him towards the staircase. The fact that it was blocked at the top had no relevance in his thinking; it led upwards, that was all that mattered. He felt the scudding at his back and ducked forward, the rat toppling over his head, but causing him to lose his balance and fall heavily. He screamed when he felt the furry bodies engulf him, the claws scraping their way through the protective suit's material. Teeth slashed across his face and as he turned his head he felt a layer of flesh come away from his cheek. He brought his gloved hands up to protect himself, striking out at an evil, leering rat's head as it bared its incisors and prepared to bite. The rat scuttled away from him, to be immediately replaced by another.

A choking cry escaped Pender as teeth ground into his forehead and he desperately tried to turn his body over to protect his face, his eyes. But they were too heavy for him; they held him pinned to the floor. He lashed out with his legs, rats clinging to them and making movement impossible. He folded his arms across his face, covering the exposed flesh as much as possible, twisting his body to prevent the vermin gripping firmly. The pain was terrible as they bit into him, every inch of his body, it seemed, caught in vice-like grips. The suit material began to tear and he knew it would soon be over, just seconds of searing pain and then blessed oblivion. His senses began to float, spiralling into a soft downward plunge, away from the terror. His eyes began to close, but they could still see the blueness above through the narrow gap between his forearms, and he was reluctant to let the sight go, unwilling to leave the world above but desperate to escape the hell below. His eyelids had almost completely closed and he was beginning to drift. Everything went black.

And the noise was deafening.

His consciousness returned with a shock and his eyes snapped open. The sky above had been blocked out by something huge and dark. The roaring sounds should have told him what was happening, but his mind was too confused, his senses not yet fully awakened from the lulling slumber they had been sinking into. The weight on his body was relieved as the vermin screeched in new panic and scattered into the deeper shadows of the underground chamber. Grit swirled in the air, driven down from the ruin above, stirring and mingling with the dust in the cellar, turning the cellar into a cauldron of thick, flying particles.

Pender choked as the dirt clogged his open mouth and his wracked coughing stirred his body, making him sit and lean forward, shoulders heaving as he tried to breathe clean air. He covered his eyes, wiping away the dust with a gloved hand. Rats scuttled over and around him, ignoring him in their confusion. His mind began to sharpen when he saw there was still a chance left. He looked up, keeping his lids closed as much as possible, squinting through the hole above. The dark shape seemed to fill the opening, almost blocking out the sky completely, and it seemed as if he were looking up into the belly of a huge dragonfly. The sound of the whirring blades thundered in his ears as they created a vortex in the shell structure of the building, making a huge chimney of disturbed air. Reason told him the helicopter was hovering over the collapsed roof of the ruined house, but he felt he could almost reach through the tunnel and touch the great machine.

He cried out in pain when he tried to rise and his hands went to his face again as a sticky substance threatened his vision. He wiped away the dust-encrusted blood and forced himself to stand. Pender caught a glimpse through the swirling mists of the crouching black creature watching him. He ran, pain forgotten, body disregarding its injuries. He staggered blindly towards the stairway, crashing into the wall, scattering the frightened rats lurking there, feeling his way along, reaching the bottom stair, dragging himself upwards, kicking down at the vermin clustered around his feet. They began to nip at his legs, striking back in fear but aware again that this was the enemy in their midst. Pender knew they would soon be all over him and he pulled at the rubble blocking the stairs, frantically clawing at the bricks, the dirt, the broken timber.

The blockage suddenly collapsed inwards and he covered his head as the debris fell around him, pushing himself up, thrusting himself through to the floor above. He rose from the rubble like some filthy, bloodied monster from the earth's underworld, scrabbling free, crawling forward, rising on shaky legs and staggering through the burnt-out mansion. The interior walls, disturbed by the fierce down-draught of air, were beginning to crumble, stonework falling to the floor below.

Pender kept going, his movements painfully slow, oblivious to the falling masonry, wanting only to be free from that dark, evil place. He did not know if the helicopter's crew were aware of his presence, nor did he care; he just wanted to be outside. He reached the room into which he and Whittaker had first scrambled in their attempt to escape the pursuing vermin, and made for the bent sheet of corrugated iron. He clambered up the debris to the opening and squeezed his body through, swiftly glancing back to see if he was being followed. He almost cried out in despair when he saw the big Black rat scuttling through the rubble to reach him. It may have come through the now unblocked stairway or, more likely, through its own escape hole – the rats obviously had their own entrance into the cellar, a hole he had been unable to see in the gloom.

Pender leapt from the outer window-sill into the beautiful, fresh, sunlit air, rolling down the incline of rubble, jumping up immediately, and running, feet dragging, but keeping going, refusing to fall. He saw the dark green van racing up the track over the field towards him, skidding when it reached the worst of the muddied area, hitting a fence post and knocking it flat. The wheels threw up showers of damp earth as the driver tried to get the vehicle clear.

Pender ran towards it, gasping in air, using his last reserves of energy to reach the van. He twisted his head to see the rats slipping through the gap in the window, running down the rubble, and chasing towards him. Almost exhausted, adrenalin pumped through his system as he redoubled his efforts to get away. He knew he would never make it, the van was too far. Pender wanted to scream in frustration and his body sagged as his knees began to give.

The sudden rush of air and whirring of the Gazelle's blades made his head jerk upwards. He turned and saw the helicopter swooping low over the pursuing vermin, making them crouch, then scatter. Bullets from the sub-machine-gun thudded into the earth, sending up fountains of blood when they struck the running bodies.

Pender groaned with pleasure at the sight and rose, stumbling onwards. The green Conservation van had freed itself from the mud and was racing towards him once again. He went down, falling to his knees, one hand resting against the ground.

'Luke!' he heard Jenny's voice scream.

He looked up as the van skidded to a halt in front of him and the door flew open. Suddenly Jenny was there, arms around his shoulders, lifting him, pleading with him to move.

Her voice shook with emotion and tears ran freely down her cheeks as she pulled him towards the van. He hardly looked human, his body and face covered in blood and dirt, his clothes hanging in tatters. Apprehension had filled her as she had headed for the lumbering, bedraggled form, for there was no telling which man it was: Whittaker or Pender? It was only when she brought the van to a screeching halt that she recognized him.

'Luke, you must move – please!' she begged.

Pender willed himself to walk and Jenny pulled open the passenger door of the vehicle, helping him to clamber in. She slid the door shut and hurried round to the driver's side, aware that several rats were streaking towards her. She slammed the driver's door just as a rat leapt. It thudded against the metal and fell back to the ground. More muffled thumps followed as the rats ran round the vehicle and jumped up at it.

'Oh, Luke, Luke, what have they done to you?' Jenny moaned, taking Pender's torn face in her hands.

He hardly had the breath or the strength to speak, but he managed to say, 'They're there in the house ... in the ... cellar. It's their ... lair. That's where ... they were ... all the time.'

Jenny screamed as the windscreen shattered and a rat perched on the jagged glass, head and shoulders not two feet away from Pender's face. With a shout of sheer rage, the ratcatcher lashed out with his fist, hitting the black creature squarely on the forehead, knocking it back onto the earth below.

'Get us out of here, Jenny!' he shouted.

The van roared round in a tight circle, crushing several rats beneath its wheels. Pender was thrown against the door and as his head hit the window, he saw the big Black rat with the strange scar crouched in the mud, its mouth open wide revealing long, yellow teeth. Its eyes glared up at him. Pender lost sight of it as the van completed the semi-circle and raced back down the track in the direction from which it had come, skidding through the worst of the mud but gathering speed.

Pender managed to turn in his seat and look through the rear windows. The helicopter was still hovering low, discharging its deadly spray. The rats, those not killed or badly injured, were scurrying back to safety – back into the house itself.

'They've got to get them now!' he shouted at Jenny. 'Now, before they have a chance to lose themselves in the forest!'

'They will, Luke! Look ahead!'

Pender looked through the opening in the fractured glass on his side of the van, the air rushing in and stinging his raw face. He managed to smile grimly when he saw the convoy of army vehicles speeding down the lane leading from the gatehouses. He looked at Jenny. 'How . . . ?'

'Denison found slaughtered deer in the reserve. He radioed the Centre. I was in the operations room when his call came in.' She carefully but swiftly steered the van through the open gate at the end of the field, rattling over the cattle-grid and narrowly avoiding Pender's parked Audi. 'I knew you and Vic were here so I came for you. I couldn't wait for them to get organized, Luke, I just felt something was happening up here.'

'Thank God you didn't,' Pender said, looking at her profile and loving every inch of it.

'They were directing the helicopter to your last location when I left. Oh Luke, I'm so glad I came straight away.'

Pender tried to touch her shoulder but either the van was jolting too much or his hand was too shaky.

The Conservation vehicle came to an abrupt halt, throwing

Pender forward. Jenny's arm shot across his chest preventing him from hitting the dashboard. He turned to face her and realized why she had stopped so suddenly. Her door flew open and Captain Mather was staring anxiously at her.

'Good God!' he said when he saw Pender.

The ratcatcher pushed forward across Jenny's lap, his face a red, grime-filled mask, a flap of skin hanging loosely from one cheek. 'You've got to destroy the house, Mather,' he said urgently. 'The ... the last of the rats are in there. Underground. In the cellar. They're trapped.'

'Luke,' Jenny cut in. 'Where's Vic? Is he still in the house?'

Pender paused before answering. He looked at Jenny. 'He's in there. But he's dead. He didn't have a chance.'

'How many vermin are still alive?' asked Mather.

'I don't know – a couple of hundred maybe.' His voice became low. 'The mutant's in there – what's left of it. The creature we searched the sewers for.'

Mather's mouth dropped open. 'So that was their hiding place,' he said.

Pender nodded. 'It was their lair – just the main force hid in the sewers. You've got to move fast, Mather – finish them off now!'

The officer turned away without another word and within seconds the whole convoy was moving forward towards the house.

Jenny engaged first gear. 'I've got to get you to a hospital, Luke. You've been hurt badly.'

He stretched out a hand, this time managing to close it over hers on the gearstick. He gently eased it back into neutral.

'Not yet. I want to see them destroy the house first. I want to see it completely demolished. Then it will be over for me, Jenny. No more rats, no more hate. Just us, from now on.'

She smiled, a sad, tearful smile, and reached for his face, careful to touch it lightly. She brushed some of the dust away from his eyes. Then she nodded slowly.

They watched the Scorpions pound the walls of the old mansion until the shell collapsed inwards, falling with a tired but almost triumphant roar. Then mortars blasted the debris until the house was nothing but piled dust and rubble, while soldiers armed with flame-throwers and machine-guns stood by at a safe distance, ready to destroy any living thing that tried to escape the destruction. But nothing tried to escape. Nothing could.

When the guns fell silent, the smoke drifting away, the dust sinking, a calmness seemed to settle over the woodlands. The green van's engine started up again and the vehicle moved slowly along the rough track through the pine forest, heading for the estate's main gate.

A breeze sprang up and it seemed to Pender, who was gazing back through an open window at the vermin's funeral pyre, that the very trees were breathing a gentle sigh of relief.

Epilogue

The rain poured from the night sky giving the forest below a heavy, glistening coat. A man crouched in the undergrowth, shivering in his blue tracksuit, his eyes on the concrete path that fringed that part of the woodland. He hadn't visited the forest for a long time, not since discovering the remains of two bodies when he had fallen into a dip. They said the woodland really was clear now, that there was no danger at all; but not many people believed them, not many wanted to take the chance. This part was hardly forest at all and certainly had nothing to do with Epping Forest, even though it was adjoining. The suburbs of the city stretched for miles in front of him, the concrete pavement the woodland's boundary. Yet still he was nervous and every so often he would glance over his shoulder and peer into the darkness.

His need had been too great to resist any longer. His mother – God, how he wished he could have fed that cow to the rats – had nagged, nagged, nagged for the past week, not stopping once to draw breath, driving him mad, driving him out. Just because he had refused to go in to school. She didn't understand: he couldn't when he felt this way – it might lead to his committing a misdemeanour there. He would be all right after tonight. For a while, anyway. The rain ran off his forehead and down to the end of his nose where it formed an overhanging droplet. He tensed when he heard clattering footsteps.

From the dark of the undergrowth behind, four pairs of small, slanted eyes watched the man. Their bristle-haired fur was sleeked black with wetness, their bodies thin and wasted as though they had not eaten well for a long time. Pointed noses twitched in the damp air, sensing prey. One began to creep towards the hidden man, its incisors bared and haunches raised, quivering.

Another of the creatures moved swiftly in front and forced the creeping rat to run. The sound of approaching footsteps grew louder.

The rats melted into the night, stealing away but not venturing far into the forest they now feared and hated. The ground sloped upwards and the vermin kept their bodies low in the grass, using every inch of cover, crawling and skulking, the only way they could survive. One led the way, the other three keeping close, subservient and dependent upon it. The group reached the crest of the hill and were dazzled by the millions of silver and orange lights spread out for miles before them. The lead rat gazed at the city, the pinpoints of light reflecting in its eyes, the raindrops finding a crude channel in the scar that ran the length of its head. The Black rat's mouth opened and a hissing noise came from its throat.

It moved forward, down the hill, heading for the lights, back to the city. The others followed.

JAMES HERBERT

The Number One Chiller Writer

Shrine

£6.99

A little girl called Alice. A deaf-mute. A vision. A lady in shimmering white who says she is the immaculate conception. And Alice can suddenly hear and speak, and she can perform miracles. Soon the site of the visitation has become a shrine, a holy place for thousands of pilgrims. But Alice is no longer the guile-less child overwhelmed by her new saintliness. She has become the agent of something corrupt. Innocence and evil have become one.

'Thrills and chills galore from the bestseller Herbert . . . his best yet . . . The build-up to the horrifying climax is subtle and sophisticated . . .'
Daily Express

REMEMBER WITH FEAR

JAMES HERBERT

The Number One Chiller Writer

The Jonah

£6.99

The shadow of his past was always with him. But he never knew what it was, or when it would strike next. Sent to a small coastal town to investigate drug smuggling, Kelso stumbles on a dangerous organization and suddenly more than just his life is at stake. It's his past, his future, his sanity. Through torture and drugs he discovers the terrifying secret of *The Jonah*. And learns, in the most horrifying way, that it can destroy him as well as others . . .

'A fresh crop of terrors bristle all through'
Daily Mirror

REMEMBER WITH FEAR

JAMES HERBERT

The Number One Chiller Writer

The Survivor

£6.99

It had been one of the worst crashes in airline history, killing over 300 people and leaving only one survivor. Now the dead were buried and the town of Eton tried to forget. But one man could not rest.

Keller had walked from the flames of the wreck, driven on by unseen forces, seeking the answer to his own survival. Until the town was forced to face the shocking, dreadful truth about what was buried in the old grave-yard. And a truth Keller did not want to believe . . .

'One of the great supernatural storytellers'
Evening Standard

REMEMBER WITH FEAR

JAMES HERBERT

The Number One Chiller Writer

The Spear

£6.99

When Steadman agreed to investigate the disappear-
ance of a young Mossad agent, he had no idea he
would be drawn into a malevolent conspiracy of neo-
Nazi cultists bent on unleashing an age-old unholy
power on an unsuspecting world – power rising out of
a demonic relic from man's dark primal past to threaten
humanity with horror from beyond any nightmare . . .

'Spine-chilling . . . violent, creepy and compulsive reading'
Daily Mirror

REMEMBER WITH FEAR